Perihan Mağden was born in Ista
of *Messenger Boy Murders* and *The
of poems. She lives in Istanbul an
newspaper *Radikal*.

Two Girls

Perihan Mağden

Translated by
Brendan Freely

With the support of the
Culture 2000 programme of the
European Union

Education and Culture

Culture 2000

A complete catalogue record for this book can
be obtained from the British Library on request

First published in Turkish as *İki Genç Kizin
Romani* by Everest Yayinlari, Turkey

First published in this English translation in 2005 by Serpent's Tail,
4 Blackstock Mews, London N4 2BT
website: www.serpentstail.com

Designed and typeset at Neuadd Bwll, Llanwrtyd Wells

Printed by Mackays of Chatham, plc

10   9   8   7   6   5   4   3   2   1

Reeds

. . . .

Finally, the winter sun cut through the darkness like a drawn knife.

The sea was more beautiful than ever.

But the first of the cousins wasn't in a state to notice this. In the crystal-clear light of a sharply cold morning, the shriek of dawn actually, he could think only of what the sea would provide. How many fish? He longed for his warm and friendly bed. He hated this fishing business. Being at the mercy of the sea. Daily bread. Destiny. It depressed him.

He became impatient. 'Come on,' he said. 'Come on, what are you waiting for?'

'Look, there's something over there,' said the second one. The one at the tiller. Not the one who was looking unhappily into the distance, the one who was absorbed, scanning the rushes.

'Whatever. Step on it. Let's get moving.'

'Look at that thing moving back and forth. I swear there's something there. Look, look. Let's go and take a good look at it.'

'What's it to us! We're freezing our asses off here. Let's get moving.'

'Just look at it. The way it's moving. That's a jacket, man! I swear there's someone there. Let's take a look and see what's what. It'll be our good deed for the day.'

They brought their little boat as far as they could into the reeds.

The moving object they'd noticed was a large, navy-blue jacket.

The corpse was floating face-down, hanging as if it was caught in the water, swinging back and forth.

Looking as if it was peering into the depths of the sea.

With its arms and legs hanging down.

The jacket was on top, above the water. Filled with air.

'Look, he's drowned. How was I able to see him from so far away? Didn't I tell you someone had drowned?' said the second one, excited.

He took the oar out of its lock and prodded the jacket once or twice. Because the jacket was caught among the reeds, like a sail, filled by the wind, it didn't drift out to sea, but moved here and there with the current.

Something had been painted on the jacket in red paint. Was it a letter? It was a multiplication sign. An X.

It was such a silly, childish mark. It made the corpse less distressing, less pitiable and less heavy. It made the situation less grave. It was bewildering. The second cousin couldn't take it; he prodded the jacket with the oar once or twice more.

'Enough already,' said the first one. 'Leave the poor thing alone. You've already screwed everything up. Fishing for dead bodies!'

They'd have to go back to the shore and tell the police. A lot of problems, a lot of trouble. But the first cousin felt an unexpected sense of joy. At least he wouldn't have to fish today. Wouldn't it be nice to go back to bed again in a couple of hours? It would.

The second cousin, the one who found the body, eagerly did all that was expected of a responsible person.

He brought the police to the 'crime scene' in the reeds. He planted himself on the beach and waited a long time for the corpse to be taken out of the water. He accompanied the corpse as it was carried to the ambulance. Until they closed the bag, he didn't take his eyes off the body for a second.

How wrinkled the big corpse's hands were (like a washerwoman's), what a strange shade of pink its face had taken on, how one of the shoes was still on, how the sock on the other foot was peeling away from the swollen flesh…(He thought of putting the sock back on. He feared that if it fell off, 'something' would be missing from the corpse.)

The corpse was that of a young man. Tall, fat, with spiky blond hair, a boy of nineteen or twenty.

The second cousin hungrily imprinted every detail in his mind.

He went back to the police station. He gave his statement. Later he went to the village coffee-house and told everyone everything he'd remembered.

At the end of his story, the men in the coffee-house said, 'Oh well, he's dead and gone.'

In the doctor's words, there were 'wounds caused by a sharp instrument' on the boy's throat and elsewhere. In other words, he hadn't died from drowning. He'd been stabbed and thrown in. Into the village reed-beds. Which was a bit of an insult. As if they'd cursed the reed-beds.

As he told the story the second cousin wept a little, but sincerely. As he was taking his fifth tea, the first cousin said, 'There's nothing to seeing a corpse. You've ruined my day. We went out fishing and came back with a corpse. It's my fault for choosing to work with you.'

'Life contains everything,' one of the wise men of the coffee-house said. 'There's death, there's life. But he was young, just a kid.'

'He was also fat,' said the second cousin. 'Six policemen had a hard time carrying him to the ambulance. He was huge.'

'In death there's no youth or old age, there's no fat or thin,' said the wise man, raising his voice for greater effect. 'Any of us could win this lottery at any time.'

'And how,' said another man. One of the less wise, backing up the wise man's words. 'A reverse lottery. One's turn to die.'

'They cut him,' said the second cousin, 'from here to here. They put a red mark on his jacket. An X.'

The second cousin's curiosity about the murder had exasperated the coffee-house.

'Never mind,' said the wise man. 'You found him there, before the fish and the birds could start eating him. That's enough.'

'Stop it, man,' said the first cousin. 'You'll go round and round with this. Some poor guy is dead. Shut your beak and let's forget about it.'

'I did a good deed. There's someone waiting for him.'

'They'll be reunited with your help,' said the first cousin. 'His corpse will go back home.'

'That's better than nothing,' said the second cousin. What he'd seen passed through his mind again, and he shivered. His eyes gently swelled with tears once again. He felt a beautiful chill run down his spine. He buried the happiness of that feeling. He kept it to himself.

The first police report stated that it was very likely the victim died from wounds caused by a sharp object before he was thrown into the water. It was established that there were twelve cut wounds of various sizes on his neck, in the region of his heart, on his arms and on his palms.

```
Sex: Male
Height: 183 cm
Weight: 102.5 kilos
```

Questions to be asked according to a forensic textbook:
1) Who is the victim?
2) What was the time of death?
3) How long was the body in the water?
4) Was the victim alive or dead when he entered the water?
5) Did the victim drown? What was the cause of death?
6) According to the death incident, crime scene investigation, autopsy and toxicologic examination, what is the origin of the death?

7)   Ante-mortem post-mortem wounds and artefacts should be differentiated.


```
The lips of the wounds are straight. Both angles of the
wounds are narrow. The wounds are wider than they are
deep. No ecchymosis was found near the lips of the wounds.
```

The police report stated that the victim was wearing a jacket, trousers, a shirt, shorts, socks and one shoe.

Dark-blue jacket: *Paul & Shark*
Lavender, red and white striped sweatshirt: *Tommy Hilfiger*
White undershirt: *Marks & Spencer*
Blue jeans: *Ralph Lauren*
Socks: *Lacoste*
White underpants: *Marks & Spencer*
Size 44 moccasins: *Gucci*
Penis size: 9cm

The symbol which had been spray-painted in red on the back of the *Paul & Shark* jacket will not be mentioned in any of the reports.

Nor the brand names of the clothes he was wearing.

Nor his penis size. Of course, that will not appear in any of the reports.

Behiye state

• •

Behiye's unhappiness has nested within her like an unwanted bird. She's wandering the streets.

It's as if she'd burst into tears if you touched her. But she doesn't know quite why she got this way. It's slightly better than the state of being distressed. No, it's much better, it's an easier state to resolve, to endure. THE STATE OF DISTRESS. The state like a blood-red balloon that's been inflated to the point where it's about to explode. It was a state in which another state existed, but wasn't allowed to fit, couldn't fit, and was strangled, constricted, squeezed by the throat, squeezing the soul itself by the throat, and pressing it down and constricting it.

That state is the worst state of all. It is the hardest to resist, to get out of, the most destructive and sickening. Makes you feel self-disgust. That is when Behiye, in that balloon of distress which swallows, suffocates, leaves breathless, wishes that she could pass into a new body.

That is when she wants to escape that used and constricting, sixteen-year-worn-out, pathetic, narrow body, throw it on to a garbage dump on the edge of the city, and pass into a new body.

Within Behiye there's also a third state: THE STATE OF ANGER. When she is in that state she could feel her head begin to throb from the nervousness. Twirling in place. Her skull, buzzing nonstop like a crazed mosquito, blinds her with anger. At these moments she is capable of anything. She can burn things down. Destroy things. Fuck things.

Because this state annoys her less, Behiye is afraid of this third state. Afraid; because she knows that when she's blinded she's capable of doing any number of things. She also loves this state. The power. Strength. This angry, darkened, loose, let-go state: the power of that state: the power of the possessed.

As she walks, unconsciously swerving from left to right, it makes her want to sob out loud to know that she's condemned for ever to the heaviness and bitterness of these three states, SORROW, DISTRESS and ANGER, that she'll never be accepted or allowed to enter any other state.

The desire to weep doesn't bring on tears. It's been like this for so many years. The desire to weep, the desire that becomes a chronic annoyance to her during her distressed state, stops up the tears. A seriously plugged state. A plug. Stone. Being.

Stonnned.

Behiye hasn't cried since she was seven and a half years old. She was seven and a half years old – she remembers the day – when she cried her heart out for her mother, because she pitied her mother, because she was ashamed of her mother, because she both pitied and was ashamed of her mother. She hasn't loved her mother since that day. She doesn't love anyone. She can't cry properly. Cry her heart out.

She only feels a great deal of shame. She feels shame for her mother, her father, her older brother, her relatives, her neighbours, her teachers, the people she sees on the streets, the people she sees on television, in fact everyone she sees. Everyone makes her feel shame. She can't stop feeling ashamed. She feels ashamed. She is the only one who feels ashamed. No one else feels ashamed.

She's fed up with being ashamed of everything she sees. But still, still, she's most ashamed of her mother. This is what she's most ashamed of, being more ashamed of her mother than anything.

In the gentle warmth of the autumn evening Behiye keeps walking and getting more massive because her self rejects any consolation. She is a mass. Black tar stone. Swallowed inside. Asphalt stone. Stonnne.

She doesn't know how long she's been walking: She walked a lot. Into the very depths of herself.

She feels very bad that she wanted to cry but couldn't cry, that she couldn't get rid of that sticky feeling of wanting to cry, that she feels so embarrassed for everyone, that no matter how much her soul is pressured, that even if she dug with a spade she couldn't find any consolation, any solace, any break, softness, sweetness within herself. Pulled to shreds and swollen. Ruined, shabby and petrified. Dreadfully sad. She won't be able to bear it. That far. Sad. Day. Behiye.

She won't be able to get out of the triangle of these three states. It seems she's chained. Nailed. Glued. Stuck. Finished. At the end. She wants to get out of this ugly envelope, this unwanted shell she's been using for sixteen years, and fly away.

Yes! She isn't going to go any further in this body.

Her sadness has increased and gone past the boundaries of distress. That big wave is going to come and swallow her now. She looked for it. It didn't stop. She couldn't stop. Wave of distress!

She has to find a way to stop. She doesn't want it. She doesn't want it!

Behiye puts her right hand in her mouth and bites it like crazy. Like crazy. Her teeth go into her hand.

When she finally takes her hand out of her mouth, she sees how much it's bleeding.

You've gone too far, she says to herself. You've gone too far. Look what you've done to your hand. Look! What you've done to your hand. Look! What you've done. You've gone too far. Enough. Enough.

Suddenly she feels her legs trembling wildly. She's very tired. She's done in. She collapses right there on the pavement.

By God, it's a beautiful pavement. A pavement with huge trees. She's collapsed under a huge old tree. She wants to lift her head and look at the tree's leaves. As if she would have understood. She wants to see what kind of tree it is.

She doesn't have the strength. She doesn't have the strength to lift her head and look. Suddenly, under that old plane tree – later she'll always remember that tree as plane; in any event she didn't know – under that old tree, with her hand still bleeding, her limbs weak from tiredness, sitting with her head against the trunk, Behiye suddenly senses a soft feeling.

THE FEELING YOU'LL BE RESCUED: This is the name of the feeling.

Things are going to happen. In three times, five times, seven times. Don't be sad. Swear, things are going to happen. You've been depressed since you were seven. Since you were seven and a half. You won't accept consolation. You've been so sad. You've waited so long. Stay in this body now. Don't go anywhere. Something very beautiful is going to come to you. Something very beautiful, good and sweet. A wonderful state will come into you; a state of wellness, a state of flying, of delight, of happiness, of going mad with happiness. It's happened already. Your blood was useful. Don't rub on your clothes. Finally, a miracle for you: The Feeling You'll Be Rescued.

Behiye feels these things within her in a strange way.

With her inner ear. Unbelievable. Very beautiful. As if that rabid dog within her had died. The asphalt stone has fallen. Water sprinkling within her. Just like that. The state of water sprinkling within her. Stone falling. Fallll.

An old man says, 'Are you all right, my girl?'

'I'm fine, uncle. I'm fine.'

'Fine, my girl. But don't get ill.'

Get the fuck away from me. Let me not shit in your mouth. So I collapsed under a tree. What's it to you?

Normally, that's what Behiye would think of saying. But this time she didn't. Instead she feels like laughing. She giggles a bit in the shade of the tree.

Later she gets up off the ground. She puts her non-bloody, non-aching hand in her trouser pocket. Somehow she has two million left. She waves down a taxi and gets in. She rides as far as a million will take her, then walks from the main avenue to the apartment building. Her legs are still trembling. But she feels better than she has for years. As light as a bird. Birrrd. Light bird Behiye. New Bird.

Without recording anything, ANYTHING, about the building, she climbs to flat number five on the third floor.

She rang the bell. Her mother answered.

'Mother, I'm going to lie down and sleep.'

'All right Behiye.'

As she closes the door to her room she can't believe her state.

She was almost going to say 'Mother dear'.

Mother dear, I'm going to sleep.

She caught herself before it came out of her mouth. Her mother probably would have fainted if she'd heard that.

Mother dear? No way!

She throws herself on the bed without undressing. She's very sleepy. She's terribly sleepy. Will this state last until tomorrow? You'll be rescued; the feeling that good things will happen to her. She tries to be frightened. It doesn't work. She's very sure of the feeling. Very complete.

As it hits in waves, she abandons herself to the beaches of sleep.

The excitement of what type of a Behiye State she'll be in tomorrow is softly there. With a sweet feeling.

Sweet? No way! Whatever.

Leman towards morning

. . . .

Towards morning, 'Mr' Şevket is dropping 'Ms' Leman off at her house. On the right just before Akmerkez. In the Petrol Complex.

Whenever 'Ms' Leman goes out, she always comes home towards morning. Before that she'll have a very long dinner with the gentlemen, she'll drink well, get merry and melancholy; internalise the songs she's requested. Then they'll move on somewhere else. Then go on to one last place. Ms Leman is still not satisfied, and wants to stay out, and because the tripe soup restaurants are the only places still open, they'll have a tripe soup session, and come home as late as possible.

Handan's mother is still on polite terms with her new 'boyfriend'. Because they're just starting out, she feels cramped. But no matter how distressed she is, no matter how real her discomfort is, once she begins drinking she throws herself into the whirlwind of enjoyment, can't stop or be stopped until she's worn out, and prepares to go home as late as possible. The duration of a night out is like proof of her job ethic, pride of her womanhood.

Mr Şevket, pulling his honey-coloured Mercedes up in front of her door, says, 'Well, my precious, that was one of the best nights. You go and have a nice sleep now, OK?'

Leman is relieved.

At last, on the third date, they've gotten to 'my precious' stage. She half turns her face. She is aware that most of her make-up is gone, and that her hair is down. But mostly, mostly she is aware that she is not that young woman, that lively flesh, not that dumb, playful thing ready for anything, and that she's tired and broken. She moves into each new relationship with more baggage, with a heavier load.

In two weeks she's going to turn thirty-five. Soon, the pages of youth and beauty would be closed for ever. She quivers. This 'Mr' Şevket, this rich ox might be her last chance. Her last stroke! She pouts. Like a baby.

'So my beauty is really tired. To tell the truth, I'd like to suggest we go to our hotel. But nowadays, family responsibilities, I mean my daughter's wedding, matters in Russia, etc., etc., it's just not possible.'

Oh, so he's finally gotten around to suggesting a hotel.

Even if it wasn't going to happen, he'd said it.

Leman feels renewed, alive. Quickly, she considers whether to ask him for money or to wait for him to think of it himself.

Mr Şevket pulls her into a sticky embrace.

Leman responds by using one of her seductress imitations.

They're no longer Mr Şevket and Ms Leman. They've gotten to 'Şevket'.

And 'Leman'. This pleases her. So she allows him to extend his kisses and reach out and touch her here and there. After all, she thinks she can get seven or eight hundred million out of him.

'I'd better get out of here. If the neighbours see, there'll be talk.' She lets out about half a dozen life-saving laughing sounds.

In order to take this stage of getting to know each other to a new level, she reaches out and wipes off the lipstick marks she's left on his face.

'I don't want you to get caught, my young bull. Dreams of most Lemans to you, darling.'

'Go on, you magnificent woman. I can still taste you. I'll call you as soon as I get back from Moscow, OK?'

With one foot already out the door, she turns and says, 'Doesn't your cell phone work in Russia, Mr Şevket?'

'Of course it does, darling precious. I can call from there. I'll be up to my ears in work. But I'll find time to call you. I swear I'll call. Don't get cross with me, girl.'

In fifteen, no, fourteen days she is going to be thirty-five. Before, the men couldn't stand to be apart from her so long. And he was going to call when he came back from Moscow!

She gets out and slams the door. She'd done all that necking in the car. And the guy didn't even cough up a penny. Her last stroke! Let the stupid ox get the fuck away from her! To hell with him! If only she didn't have to think about Handan's expenses…

She feels a terrible bitterness sink into her. The kind of bitterness she feels, when she's not on the job, after drinking this much. An obliterating, crushing, belittling pain: a state of patheticness. Occupational pollution. The weight of it. The bad smell that invades the soul.

She pushes open the front door of the building. She climbs to the second floor.

No matter how hard she digs she can't find her keys.

Damn it! Why can't the keys just jump out of the bag when you need them?

Collapsing in front of their door, she takes off the shoes Handan calls her witch's shoes and flings them away. What a relief! With those square high heels it was like walking down a steep hill, and it killed her legs. She has a little crimson bag. Where could her keys have gone in that little crimson bag?

Annoyed, she empties the bag on to her lap. Her silver-backed mirror grins at her. She can't stand it. Leman is one of those women who can't resist when seeing a mirror. She takes the mirror and holds it up to her face.

Is this Leman? Is this what became of her?

Has this happened to beautiful Leman? Even her eyes are less blue. Leman is gone: but where? Of course a man would call this tired, lifeless, worn-out woman with bags under her eyes when he came BACK from Moscow. He wouldn't politely squeeze seven or eight hundred million into her bag, either.

Doesn't she deserve it, though? Is she in a state to be wanted? Is she in a condition to provoke strong desire?

She begins to cry delicately. Silently. When she sees her crying face in the mirror she cries even more. The crying increases. It gets bigger. The crying swallows Leman. She has no control. None. She's so helpless, so weak.

Her nose is running. As her nose runs, she comes back to herself. She finds one of the restaurant's big paper napkins in her bag. She blows her nose.

What are you doing blubbering in front of doors in the wee hours of the morning? You're a grown woman, you should be ashamed of yourself. You're the mother of a young girl. You're big, Leman. Shame on you, really!

Repeating this to herself, she finds her keys. She puts everything into her bag and rises to her feet.

She opens the door, enters. She forgets her square-toed, square-heeled witch's shoes in front of the door.

Whatever. She's inside now.

The familiar smell of her home, her own home, her tiny house. How good it is to smell that smell.

This is mine. With its smell, with the furniture, every centimetre is mine. My daughter's and mine. This is our nest. Our nest.

MY DAUGHTER'S.

She's looking at Muki, asleep and wheezing on the pull-out bed in the sitting room. She's taken out her false teeth and is wearing a nightgown with a rabbit design, and she's lying there like a dead person, her mouth sunken, a dry bone. How pathetic, how pitiable, how lovable, how wretched, Muki is sleeping there, wheezing away.

The door of Handan's room is standing half-open. Handan never sleeps with her door closed. She's watching her daughter lying there in her narrow wooden bed, which is painted pink each time the house is painted. Her brown hair is spread out on the pillow, like a baby, she's sleeping on her back the way she did when she was a baby. Her long, curling eyelashes are moving continuously on her cheeks. Her big lips, too. Her big lips are moving as if she's whispering something. Leman looks at her daughter's cheeks, lips, eyelashes, eyebrows, her little button nose. Later she looks at her long fingers, her hands, her meaty but thin arms, the breasts that are apparent through the cotton blanket, her waist, her legs.

She's looking at her baby, sheltered in that room, grown but still growing, beautiful but becoming more beautiful. The most beautiful baby, the most Handan baby in the world. Her baby. Leman's baby.

She was sent to me. My guest. God, look at how beautiful she is. Ever since she was born she warms me inside. What did I do to deserve such beauty? God, look at how beautiful my daughter is. How did I deserve you, my baby? Did they send you from above to this broken woman? The most beautiful baby to this defective woman? Having you was the best thing that could have happened to me. You're the most beautiful thing. You are the most sweet thing. You were sent to me. You were given to me.

Leman starts crying again.

What did I do to deserve you? I loved Harun. I loved Harun so much. They sent you to me from Harun.

Without opening her eyes, Handan says, 'Mother, are you back?'

Leman kisses Handan on the neck and cheeks, smelling her as she does so.

'Mother, I'm sleepy.'

'Sleep, my baby. It's still very early. Sleep, my baby. Go on sleeping.'

She wipes off the tears she left on Handan's face. She can't keep from stroking her cheeks.

My beautiful child. My beautiful gift. They sent you to me. They sent you.

She goes to the toilet and takes a piss. Carefully, she brushes her teeth and takes off her make-up. She puts lots of almond milk on her eyes. *Bebak*, bitter-almond milk. She wipes her eyes with wet cotton. She wets more cotton and wipes again. The cotton becomes completely black. The cotton she wipes her face with becomes earth-coloured, from the foundation. Red, from the lipstick.

The little basket by the toilet is filled with soiled balls of cotton. She looks at her face without make-up, her exhausted face: better. It's prettier and calmer than that messy face. Leman face.

She takes a long time brushing her hair. All of these rituals, like the smell of the house, Muki sleeping on the pull-out bed, Handan sleeping on her bed, makes her feel better.

She takes off her black lace panties and throws them in the laundry bag. She goes to the bedroom and puts on large, clean, white cotton panties. She wears them when she isn't meeting men; what Handan would call 'young girl's panties'.

Then she puts on her baby blue pyjamas. When she wears them Handan calls her 'my baby, my blue rabbit, my mother-baby'.

She wears them so that Handan will say these things to her in the morning.

She loves her daughter when she's sleeping at night.

Her daughter loves her during the day. Makes her feel good.

Have I loved my daughter less than I could have? Was my love defective? Am I lacking? Am I broken? That's how I am. I'm defective. Harun, you gave me Handan, then you upped and left. You dropped me and left me, and it still hurts. Not because of you, not because I miss you. I don't even remember you. It's the same with the Leman I was then, I've forgotten her too. But pain has a life of its own. I hurt inside. I feel empty. Since I can remember.

Leman starts crying again. But she's tired, she's drained. She can't keep up with her crying, can't give in. She lets her crying go wherever. She wraps herself in her quilt. She throws one leg out. She dives into sleep. Like a fish. She's already asleep.

Behiye home

. . . .

Behiye wakes to crashing sounds from the kitchen. Her room
– in fact a section of a room that had been partitioned off – is
right next to the kitchen. For ten or fifteen minutes she'd been
on the border between sleep and wakefulness, while her mother
went in and out of the kitchen. With the noise of breaking plates,
she crossed the border. She's fully awake.

'It's started again: my tormenting mother's kitchen antics.'

She feels an almost physical reaction, a desire to rush into the
kitchen to scream at her mother (she'd said it a million times:
don't do anything in the kitchen, mother. Don't, mother. Don't!).
As if terrible things were stuck in her mouth and she had to spray
them out, she couldn't stop them, she couldn't hold them in,
she had to spit them out right then and there, to get them out.
Something like that. Just like that.

This woman, this wretched bird, can't set the table without
dropping something and breaking it. She's certain to break
something, drop something, burn something, and will
undoubtedly, but undoubtedly, hurt herself. She'll burn her hand,
or her hair, or her eyelashes, or cut her fingers, or bang her elbow,
or spill something boiling on herself, or hit her head against
something: Kitchen accidents.

Her mother is a constant victim of kitchen accidents. A perverse victim. A serial victim. A victim who never tires of being a victim. A victim who's her own murderer. A perfect state of completing herself.

In an instant Behiye is at the kitchen door. She has that piercing look in her eyes, that look, reserved for her mother, that combines sarcasm and disgust. Her lips have disappeared. Her upper lip and her lower lip are pressed into her mouth. Her mouth is also slightly turned down, as if she's grinning. A grin that seems to say, 'How disgusted I am with you. You've made me lose my temper; at the same time you're such a pitiful little thing, you are not worth a thing.' A grin. A grind. Weigh. A weight that's called your mother.

'Behiye, my child, did I wake you? I'm sorry, my daughter. You know your mother.'

You know your mother.

Your mother is your geography. You're as much as your mother. Just that much. Be bored, cramped, depressed from here to Jakarta if you want. Suffocate from distress. Unable to breathe. You're your mother's daughter. An extension of your mother. Your mother's kitchen is your life. Your life is that kind of place: a place that engenders accidents.

There's no real damage. There's no real destruction. Not enough to have to make a new start. A fire, a tornado, a flood, an earthquake – no! Only just enough damage to keep managing, spreading through daily life. Small kitchen, house accidents. A little wounded mother. 'Could you pass the ointment?' That's all. But: all the time. Continuously. Little Accidents. Spreading.

'Mother, why are you working in the kitchen? Didn't I tell you a hundred thousand times? Mother didn't I tell you repeatedly? Leave it, Mother, I'll do it!'

Suddenly one of her hands becomes a fist and descends on her head. On her voice. Quiet Behiye! In order to say quiet Behiye to herself. The hand, her own hand, her right hand becomes a fist and is descending on her head. She's been screaming and shouting at her mother. Shouting is the most dangerous.

Shouting is the most dangerous thing.

The most dangerous thing is shouting.

It had happened, after all.

Her mother dropped the pink plastic dustpan on the floor and sat at the table. She'd collapsed. She took her head between her hands. Then she couldn't hold her head. She hit the table with her head. She pushed the plate she'd laid for Behiye – The New Plate, the white plate with a border of little squares – with her arm. The Old Plate consists of the broken pieces that scattered from the dustpan onto the floor.

She pushed it with her arm when she put her head on the table.

Behiye found herself leaping towards the table to save The New Plate That Had Been Laid for Behiye. Otherwise that would have broken too. Would that plate have broken too?

Behiye is looking. At the broken pieces of plate that fell out of the dustpan. At the margarine on the table, at the olives and jam – rose jam – which had been put out for her, at the slices of fresh bread that had been cut for her. The salt shaker in the shape of a female cat, the pepper shaker in the shape of a male cat. At their little kitchen. At the cheap kitchen cupboards. At the cracked tiles, at the plastic thing for drying dishes, the tray underneath it, the cloth bread-bag hanging from the wall, the misshapen carpet on the floor, at the toaster with the burnt handle, the grumbling old refrigerator, at the worn-out Fenerbahçe decals on the refrigerator, at the pitiful, miserable curtains with the ruffled ends and blue heart designs on a white background that was trying hopelessly to cheer up the kitchen. At the kitchen curtains her mother had made. At their impossibility.

Her mother is crying, crouched at the table.

The thing she'd least wanted had happened. This was what she'd feared most.

A Crying Session. How long is her mother going to cry this

time? What will Behiye have to say? What will she have to tell her? What will she have to do?

She'd saved the plate. The New Plate is safe and sound on the table. She's accomplished this. But her mother's crying? How is she going to stop that? If she went and grabbed a towel. If she started pressing it on to her head. Will she be able to stop the crying? What will she do, how will she stop it? Why is today beginning like this? Why did most days begin like this in a thoroughly fucked-up way? Why did they begin with damage and leave Behiye unable to breathe?

'Mother! Mother, I would have set my own breakfast table. Mother, I didn't say anything bad. Mother, look, if you don't cry...'

Eh? She has to say something here. Things will get better? I'll buy you some shoes? Stop here: I'll suffocate. I'm going to suffocate. One day, one moment, I won't be able to stand this anymore, this racket you make when you break something and your crying. I won't be able to stand it anymore.

'Mother, I won't be able to stand it.'

She cries even more. Even more. Can you believe it?

Should I fill the sink with water? Put the plug in. Stick my head in. Or else stick her crying head in. Would she struggle? She'd struggle. Would she splash water all over the place? She would.

As she's drying the floor on all fours, Behiye is thinking of herself.

Is it possible for me not to make you cry, Mother? And now is it possible for me to get you to stop? What am I to do, Mother? What's to be done with you? How can I get you to stop?

'Will you be quiet?'

Her mother lifts her head and takes a napkin from the wooden napkin holder in the shape of two birds kissing. She blows her nose. This is good. This is a good sign. The sound of her blowing her nose.

Abruptly, Behiye grabs the broom from under the sink.

She sweeps the broken pieces into the pink plastic dustpan. There's nothing left of The Old Plate. Crumbles. Broken. Pieces. Molecules. Nothing left. On its way into the garbage.

'Mother, I...' She could still press a button connected to one of the unknown wires that would start another crying fit. Hundreds of thousands of wires. Hundreds of buttons. Thousands. Lots of buttons. Lots. But. Tons.

'My fault, Behiye. I'm always dropping things. My fault.' A hiccup.

Behiye's heart is in her mouth from fear. That she'll start crying again. Let her go. Go. Just let her leave the house. Let Behiye have the house to herself.

'Mother, you'll be late. It's already ten o'clock.'

'Is it ten already? I'm late. Make yourself some breakfast, my daughter. I'll go buy fruits and vegetables and come back. I mean, I'll tell your father and he'll go to Eminönü to get them. You enjoy yourself today. It's not long before you start school.' An indrawn breath.

Behiye's heart is in her mouth again. Fear of making cry. Fear of the crying mother. Horror. Fear. Tunnel.

Her mother fastens the buttons of her shit-coloured cardigan. She's taken off her nurse's slippers and put on her nurse's shoes. She's put on her scarf. Her mother is ready to go to work. To her shop, to her box. Tailoring alterations. On the third floor of the arcade, she spends all day shortening trouser legs, pressing jacket sleeves, measuring for skirts, taking in waists. They're mostly sent from the shop where her father is chief clerk. Squeezed into her little box, she makes tea for herself on her little burner. She'll make tea. She'll drink tea. Then she'll sew. Yildiz the seamstress.

Her mother's name is Yildiz. How could that be? Such a merry, cheerful name?

Her name should be Accident. Wounded. Lame. Burnt. Her name should be Snail. Even that's cute!

Her mother quietly closes the door and leaves the house.

God, at last I have the house to myself!

Should she drink tea? Will tea soothe her shattered soul? Will it sew the pieces together? Will it ease the weariness of her soul? The shrinking of her heart? Will it heal her? Will tea heal her?

Behiye loves to drink tea. But now tea is something associated with her mother.

It belongs to her mother. Behiye is disgusted by anything associated with her mother. Anything that reminds her of her mother. Anything connected to her mother. Motherthings. Mothertouched.

That kitchen too. The place where her mother wounds herself. But the kitchen is a place that soothes Behiye. When she leaves, it becomes Behiye's. She puts away the things on the table. Into the refrigerator and the shelves. Only the wooden napkin holder in the shape of two birds kissing remains. The male and female cats remain. The jug remains. Those belong to the table. And the new plate. The plate her mother had cried into. The new plate she'd put out for Behiye, remains.

Behiye is disgusted by that plate. Her mother cried into that plate. She didn't cry into it, she pushed it. She touched it with her arm. Just before she started crying. She picks up the plate and throws it on the floor. Let it break, let's be rid of it. The plate doesn't break. Stubborn plate. Bad plate.

Never mind: The plate won.

She washes the plate. With lemon *Pril*.

She scrubs the sink. With *Cif*. The one that has ammonia.

She makes the tiles shine. Later she mops the kitchen floor. She mops the stone. It soothes her to mop the stone. She sanctified the kitchen. It's as if her mother hadn't set foot in the kitchen. She's made the kitchen spotless. She's chased out the demons of distress, nausea and crying. The kitchen has become hers.

Now the kitchen is brand new. Now the kitchen is ready. Ready for the ceremony of good cooking. She can go in and cook the evening meal. She's cleaned the kitchen and made it her own. New kitchen. Behiye Kitchen.

She tidies up the sitting room a bit.

She makes her mother's and father's beds. They sleep on hard, narrow, single beds with a small commode between them. She folds her father's cotton pyjamas and places them at the foot of his bed. Salim's pyjamas, the poor, poor man. Salim!

The door of her older brother's room is closed, as always. She opens the door. No! She's not going to go in and make his bed. She spits towards the Fenerbahçe poster above his headboard. This is part of her morning ritual. Sometimes she pokes two fingers in the eyes of the photograph of Tufan the soldier commando hanging on the wall across from his bed. At the glass. Sometimes. Tufan the stockbroker. Office boy. Tufan the nationalist office boy who thinks he's a stockbroker. Made of straw. With a brain the size of a lentil. A brain that small. Lentil-brain Tufan.

She closed Tufan's door. Tufan is finished for today.

She's hungry. But she's not going to eat. She's going to lose a lot of weight. There's no other way to get out of this boredom capsule. She has to be thin enough to pass through the eye of a needle. Behiye has to lose weight. She's not exactly tall. But she's not short either. But when she loses weight she'll look taller. Just like a ribbon. Like a whip. Like a ruler. Like a stick. A lot of things.

She's not going to eat. She's just not going to eat food.

As she feels pleased with this idea, the idea of never eating again, she's reminded of the feeling she had yesterday. THE FEELING YOU'LL BE RESCUED. You'll be rescued from being a bug who loves no one and is loved by no one. Wonderful things will happen to you. Feeling.

She'd been shaken up since she woke that morning. So much that her head spun from it. Wrath, anger, disgust, nausea, boredom, ritual: ritual of cleaning, sanctifying, straightening, ritual of hatred, The Feeling You'll Be Rescued, the memory of The Feeling. She remembered. It felt good.

Her head is spinning. She has to get out of the house at once. She puts on her big purple boots. She bought them in the *Atlas Pasaj*. She's wearing a long-sleeved black T-shirt and black jeans. Size 42. Embarrassing. Soon she'll be 36.

She puts on her black, hooded jacket. She flings away the backpack she'd grabbed. She didn't want to, but that is also purple. She looks like someone who only wears purple and black. But it's true. That's all she wears. She doesn't want people to think that. But they're right to think that.

The bus came. She jumped on the bus. Taksim. Yes, that's fine. She knows the place. She can't know every place. You can't know every place, Behiye.

The Feeling You'll Be Rescued.

Will you come and rescue me? Or will you leave me here; will you leave me in this dark, wet place?

Alive. Buried.

Buried. The sun is shining. With all her strength, Behiye tries to hang on to The Feeling You'll Be Rescued. It could happen, perhaps.

Handan home

· ·

When Handan wakes towards eleven, she finds her mother in the kitchen, with her Nescafé Gold and her Salem Lights, singing along with a song that is playing on the kitchen radio.

Nana nan
Nana nanan
Nanana naaa

'Careless whispers,' says Handan.
'What? What do you mean?'
'That's the name of the song: It means thing, careless whispers. Some nonsense like that.'
'Careless whispering?' Leman says to herself with the self-confidence of a deep-sea diver who has dived deep and come up with wonderful pearls.
Suddenly, she pulls herself out of these meaningful depths to the daily shallowness.
'How's my most beautiful baby Handan this morning?'
Her mother's voice that first cracked because of all the coffee and cigarettes since she was seventeen, and then smoothed,

mended, thicker and more beautiful, the voice of a woman who'd seen difficult times and gotten through them. A nasal voice that delighted Handan.

'Has Muki gone, my coffee-drinking, cigarette-smoking blue baby rabbit?'

'It was seven or so in the morning, I was in bed; she said bye-bye and left. It's a problem for her to stay with us during the week, you know. My dear Muki. At her age she's still wearing herself out cleaning houses. Handan, your mother Leman isn't worth two pennies. Think of it, I couldn't help out the person closest to us, this reminder of your grandmother. Shame on you, Leman! Shame, shame.'

'Mother, pleeease. Don't get started on this guilt trip again. You've done the best you could. You raised me by yourself, you kept this house going…And last year who paid for Muki's operation and hospital expenses? What more could you have done? My blue rabbit, you've worn your blue pyjamas again. How loveable, how kissable you look.'

She gives her mother many kisses on the cheeks and neck like a little kid. She perches a little on her lap.

'Why did you ask about Muki? If she was here, what nice eggs she would have made. Isn't that so? That's why you asked.'

'Yes. I miss Muki's eggs. I'm also as hungry as a wolf. What do we have in the house for breakfast?'

'Wait, let me call Cetin. He'll bring us some things from Hayri's. Would I let my daughter go hungry?'

As she walks back to her room, Handan sighs and says, 'Neverrr.'

It would be difficult to find a child who'd been left hungry as much as Handan. Leman had never so much as fried an egg in her life. Sometimes she buys unnecessarily expensive cold-cuts, or rather she orders them by phone. They don't eat most of it, and it goes bad, and is thrown out.

She doesn't think about food until it's time to eat; then,

ordering by telephone from restaurants and delis and kebab shops becomes an urgent problem. The problem is solved by ordering out; and she doesn't think about it or do anything until the next time someone's hungry.

Throughout the day, Leman never gets hungry, and gets by on cigarettes and coffee. It never occurs to her that anyone else might get hungry, so she always faces the indescribable calamity of having to order at the last minute. The Leman Method.

When Handan returns to the table with her hair in a ponytail, her beautiful behind squeezed into blue jeans and her breasts small and pert under her pink T-shirt, her mother reaches for her Salems, thinking about all that might befall this young girl who could turn heads in the street with her beauty.

'Don't smoke now. Smoke after we've eaten something, my blue rabbit.'

The doorbell rings. Leman looks at her feet, which she's swinging in her transparent plastic high-heeled slippers, and which shout, 'Pedicure!' Immediately she feels depressed. In fact, summer is almost over. But her feet look terrible without a pedicure. She can't look after herself. She just can't find the appetite, the energy to look after herself.

'My bag is in my bedroom. Take it from there, baby.'

Opening the door, Handan says, 'One minute, Cetin.' She runs to the bedroom.

'Mother, there's no money in your bag!'

Leman gets up and hurries to the door, swinging her hips.

'Cetin, tell your brother-in-law to put it on our account. I forgot to take money out of the bank.'

Looking at the floor so as not to look at Leman's breasts, Cetin says, 'My brother-in-law Hayri wants you to pay what you already owe.'

Leman takes two more steps and nails Cetin. 'My darling boy, has your big sister Leman ever left even a penny's debt unpaid? Who's been your best customer all these years?'

'You have, sister Leman.' He finds the courage to glance at Leman's blue eyes.

He first began to masturbate, fantasizing about Leman. Still his 'big sister' Leman is a hundred times more exciting than all those look-alike girls on the paparazzi programmes. Her voice, her smell, her face, her body is so very exciting.

'All right, big sister Leman. Excuse me.' His voice is on the ground, with his eyes.

'Oh, Cetin, I've watched you grow up since you were this big. How could I ever be angry with you?' She reaches out and strokes his hair, on which he's put about a quarter of a bottle of gel.

Cetin thinks, she watched me grow up? Do you know, Leman? I mean, does she understand? Doesn't she know how improperly I've fantasised about her?

He blushes from head to toe. He runs down the stairs. That evening would be devoted to big sister Leman. Without a doubt.

'Mommie, you were going to find the money for my course by this weekend.'

'How much is the course?'

'The best is the one that's four days a week. It has study sessions too. One billion seven hundred and thirty-four million.'

'All of these numbers straight in the morning. Mommie will find it somehow. Let's sit down and have a nice breakfast.'

'Let's have a snack, you mean.'

'You know that ever since your father insulted me when we got married I can't do anything about food. Why are you giving me a hard time? Am I a mother who'd let her princess go hungry?'

'Come on, let's not go into this old melodrama.'

'Don't make fun of me,' says Leman in a flirtatious way.

She takes out a cigarette and lights it. She doesn't have a penny in the bank, for God's sake. They've hit bottom completely. All those debts, including the credit cards.

'We'll see if you can register without paying. I'll go talk to the course director. We'll pay it in five–ten days. We're not going anywhere, after all.'

'Mother! You're not going to go and fool around with him? Please don't go. I'd be so embarrassed. I wouldn't be able to look anyone in the face.'

'Handan! That's no way to talk to your mother!' There's a lump in her throat. Her own Handan! How could her baby say something like that? She's changing. As she grows up she's becoming malicious; she's wounding Leman.

What's happening to sweet Handan?

'Look, Mother, you're not going to go talk to the course director or anything like that. We either find the money in two days or we forget the course. I'll start working at a shop in Akmerkez. So what?'

'My Handan becoming a shop girl! I won't have it! Don't be silly, Handan. Don't upset me. Did you get that idea just to ruin my day?'

'It's better than being a mistress,' she says, swallowing the words from her lips.

'Excuse me? What did you say?'

'Nothing. I didn't say anything. It's impossible to eat with you.' With a moustache of orange juice still on her lip, Handan gets up from the table, goes to the sitting room and sits in front of the television.

Leman finishes her 'cigarette of pain'. After painful incidents she always smokes a cigarette of pain. There are also cigarettes of joy. Cigarettes of consolation. Cigarettes of sadness. Cigarettes of longing, of patience, of stubbornness. Cigarettes of waiting, of calming down, of sun, of rain. There's a cigarette to accompany the emotions of every stage of life, every period of time, every feeling, and they have a name. Leman Cigarettes.

She puts water on for one more nescafé. Later she throws away the food on the table. She can't stand to see it sit there waiting to be eaten.

After all that work, she sits down in front of her coffee. She lights a tiredness cigarette and thinks about whom she can get money from for the course.

Who can she ask? There's only Cevdet. She and Cevdet separated when Handan was twelve. Has it been four years already? Cevdet bought this apartment for them. He's the one who rescued them from that house in Bomonti, and from those nosy, interfering neighbours. Cevdet was Handan's 'uncle'.

Later there was that blade of a relationship. Ayhan, who all but destroyed Leman, ate her up, burned her. She doesn't even want to think about him. There were two or three people before and after Ayhan, two or three impossible pricks. They wore Leman out.

She can't call Ayhan. The balance and strength she'd established would be turned upside down, she'd fall into the fire again. There was also the oath. After their last telephone conversation, she'd sworn on Handan's name never to call him again.

'Here you are again, Cevdet. Who else do I have in my life?' The thinking cigarette after the tiredness cigarette worked out fine.

In the sitting room, Handan had turned on that foreign music station, with its thumping sounds. Never in her life had Leman even said, 'Turn the television down' to Handan. Thinking about this, she realised she'd never in her life scolded Handan for anything. Her grades, when she came and went, when she went to sleep, who she saw, the telephone, what she ate and drank, what she wore, what she did when…

My poor baby. My Handan. My guest from God. You brought yourself up. My most beautiful gift. My daughter.

She feels a terrible longing for Handan. She goes to the sitting room.

'I've found who I'm going to ask for the money for the course.'

'Where? Are you going to ask Hayri the grocer on the phone?'

'My baby…Don't be cruel to your mother. What's the date today?'

'How should I know? The end of September.'

'My baby, today is Thursday. The day of the Ulus Market. We haven't gone to the new site yet. Let's jump in a taxi and go. We'll buy ourselves some nice new clothes. We can buy winter clothes, for instance. Won't that be nice, my baby?'

'Mother, you don't have any money, what are you going to buy them with? And who are you going to beg the money for the course from?'

'Handan, please…they take credit cards at the market. You're going to ask your uncle Cevdet for the course money. Tell him it costs three and a half billion. We'll use the rest to pay off our debts. But we can't tell him that, can we?'

'Mother, be reasonable! We haven't seen his face for years; we are still abusing him to the hilt. And aren't you ashamed of using me? Besides, aren't you aware of how much interest we pay each month on your credit cards?'

'I'll call him, Handan,' says Leman. Tiny tears form in her eyes. She collapses into an armchair and reaches for the pack of cigarettes on the coffee table.

'Go ahead and break poor Leman's heart. If there's any place left to break, go ahead and break it.'

'My little blue rabbit,' says Handan, jumping on to her lap. 'Don't be upset. All right, I'll call Uncle Cevdet. But I'll only ask him for the cost of the course. Come, get dressed and we'll go to the Ulus Market. We'll buy you one or two nice things to cheer you up. I could eat some of that lady's olive-oil dolmas. I'm starting to get hungry again. Do we have any money left in the jar? Money for the taxi and the dolmas? Has my little blue rabbit spent all the money, or is there any left?'

She smothers her mother with kisses. Her child-mother. She can't help it. She suffers, she gets worn out, she collapses, but she never grows up. Girl-child. Handan has never loved anyone so much in her life. She can't help what she does. My child-mother. She stays that way. My girl-child mother. Leman baby: my mother.

Taksim

• •

Behiye is in Taksim now.

In front of the place where the water flows over the stones
– FALSE WATERFALL – near the newsagent's. Blind people are playing
music on electric keyboards, magnified by huge speakers.

They are, really.

A blind boy is playing, seated on a white plastic stool. A blind
woman is singing into the microphone at the top of her voice.

Growing accustomed is more difficult than love
Growing accustomed is like a bleeding wound.

'Shitty blind music,' says Behiye. The weather is hot, after all.
This noise seems too much. It's as if these blind people's music
makes the weather hotter. It's suffocating Behiye. As if her mother
has brought a sweater from inside, and is trying to wrap it around
her neck. That's what the blind people's music feels like to her.
She wants to kick the electric keyboard with her big purple boots.
To wreck everything, the speakers and all.

These people are blind. And they make music. They seem
better off than me. As if everything is going like clockwork for
them. They're in a better situation than I am.

Situation. Strange word. This is the situation. Everyone is in a better situation than I am. I'm the most distressed. The most depressed. In this situation.

As she left the house she was trying to remember The Feeling You'll Be Rescued. It would make her feel better. Today, today for once, she wants to be better. She wants that feeling to flow through her like lemonade. She takes off her coat and ties it around her waist. Taking long strides down Istiklal in her big purple boots, she feels a little cooler. She's also hungry. As she grows hungry, her demons begin to flock around her.

A number of demons, hooded like the ones in fairy tales, flock around her head and land on her short red hair. Imagining this scene makes her smile. As she smiles, she wrinkles her nose. That's what happens when she smiles. When she smiles her nose always wrinkles. It makes Behiye look sweet. She has hundreds of little freckles on her nose.

Behiye has red-orange hair. She has brown eyes, and hundreds, thousands of freckles. She cuts her hair short, and is embarrassed by its color because so many people are dying their hair red now. If she wasn't afraid of hairdressers, she'd have her hair dyed black. She's embarrassed by her freckles too. Because they take her out of the ordinary. She doesn't want to be a 'red-haired girl with freckles'. That's why she goes around as an awkward, hunched, short-haired, long-faced girl. The girl no one notices. Yes, this, it's better.

What does she have that would attract notice? It's best not to be noticed.

Behiye's favourite bookstore is near the end of the avenue. Her favourite bookstore.

It's a very good bookstore, because the people who work there are nice. A nice girl works there. She knows that Behiye steals books, but she closes her eyes to the situation.

Books are very expensive, though. Since she was twelve, Behiye hasn't been able to get her fill of reading. She couldn't, or she'd die. She'd have killed herself. She wouldn't have been able to bear that balloon of distress called home. She reads constantly, she has no other recourse. Books are her medicine. There's no other way. Otherwise she would have died.

At this bookstore, there's a place on the top floor where you can read the books. When Behiye climbs up there and pretends to look through the books, she takes out her little pocket-knife and pries off those plastic things stuck on to the covers. Only from the books she's going to steal. Not in big numbers. After she takes the plastic things off, she throws the books in her bag. The bag she never closes. The nice, good-hearted bag. It's quite old.

Later, she goes downstairs and puts some of the books back. The 'I looked at all of them. I'm only going to buy this one' game. At this point several of them, freed from their plastic things, lie like babies in her bag. She goes to the cashier and buys the cheapest books. The alarms don't sound for her. Once, they did sound. But because of the plastic thing on the book she'd paid for. They said they were very sorry. It was pleasant.

She bought Alberto Moravia's *Jealousy*; that was the cheapest one.

She stole Kafka's *America* and Sartre's *Nausea*. She couldn't do without these. She'd rescued them from their plastic things. She's had to.

Outside, she walks down Istiklal to the sound of Tarkan's *Lamb Lamb*.

> *Throw me out if you want, kiss me if you want*
> *But first listen, look into my eyes*
> *Believe me, this time*
> *I've understood the situation, I've made vows.*

What the hell, says Behiye. What's this? If it was up to me I'd throw you out. I'd toss you on to the endless garbage heap of kitsch.

Behiye has such a garbage heap. She'd like to throw so many things around into her endless garbage heap.

Behiye doesn't listen to Turkish music at all. Turkish music brings her down. She buys pirate CDs; for a while she's been stealing CDs. But stealing CDs is difficult. Much more difficult. So she waits for most things to be pirated. Late, but clean. What can she do?

Lamb Lamb is blasting from every shop on the avenue.

TARKANPRESSURE, says Behiye. But the song has a looseness to it that does a person good. It doesn't drive you as crazy. It creates a joyful atmosphere.

I own three books. I have three wonderful books. This makes for three wonderful weeks. I have three books. Three! Three!

She has the urge to run shouting down the street.

Put the brakes on, Behiye. Drink a tea. What time is it; you still haven't eaten or drunk anything. Get a grip on yourself. A grip.

'What time is it' reminded her of Çiğdem. They were supposed to meet in front of the course in Beşiktaş.

This year they'd graduated from the same school. The same high school. The girls' high school: across from the tramway stop. They'd gone to the same middle school, the same primary school.

Behiye can't escape Çiğdem, and carries her from here to there like a suitcase full of unneeded things. She's fed up with Çiğdem; but what would she do without her? She's her only friend in the world. Çiğdem has no idea about many of Behiye's thoughts and feelings. She talks constantly, and Behiye listens. When she talks, it's necessary to give advice. Constantly.

Çiğdem takes this advice and cuts it into little bits and pieces with her scissors. Turns it into a bird. She adapts it to her own thoughts. But she never stops taking advice from Behiye. She's constantly asking for advice. But then she forgets it. Or rather, she translates it into her own ideas.

Behiye knows that no matter how thorough she has been with Çiğdem, she's never quite reached her. But their relationship started when they were children. Çiğdem is the only reason Behiye is not alone one hundred per cent of the time. That's why she values her. She behaves badly to her. She puts her down, tells her off, pushes her and shoves her. But she doesn't throw her out of her life. She holds on to her. Her one and only Çiğdem. Out of necessity. Out of need.

Çiğdem hadn't been able to get into university. When she was filling out the form, she'd reached beyond her abilities. She was stubborn; didn't listen to Behiye. She'd been left out in the cold.

Now she's chosen a private university preparation course in Beşiktaş. The nearest ones to where they lived were in Aksaray. But no, she had to choose one in Beşiktaş.

'A better class of people go there. Let's escape from the Çemberlitaş–Beyazit–Sultanahmet–Eminönü–Aksaray triangle.'

'A pentagon; it's five sides,' corrected Behiye.

She waits for Behiye: in order to choose a course that will last a year. At two o'clock. On the right, at the foot of the hill, in front of her first choice of private courses.

It's half past two. She forgot. Çiğdem is something to be easily forgotten: a broken umbrella, a threadbare shawl, a heavy and bulging suitcase full of boring things.

Çiğdem is used to Behiye being late. Behiye always comes at the last minute. Çiğdem always waits. It doesn't bother Çiğdem to wait for Behiye. In the end Behiye always comes. She may be a little late, or very late, but she always comes.

Behiye goes and jumps on a Sariyer minibus. She gets out right in front of the school. Çiğdem is not on the front stairs. She's not at the door. She goes and looks around in the registration office on the left just past the entrance.

She sits at the foot of the stairs and begins to wait. The school candidates aren't horsing around. Thank God. She can sit comfortably.

The weather is hot and everything is going well. Then she sees a girl. A girl walking straight towards her. Bouncing a little. Looking into her eyes.

Her hair is gathered into a ponytail on top of her head. She's wearing a tight pink T-shirt and loose, low-waisted blue jeans. On her feet, thick-soled, grey-white sports shoes. She is bouncing. Towards her.

Between her T-shirt and her jeans, three or four fingers of flesh are showing. Not much. That's all. And her eyes are so beautiful. They're big eyes, but also slanting. Cat's eyes. They shine. Or at least it seems so to Behiye. They shine, as if they're scattering light.

She's wearing a pink cardigan over her pink T-shirt. A furry one. The kind they call mohair. One of those little cardigans they make for babies. The sweater has no collar. In front, two mohair balls hang by pink threads. It closes with a bowknot like a baby's sweater. Two pink balls. Bouncing in front of her.

By God, what a beautiful creature! She's coming toward Behiye! She waves to Behiye.

Behiye blushes. She feels hot. Where does this baby-sweatered girl know her from?

She gets up and leans against the banister. Her legs almost give out from under her. They're shaking like mad. Her knees are knocking together. She's very excited. But why?

'Shhh. Are you here at last?'

With a jump, she looks behind her.

Çiğdem! The girl climbs the steps two at a time and joins Çiğdem.

'She's here at last. We've gotten hungry waiting for you, Behiye. Why can't you be on time for once? Look, this is Handan.'

'Hello,' says the girl with the baby cardigan. 'We want your opinion about something, Behiye.'

She knows her name. She's learned her name. Her name: Handan. My name: Behiye. She said my name. She's learned it.

The Feeling You'll Be Rescued flows through her as if it's being pumped from her toes to the top of her head. The Feeling You'll Be Rescued. An unbelievable sense of delight invades her soul. She submits to it. How does this beautiful creature, this baby girl, know her name? And I know her name. Her name: Handan. Her name: The Feeling You'll Be Rescued. She's come to rescue me.

Getting acquainted

· ·

'Come, let's go sit somewhere,' says Handan.

In her baby girl voice. In her breathy, warm voice. A pink wool voice, soft to the touch.

Behiye wants to eat Handan's voice. The cardigan, the ponytail, she wants to eat them all. The way people feel when they want to eat babies, that's how this girl makes her feel. She wants to sit on her lap and kiss her and caress her.

It hasn't even been five minutes since she set eyes on the girl. Perhaps you've gone out of your mind. She feels as if she wants to kidnap the girl. Don't be silly, Behiye. Go drink some tea. Come to your senses. You've gone mad.

But she can't keep from smiling. Her nose gets all wrinkled; how delighted, happy. She wants to jump for joy. She wants to shout. To embrace and kidnap the baby girl.

Thank God, Çiğdem doesn't notice. Çiğdem lives in her own world. She's always involved with her own big problems. If they were sitting at Behiye's and Behiye becomes mad at her mother because her mother had broken something in the kitchen again and cut her finger, and Behiye had grabbed a bread knife because she wanted to be free of all these little accidents once and for all, once and for all, Çiğdem wouldn't notice. She just keeps talking about whatever she's talking about. She doesn't sense anything about Behiye. She doesn't notice. Limited Çiğdem. Çiğdem Limited: she doesn't care about anything except herself. Reserved: There's no room for anyone else's feelings on that full table. Full Çiğdem. Empty-headed.

'Let's go to the pastry shop across the road,' says Çiğdem in her pipe-like voice. It's like a frightful stand-pipe, and it brings Behiye back to herself. Pipe Çiğdem.

'Fine,' says Behiye. 'I have time.'

The baby girl orders a lemonade and a pastry for herself.

Behiye orders the same thing, because that's what the girl ordered. Çiğdem orders some of those little, little pizzas. She orders a plate of those tiny pastry shop pizzas and a tea. Autonomous Çiğdem. She's gotten hungry thinking about her big problems. Dwarf pizzas will restore her.

'Handan and I met at the orientation meeting the other day. What a beautiful girl, isn't she?' she says bluntly.

'Oh, Çiğdem, please,' purrs the baby cat girl. She closes her eyes briefly and lowers her head.

She's embarrassed. Of course, everyone finds her beautiful. When we entered the pastry shop and sat down at our table, a number of heads turned. What a strange thing that is. Everyone sees her. Everyone looks at her. At this beautiful creature. But for me she's The Feeling You'll Be Rescued. She's my good news, not theirs. It's me she's come to.

Again she feels as if she wants to kidnap Handan. The way some women feel when they see a baby and say, 'What if I kidnap this baby and kiss it and smell it?' The way some animals feel when they see baby animals.

'Behiye got into Bosphorus University,' says Çiğdem in her 'you're beautiful but my friend is intelligent' voice.

'Bosphorus University? I don't believe it.'

'In a shitty department. My verbal score was good, that's the way it worked out.'

'What I want most is to get into the translation department

at Bosphorus University,' says the baby girl, with a touch of sadness in her voice. 'I only got pass marks in verbal and foreign language.'

'But they weren't good enough to get into the translation department,' neighs Çiğdem. Horse Çiğdem. Her laugh sounds like a horse neighing.

Handan lowers her head and says, 'They weren't good enough.'

Behiye wants to slap Çiğdem's meaningless face. She wants to pull her chair out from under her. Falling to the ground might knock some sense into her. Stupid pig. Pig Çiğdem.

'Your wonderful marks weren't enough to get into Bosphorus either,' she says, squinting her eyes. Behiye tends to squint her eyes when she gets annoyed. Then, her small eyes all but disappear.

'Didn't Bosphorus start this Monday?' says The Feeling You'll Be Rescued.

Behiye's face relaxes again. Her nose wrinkles. She can't keep herself from smiling. The girl's voice does something to her. 'It opened,' she says. 'I didn't pass the English exam. I have to spend a year in prep. I thought it wouldn't matter if I started next week. After all, the situation is going to be confused during the first week.'

'I don't believe it!' toots The Pipe. 'Your foreign language marks were excellent. It's not possible that you didn't pass the exam. You did it intentionally. I swear, Behiye, you did it intentionally.'

'I thought I would take it easy for a year,' says Behiye. She starts to laugh. Because of Handan! Otherwise she would have died before admitting this to Çiğdem. She doesn't understand these kinds of things.

'In other words you'll honour your new school with your presence next week. You're something else, Behiye. I told you. She's super.' Çiğdem is neighing again.

It gets on Behiye's nerves. If she had remote control, she'd like to press a button and make Çiğdem disappear. Disappear. For ever.

'If it were me I'd want to start at Bosphorus right away,' says Handan. She settles her eyes on Behiye's eyes.

Behiye lowers her eyes.

Her eyes are green. Brown. Her eyes are both green and brown. The most beautiful cat eyes. Her eyes are so beautiful. So beautiful she can't look at them. She blushes, and so forth.

Çiğdem won't notice that I'm blushing. She won't notice how happy I am. She can't know I've finally met my Feeling You'll Be Rescued. Handan is not something she could understand. Handan.

'Handan.'

'Yes,' she says, searching for Behiye's eyes with her cat baby eyes. 'Yes, Behiye.'

She has nothing to say to her. But she wants to hear that voice say her name. For those eyes to touch her eyes. Inside her, unknown birds fly. As if they might lift her into the air out of her seat.

I might fly. I might levitate into the air from my seat. She has come.

'Should we register here, Behiye? You know about these things.'

She turns and looks at Çiğdem's twitching, glass-blue eyes. At her fat, meaningless face. Nevertheless, she knows; people find Çiğdem beautiful. They like that potato face. What nonsense!

'Yes, this is a good place,' says Behiye. 'I'll help you study. I won't have to work hard at school this year. I'll be practically free. Both of you... I mean, I can help you.'

'You're one of a kind, Behiye; you're my super friend. Tuesday, Wednesday, Thursday, Friday, classes from half past eight in the morning until noon; study sessions until seven in the evening. That's what they said.'

'Yes, we can ask questions during the study sessions,' says the girl with the baby cardigan. 'It would be wonderful if you could help us.'

'Let's go,' says Behiye. 'I'm going to go home and make dinner.'

She doesn't believe she said this. She doesn't want to part from Handan at all. She wants to put Handan into her bag with her stolen books and take her with her. Not without her. With her. But she's on fire, and wants to run through the streets. She can't sit still anymore.

Opening her cat eyes wide, Handan says, 'Do you know how to cook? In my house no one knows how to cook. Neither me nor my mother. We're practically dying of hunger.'

She's laughing. Such a sweet laugh. Like a baby's laugh. An inward laugh. As if she wants to keep it and not let it escape. Her inner laugh. Just for herself. Her laugh. Rose.

'What do you like most?' asks Behiye. 'What food do you like?'

'I like lemon kofte,' says Handan. 'I like tomato pilaff. Dolma. Potatoes with meat, chickpeas. Aubergines. Mmm, I like all sorts of home-cooked meals. My mouth is watering.'

'I'll cook for you. I'll make you lemon kofte. I'll make whatever you want.' At that moment she would have run miles to make lemon kofte for Handan. The desire is so strong it's coming out of her ears.

Hungry baby. Hungry little girl baby. She hasn't been fed. She's been left hungry. I'll feed you. I'll look after you.

'Will you, really? How lovely. Perhaps we'll be very close friends. Wouldn't that be nice, Çiğdem? The three of us.'

She could see the cloud of jealousy in Çiğdem's face; she's taken her in. How sweet, what a baby. Let Çiğdem just fuck off. Let her get lost. I'll stay with you. You came to me. To rescue me. You came for me to love you. So I won't have to be an insect any more. Handan.

She opens her little pink backpack and takes out two mussel shells. She gives the purple one to Behiye, and the smaller brown one to Çiğdem.

'Let them be a reminder of this day. I love mussel shells. I just got these in Beşiktaş.'

'You didn't gather them yourself on the shores of Malaysia?' says Behiye. Her voice rings out. Trying to be funny.

The baby girl lowers her eyes again and says, 'I didn't gather them.'

What have I done? How rude I've been! I'm like a bulldozer. Like a machine in a doll's house.

'That's not what I wanted to say. I – this is the most beautiful gift I've received in my life. I was just trying to make a joke. I'll make lemon kofte for you. I'll make whatever you like. Dolma, chickpeas.'

Behiye stops. Çiğdem is staring at her with cow's eyes. Çiğdem has understood. That's all I need. I've made a mess of things. I'm going to frighten her off. What a hopeless, stupid, boorish tanker I am. Tanker. Bulldozer. I'm a. Bull. Dozer.

She finds herself reaching out and taking Handan's hand. She did it without realising. Otherwise she'd rather die than do something like that. She dies of embarrassment when she sees herself holding her hand. That light, elegant, white hand. She's very embarrassed. But she doesn't let go of the hand. It's so light, like a bird. She's gone all red again.

'Come on, Behiye, aren't you going to be late?' says the stand-pipe voice.

'No. It's not that important. It would be nice if I'd gathered them myself. But I bought them from a shop on the Ortaköy road.'

She's smiling. Showing her dimples. She didn't write me off. She understood. She knew. She knows me. She's getting to know me. She knows me.

They make plans for the following day. Çiğdem and Handan are going to come and register. Behiye is going to come too. 'I'll come too,' she said. It's done. Otherwise she wouldn't have gone home. Not without knowing if she'd see Handan again.

The baby girl's cell phone rings. 'All right, mother.' 'Yes, mommie. I'm registering tomorrow.' 'Of course, mother baby.'

Mother baby? She purrs as she talks to her mother.

'Sorry,' she says as she hangs up. She's so polite, like a fairy-tale princess. Her favourite food is lemon kofte. In the world.

'I'll see you tomorrow,' says Behiye as they part. 'At one o'clock. In front of the door.' Her freckled nose wrinkles. She laughs.

'Bye bye,' says the baby girl. 'Take care of yourself.'

Behiye hates this phrase. What an asinine farewell. But when she uses it, it becomes something else. She takes a disgusting phrase and turns it into something beautiful.

'I'll take care of myself,' she says.

'Come on, Behiye,' says Çiğdem. In a haughty tone of voice. Her tomato lips are pursed. Her expression says – I'm not at all happy: what's going on here?

Feeble-minded pipe. It's up to you.

I found you. It's you I found. I found you in order to love you. Behiye wants to shout this.

But she holds herself back. You've gone mad enough. What nonsense you talked. You went completely mad. In front of that ox Çiğdem. Furthermore. Furt-her-more.

On the bus, she wants to sing at the top of her voice. It's embarrassing, but she wants to sing *Lamb Lamb*. She can't stop smiling. She's laughing. She's talking nonsense to Çiğdem. She's talking so that she can smile comfortably.

'It's come to me,' she says at one point.

'What's come?'

The Feeling You'll Be Rescued, she says to herself. Blockhead Çiğdem. What could you know about my Feeling You'll Be Rescued?

'Whatever,' says Behiye. Suddenly, like an hourglass that's been turned, she feels an unaccountable love for Çiğdem. Poor Çiğdem. Goose brain.

She kisses Çiğdem on the cheek. 'Let's jump off the bus here.

Let's run home. Look how beautiful the weather is; a person can't sit still.'

'What's going on with you, Behiye?' says Çiğdem, smiling. 'You're very peculiar today. You're like a child.'

'There's nothing going on. Come on, Çiğdem, let's race like we did in primary school. The first one to reach the corner wins.'

Behiye begins to run. She turns around and shouts at the top of her voice.

Stupid Çiğdem; clumsy Çiğdem
Catch me if you can

She's laughing as she runs. There are tears in her eyes from laughing. She stops and wipes her eyes. She can't remember the last time she was this happy. She can't remember.

Family evening

• •

The door of the apartment building has a nylon string. A dirty nylon string tied to the latch. When you pull it, you find yourself enveloped by the smells of the building: Smelly Building. The smell of cooked onions. The moment you enter, it blankets you. Blanket Building. Behiye entered. It enveloped Behiye. The Blanket of Smells Building.

There are shoes in front of every door. This way, you know how many people are inside (except for babies). The babies don't have shoes. You can't know how many babies are inside.

As she climbs to the third floor, Behiye counts fourteen pairs of shoes. Once, on a holiday, Behiye counted all of sixty-two pairs of shoes. And this didn't include babies. Because the number of babies are unknown, they're represented by X. Unknown.

Most of the shoes are worn out. Old and battered. Gnarled and misshapen. Throw me out, please throw me out, they seem to beg. The backs are crushed, the toes are scuffed. Dusty, muddy, neglected, miserable shoes.

How many times, how many times, has Behiye wanted to gather all those shoes into a garbage bag (*Koroplast*, blue, 80 × 110cm, jumbo; Behiye's favourite) and throw them all into the garbage. To rescue the owners from those frightful shoes. So they could be free of those depressing shoes, and be happy. So that every time she enters and leaves her house Behiye will be saved from counting the shoes, of thinking how miserable and depressed these shoes make their owners.

But it would be impossible for Behiye to throw all those shoes away and replace them with new ones. Impossible Behiye. She can't throw those shoes away and replace them with fairy-tale shoes. After all, she's not a witch. She's not a magician; nor is she rich. All that she is: Impossible Behiye.

Behiye's mother doesn't make people take their shoes off at the door. How many times. Who knows how many times her mother asked the next-door neighbours not to leave their shoes in front of their door? In order not to seem like 'bad people' to this strange woman, they don't take their shoes off at the door. That is, when they remember not to. This embarrasses Behiye too. As if they were that well off; as if they were one of those television families who wear their shoes inside…The same way her mother won't buy plastic dishes in order that she won't break them all the time. As if it wasn't a house of damages, and she wasn't an unhappy, accident-prone woman. As if she was a step higher on the social ladder. Embarrassing.

Today, as she climbed the steps through the smell, she didn't count the distressing shoes. She wouldn't allow herself to count. Outside the neighbour's door there were two pairs of children's shoes and one pair of woman's shoes (all together: three pairs). She just looked. One of the children's shoes was red, patent leather and in good condition. At least. Least. Finished.

To think that she'd finished high school; that she was free of that awful girls' school pleased her terribly. And today there was something more important than the building's scruffiness, its signs of poverty that distressed and depressed her: Behiye has met her. She's found her.

As she thinks this, it's as if bells are ringing within her. She feels alive. She feels very well. She feels wonderfully well, and happy. She feels very well. She feels as if everything is possible. Possibility Behiye.

It's five o'clock now. For an hour, an hour and a half, until the Armed Occupation Forces enter the house, she cooks in the kitchen, her small but clean country, unstained by her mother's accidents, for a brief time her own poor but healthy ground. While she cooks, she thinks about Handan. She's so happy.

In a circle of happiness. No one could enter this circle and break it. A halo. Surrounded by a halo of happiness. She'll see Handan tomorrow. Tomorrow and every day. She'll see Handan every God-given day, every God-given day. A day won't pass without Handan. She knows this as she knows her name. She knows this as she knows her name: Behiye.

There are six large courgettes in the refrigerator. She makes courgette moussaka with them. She's making red lentil soup. And cracked-wheat pilaff. Her father's favourite dishes. Tufan also likes lentil soup. If she should stick her finger in his plate while passing it to him. Wearing surgical gloves, with a special virus spread on that finger. Ebola. Anthrax: animal disease. AnthraxTufan. Catch it.

Behiye starts to smile. It's not that easy to get rid of Tufan, even with the rarest virus. Tufan just won't get the fuck out of this crowded house. He just won't leave this house where everyone's on top of one another, just won't make room.

But Behiye doesn't want to think about him. She doesn't want to think about her sleepy, melon-like father either. Her poor father. Salim.

As she cooks, Handan is constantly on her mind. *Metallica* is playing at top volume on the stereo in her room. She's not as crazy about *Metallica* as she used to be. It's been some time since she listened to it. That's why she's listening loyally, from her heart.

Behiye is very well. Her soul is well inside her body. This sheath seems just right for her. This sheath is good enough. Let it stay. The sheath and the inner suit each other. They're in harmony.

She looks below her waist. I'm going to lose ten kilos, ten kilos. I'll be able to pass through the eyes of a needle. I'll be like a whip

next to Handan. Handan. I'll cook for you. I'll protect you too.
Are you alone and hungry in this world, Handan? I'm well now.
You came, and I got well. I'M COMPLETE. I'll protect you from the
winds and giants and black-magicians and scoundrels and evil
puppets; from waves, storms, pirates and belly-dancers. You've
made me happy. You made me complete. And I'll look after you,
Handan. I'll make you lemon kofte and other dishes. I'll protect
you and watch out for you. I'll be good for you. I'll do you good.

'What's all this noise, my daughter?'

Her mother is hanging up her cardigan. She's put on her
slippers. She hadn't heard her come in.

'All right, mother.' She goes and turns off the cheap stereo.

She decides to make tomato and onion salad. There are two red
onions and four or five tomatoes left in the house. Her father likes
this salad very much. Wretched Salim, I'll do something nice for
him...chief clerk Salim. Headwaiter. 'My dear sir, my dear madam.'
That's how he talks all day to the customers in that démodé shop
where he works. Licking everyone's ass until evening. That's her
father's job. Her father's job is to lick ass and sell things.

Her eyes are watering from the onions. They watered from
the onions for the moussaka too. But this is different. Red onion
tears. House suffocation tears. Red onion plus crying tears.
Suddenly, as she's slicing the onions, she cuts her finger. It's a bad
cut, a deep cut in her left index finger.

Behiye looks at it.

She's cut her finger. She turns on the tap and puts her finger
under running water. It's bleeding a lot. Is this normal? Could it
bleed this much? Fucking knife. How it cut her!

Should she call the professional mother? Let her mother
wrap it in a bandage. Tightly. Though her mother doesn't cut her
fingers this badly. The flesh is protruding. It turns her stomach to
see the protruding flesh. She runs to her room. What a strange
thing blood is. Hot and flowing.

Behiye takes some old black underwear from the laundry

drawer and tears it. She wraps her hand tightly. To stop the bleeding. Should she shout 'Mother!'? Her mother can come with the first-aid kit –

No. She can't cope with her mother saying, 'How badly you cut yourself.' She doesn't want that. She's very much up and down today. Happiness is difficult too. It's like those crazy rides at the amusement park. It's like the *Kamikaze*. It turns your stomach. You go up and down very quickly. It's strange; that's difficult too.

She tries to lie down on her bed and rest a little. She wants to feel Handan again. She wants to feel that coolness within her, so that the birds can fly again. She doesn't want to live in this house any more. She doesn't want to be a piece of this house. PIECE. Subdivision. Division. Divided Behiye.

Since Handan had come into her life, she'd found Handan; why couldn't she live with Handan? Every day. Every God-given day. How many hours until tomorrow? How many hours until one o'clock tomorrow?

It's seven o'clock. Let's say it's seven. In five hours it will be twelve. In thirteen hours it will be one. Thirteen and five makes eighteen hours. It's a lot. It's long.

If she can manage to get through eighteen hours, if she can manage to get through eighteen hours, it will be one o'clock tomorrow: Handan time. My God, how beautiful!

The doorbell has rung. Tufan noises. At home Tufan claims that he's a 'dealer'. Even though he's just an office boy at that stockbroker's office in Şişli. Some kind of bodyguard/office boy. But every evening at home he's fucking their brains with his stock market stories. He bought this, sold that. They made a killing in such and such a way. They'd been cleverer than anyone else had. Dealer my ass. Nationalist fascist commando Tufan.

Her father has also arrived. Coming into his own house as if he were a guest to be endured.

From inside his timid voice: 'My dear Yildiz. Dear Yildiz.' He's not man enough for her mother or for any woman. Does her father know this? How well do her father and mother know each other? What do they know; how much are they able to understand, how much are they unable to understand? Behiye doesn't know. She doesn't want to know, doesn't even want to think about the subject.

Her father has done the shopping at the market. She can hear him putting things away in the refrigerator and in the cupboards. The long-suffering father has brought a number of plastic bags home.

Behiye buries her head under the pillow to try to escape the noises of the house. NOISE HOUSE.

My Feeling You'll Be Rescued; will you come and take me out of this hole? I don't want to be with them; don't want to see them, hear their noise. So who do you live with? Who's your mother? Will you take me in with you, wherever you are? Will you come and rescue me from this place? From this dark and sticky hole?

'Behiyee! Come to the table.'

She puts her hand in her back pocket. She straightens her hair a little with her right hand. Behiye cuts her hair very short. Stubborn, short hair. She usually doesn't do much with it, and lets it stay however it is.

'What delicious food you've cooked for your family, my daughter.'

For your family? This is the kind of nonsense that comes out of her father's ass-licking mouth. Like that. It just falls out. On to the floor, on to the table, into the lentil soup. It flows out.

'Let's not forget that our girl is now a Bosphorus University student, father.'

She gives Tufan a 'you're nothing but a piece of shit' look. A 'back off or I'll show you' look. Those are two of the disgusted looks from the menu she'd developed while living with Tufan.

'What's the matter, carrot-top? Aren't we allowed to take pride in our super intelligent sister?'

'Shut your mouth,' hisses Behiye.

'Who are you telling to shut up! Who do you think you're

talking to? Do you have any idea how many terrorists I got rid of when I was a commando? It's only because of us that worthless people like you can live safely in this country! You shut your own evil mouth!'

As he shouts, the swollen veins on his throat twitch. Back and forth. Back. Forth. His eyes are popping. Behiye wants to stick two fingers in his eyes, the way she did to his photograph. What can he possibly see with those eyes? What are they good for? Behiye wants to take out those ugly and useless eyes and give them to someone who needs them. At least the retinas. To a blind child, for instance.

'Tufan! Behiye!' said her mother in her 'I'll fall down and faint now and then you'll see' voice. Very low and strained. But at the same time piercing. A voice like a drill. A drilling mother's voice. Drilling Mother.

'Look how upset your mommie is!' Her father; he's cried, he's going to cry, he's frightened, trembling. He'll cry in a moment. Crying father. Sorrowful Salim. Melon.

'I'm not going to eat. I ate out. I'm full, Mother.'

She raised her eyes and looked at Tufan again, giving him her 'I'm not the least bit frightened of you' look. These looks drive Tufan crazy, more than anything else. She knows, from years of training.

She closes the door of her room. She puts on her earphones and listens to music. She's listening to *Linkin Park* now. This music and these books have held her together.

Otherwise Behiye wouldn't have made it. She'd have flown off. Got lost. Disappeared. The lyrics of these songs are the marks of her fingernails. Her fingernails on the concrete wall of life, she got by with them.

She imagines a cat's long claw marks on freshly poured cement. She doesn't want to be that way, but at the same time she does. She doesn't know what she wants. In the end.

She lies on the bed, holding both sides tightly.

Where are you going to take me? How can you rescue me? Perhaps I have to rescue you first. I'll be rescued as far as I'm capable of rescuing you. Not to be calculating. I'll also rescue you. Your arrival has changed everything. I know: EVERYTHING has changed. Perhaps we can run away together somewhere, Handan. We can run away to the other end of the world. We'd be fine there. There won't be animals like Tufan there. If there are, I'll get rid of them. I'll pick them off one by one. I'll put an X on them. We'll be fine there. We'll be very fine. Tomorrow you'll be there, thank God. Tomorrow's guarantee: your presence. Handan lesson. Handan day. Handan and Behiye. That's what we'll be. For ever.

She shuts off the stereo and takes off her earphones.

She's tired. She falls exhausted at the door of her new life. She pulls a corner of the blanket that lies haphazardly on top of her. She's falling asleep. She's completely worn out. The kind of deep sleep that comes after crying. Pulls Behiye inside like a baby.

Meeting

. . . .

Behiye woke up.

In the room right next to the kitchen. The house noises have started reaching out. Toilet noises. Someone has turned on the tap and washed his face and is brushing his teeth. It's Tufan. Listening carefully, lying there unmoving like a cat, you can tell who's doing what from the noises.

Her father has opened a drawer. He's looking for socks. Poor socks. A pair of poor Salim socks.

Tufan has sat down and is taking a shit while reading his *Hürriyet* newspaper. Tufan shit. After that, it's better not to go into the toilet. For at least half an hour it will smell of Tufan Shit. No one else's shit smells that bad.

Behiye doesn't want to have to use the same toilet as Tufan. She doesn't want to live in the same house as Tufan. Tufan is a thing that dirties and ruins the house and makes it smell. A foreign object. Disgusting. Tufan is a frightful substance. Waste matter.

Her mother has gone into the kitchen. She's making breakfast for her son Tufan and her poor, useless husband. Breakfast noises. Mother noises.

Tufan has shaved. He's dressing in his room now. Her father has dressed already.

Behiye won't get out of bed until they've gone the hell off to work. She'll stay there without moving. So they won't know she's awake. She doesn't want to hear a sentence with the words 'daughter', 'breakfast' or 'today' in it. Behiye doesn't want to snap at her mother. She doesn't want Tufan to take revenge for last night (nationalist fascist commando dealer). She doesn't want her father to have to interfere like a buzzing fly. Salim. Don't make him buzz.

She has a terrible need to piss. Behiye holds it. Even if she has to piss the bed she won't get up. She'll hold it. She can hold it. Piss. Pissss.

She's not going to see them this morning. She's not going to allow them to spoil the day, to soil it, scratch it. They won't be part of her day. After all, she's going to be rescued from them. She's going to be with The Feeling You'll Be Rescued. That's all.

She won't get out of bed even if her mother breaks a plate, a glass, a teapot, a flowerpot, a jug. Let them do whatever they want. Let them be whatever they want to be. On their own. I'm not actually here. I'm not actually in this house. Behiye doesn't live here.

She has an urge to open the door and shout, 'Behiye doesn't live here!'

She holds herself back. She holds her piss back. Lying in bed, she squeezes her legs together.

Her mother didn't break anything. In the kitchen.

Tufan left first. Then her father.

Then her mother. First she hesitated a bit outside Behiye's door. Trying to decide whether to wake her or not.

She didn't dare to. She left quietly, closing the door behind her.

Behiye runs to the toilet. She takes a long time pissing, enjoying the wonderful sensation.

She washed her face. She brushed her teeth. She lights the water heater. It would be good if she washed before seeing

Handan. She should be very clean. A brand new Behiye. She hasn't seen anyone. She isn't broken. Because of them.

Han-dan! Handan! Handan!

She trembles within as she repeats the name.

She's completely clean. She smells nice. She smells like a baby. Soap and mermaid. Princess and jasmine. Strawberries and chocolate. Nice. Handan smells of everything. She wants the smell to come, to lick her soul. Handan's smell. Let it come to Behiye.

How long until one o'clock? It's two and a half hours till twelve. One more hour: three and a half hours. How is the time going to pass three long hours waiting for Handan! It won't be easy.

After all, last night passed. She passed many hours sleeping. Behiye is happy about the hours she's put behind her. There's only a short time left until Handan. In three and a half hours it will be Handan time. Baby cardigan girl. Handan Time.

Will she arrive today with two pink woollen balls swinging in front of her? Pink?

Behiye decides to make some food. She'll wash later.

The telephone rings.

The one on the cabinet in the sitting room. The telephone seldom rings in the house. It always startles Behiye. She's not used to the telephone; she doesn't like its ring.

Çiğdem.

'No. You go, Çiğdem. We're meeting at one in front of the school. OK. That's what I said. What's it to you? Come on Çiğdem. All right. Bye bye to you too.'

She got rid of Çiğdem. How will she get rid of her later? She'll get rid of her. Çiğdem-ridder Behiye. It will happen.

Behiye cooks stuffed tomatoes and peppers. After cleaning the kitchen, she takes off the tops, scoops out the insides, fills them, fries finely chopped onions in oil until they soften, and throughout the making of dolmas Behiye feels very happy.

'Over a medium flame.'

Behiye is happy to be cooking, happy to be a good cook, happy to be making the evening meal.

I'm cooking now, and my hands, my fingers, my hair and my eyelashes smell of onions. Every part of me smells of food. Later I'll wash, and be very clean. Then I'll be with Handan. I'll be with her. Handan!

I'll be right next to her.

My last meal in this house. Later Handan, later for you. I'll only cook for you. My hungry baby princess. You're good for me. You did me good. You made me happy. You made me COMPLETE. How wonderful!

'Mother, I won't be home this evening. I'll be at Çiğdem's.'

She wrote and left it in the kitchen. Under the wooden two birds kissing napkin-holder. Her mother wouldn't call Çiğdem's, would she? She wouldn't call. She'd feel shy. Behiye might call later. Mother talk. With her, 'But my daughter...' Perhaps she won't call. After all, she wrote a note. She doesn't want to think about her mother at all. She doesn't want to ruin the day, to narrow it.

She rids her mind of Mother who has to worry. This is a wonderful day for getting rid of trouble. Today she's an incredible trouble-shooter. Shooter. Shooooot.

The bus brings her to the bottom of the hill in Beşiktaş. Two paces from the front of the school. Çiğdem is there. And Handan.

She struggles to tell herself that this is a normal thing, an everyday thing. Çiğdem is there. And so is Handan.

She repeats this to herself as if it were a prayer.

She's let her hair down. It falls over her shoulders and covers her breasts. My God, how beautiful she is! She knew that she was beautiful. But she'd forgotten just how beautiful. My God, she's so beautiful. You can't take your eyes off her.

Enough to make you want to reach out and touch her.

Are you really there? Are you real? Do you exist? If I touched you would you still be there? Would you stay and not fly away, Handan? Handan. Handan.

Behiye wants to cry. As they register at the entrance, she wants to cry. She's so happy. She's beside herself. She's giggling. She can't believe Handan. That she's found Handan. That feeling she felt under the tree has come true. Behiye can't believe it.

Believe. Believe.

Later, everything goes more quickly.

Later things will go even more quickly.

Even more.

Çiğdem isn't with them anymore. Somehow they freed themselves of Çiğdem. They're walking along the Bosphorus. Handan and Behiye.

They passed Ortaköy. They passed the park. Passed Kuruçeşme. Passed Arnavutköy. They're in Bebek. They're talking. Talking constantly.

Behiye is laughing a lot. And talking. She feels like laughing and talking. But she doesn't fully know what she's saying, or what she's laughing about. Not fully. Half. Fully half.

But she knows what Handan has said. Handan is talking about her mother. Her mother's name: Leman.

In our house no one ever cooks. In our house one can't sleep through the night. Life never stops in our house. In our house. In our house. My mother. My baby mother. Leman. Little blue Leman. My Muki. My dear Muki. Muki who knew my grandmother. My mother's nescafé and cigarettes. My mother goes out at night. Money flies out of the house the moment it comes in. A tiny little flat. In the Petrol Complex. On the right just before you get to Akmerkez.

Behiye listens to Handan with five hundred and ten thousand ears. She records it word for word. She doesn't hear what she herself says. She doesn't hear what comes out of her own mouth. She knows that she's giggling. She can't keep from laughing.

They're at Asiyan now.

'The cemetery here is very beautiful, Handan. Shall we go in and wander around a bit? Almost everyone is buried here. Writers and so forth.'

'Won't it be frightening? I'm not sure if I'll like it.'

'Don't worry. It's the world's most beautiful cemetery. I love it here. I discovered it the first day I came to the university. I've wandered through it at least ten times.'

They're wandering around the cemetery. On a hostess's tombstone, her family blames the man who killed her in a car accident. The man who caused the accident. The girl's lover, apparently. An Iranian.

An inflated boat has been thrown on to one grave. It stands there full of rainwater. As if the person buried there had died inside that boat. Not really, of course. But why is the boat there? Strange and slightly spooky.

On another tombstone, a man is calling to his wife who killed herself. There's a black and white picture of the two of them dressed for a masked ball. The two of them young and beautiful dressed for the ball. The man doesn't blame his wife for committing suicide. He's just sad. That's all.

There are rich people's graves. They look like marble layered cakes. There are railings, steps and fountains. They used as much marble as they possibly could. Cake graves.

'Shall we sit over here?'

They sit on a marble railing. The Bosphorus is offered in a tray below them.

'Isn't it beautiful here? Do you like it?'

'It's beautiful. But it's still a cemetery. But yes, it's beautiful. You're right, Behiye.'

'Look, Handan. Do you notice how it seems as if we've known each other a long time? It's as if we hadn't just met, but as if we've known each other a long time.'

'Let's get out of here, Behiye. I'm hungry.' She reaches out and strokes Behiye's right cheek. With her bird-like hand. 'Behiye?'

'Yes?'

'I can't count how many people I've met, but I've never met anyone like you. What you say is true. It's as if you've been in my life for a long time. As you said just now. You're right.'

As they walk down the hill, Behiye puts her arm around Handan's shoulder. Even though Handan is a bit taller, Behiye puts her arm around her. Surprising herself, but in a natural way. She catches the smell from the nape of Handan's neck. Handan smell. The most beautiful smell in the world. Like an animal, she knows she couldn't exist without the Handan smell. She feels in her bones that there's no turning back now. They've become Handan and Behiye. Until Judgement Day. Judgement? Whatever that means.

Forest

· ·

The winter sun rose heavily crippled over the seclusion of the forest. The cold, though not biting, made its presence felt. An early winter cold, reminding itself all over again, polite, but sure of itself.

The young woman, wearing a woollen headband which served both to keep her hair out of her lightly made-up face and to frame its beauty, as well as to guarantee that her ears would definitely be kept warm.

She wished she'd worn a thick turtleneck sweater instead of the *DKNY* sweatshirt, or rather she wished she'd considered this possibility.

It was important to her to estimate the probability of all life's possibilities. It was essential for her not to have to analyse herself all day, not to feel guilty or defeated.

'If only we'd been smart enough to dress more heavily. You feel the winter cold more in the early morning.'

The young man made the noises of a young man who was sure of himself, at peace with himself, successful, handsome, continuously on the rise and who had a winning smile.

'Typical horoscope sign of a planner,' he said. 'A case of occupational deformation.' He pronounced each word carefully, speaking in a wonderfully measured tone that had a touch of irony.

The young woman said, 'Don't make fun of me.' She ran up beside the young man and pushed him. She showed him her playful side too. They pushed and shoved each other a little. They made laughing sounds. They were 'bringing out the inner child', 'going where their soul takes them' – doing all that 'stuff'. Later, they began running along the track, as they did three mornings a week.

They felt superior to, better-looking and fitter than all of those poor layabouts, those losers who sacrificed their lives in order to sleep an extra half-hour, who allowed themselves to become overweight, undisciplined, to fall prey to all the ills of indolence and who lacked energy. At every metre. As they ran.

Badi too, running along with them. As is necessary for all golden couples. Their beloved golden retriever, their only son: Badi.

Badi, with his tongue hanging out and his tail in the air, running left and right alongside them, was breathless with happiness at these wonderful excursions into the forest with his masters. Badi exuded unconditional love and boundless delight. Just as he should. Everything was as it should be.

From time to time the young man said, 'Come on, Badi, come here, son, go there, son.' Father and son. Giver and taker. The golden couple and their beautiful golden dog out for their morning run. This is the scene.

Badi left the path, as he often did, and went into the forest. But now he doesn't come dashing back to his masters panting with mad delight.

'Come on, Badi. This is too much. Badi! Badi!'

The young woman joins in, 'Badiii! Come on, baby. Where are you?'

The young man became quite annoyed. He left the path and dived into the forest. 'Look, Badi! Come here! I'm getting angry!'

Badi comes running. He's filled with delight to see his master.

He presses himself against his trousers. He's not in a state to pay attention to 'Badi stop.'

He runs in circles around the young man, barking madly. As if to say, 'Come with me. Come quickly. Look what I found for you. What a gift I have for you.'

The young woman joins them. 'What does he want to show us? He must have found something. Let's not look. Come on, let's turn back, darling.'

'It must be a dead bird or something. He's a hunting dog, after all. His instincts have emerged in this wild nature.'

They make synchronised laughing sounds. They start turning back to the path. Badi is past being calmed; he can't stop or be stopped. With a crazed energy, being useful perhaps for the first time in his short life, he dives back into the depths of the forest.

'This is too much. Badi! Badi! Look at me. You're going to get a beating. Come here. Come, I say.'

The young man and the young woman have to go after Badi. The young man mutters angrily to himself: 'What could he have found in this poor excuse for a forest? It must be a duck or a rabbit carcass. Silly dog. We're going to have to go back without finishing our run.'

They didn't have to go very far.

A little further along, Badi is circling excitedly, and they see what he was trying to lead them to: a corpse. The corpse of a young man of nineteen or twenty.

They saw it. No matter how much they wished they could go back and not have seen the body, not to have the image of a dead person lying in the forest impressed on their minds, it was done. They'd seen the body.

He was lying there. On the forest floor. As if he was sleeping. But his throat was cut from one end to the other.

The young woman's legs give out from under her. She collapses under a tree. She starts to cry.

The young man wants to kill Badi, to make him disappear, for having done this to their day, to their lives. After all, they'd seen a corpse. Until then they'd never seen a corpse. Never. They'd seen a body, someone who'd been killed, someone whose throat had been cut, someone who'd been dumped in the forest.

Badi, still in the grip of excitement, bites at the corpse's trouser leg, and writhes as if in celebration. He's still wagging his tail, running back and forth. 'Look at me. Look what a wonderful thing I've found for you. What about some affection, some praise.' Patiently. Stubbornly.

The young man gives him a big kick in the behind. 'Fucking dog. God damn you.' Badi yelps with surprise rather than pain.

The young man can't keep himself from looking at the corpse. The first corpse he's seen in his life. It's not that bad after all. This too is something to be seen, to experience.

A very handsome young man with black, gelled hair and a white complexion. He's lying there on his back, with his arms spread, as if he's taking a nap in the forest.

Everything is as it should be. Everything is in order. He even looks good. Except for the area around his throat. He even looks beautiful.

Just below the boy's chin there's a gaping wound. In the shape of a boat. It stretches from one side of his throat to the other, and it's apparent that at the centre it's very deep; a deep and fatal wound. The young man can't help looking in admiration. It's the biggest, deepest, most wounding wound he's ever seen: in the shape of a boat.

Later he looks at the corpse's anorak, sweatshirt and very nice blue jeans. When he sees the shoes, he feels as if he's been punched in the stomach. The boy has a pair of *Killer Loop* shoes on his feet.

In a moment of terror he looks down at his own feet.

No! It can't be! For his run he'd worn his latest *Nikes*. But at home the young man has the same *Killer Loop* sports shoes – the same colour, the same model – as the boy. He has exactly the same shoes in his closet. They're there.

He feels a shudder within him. Akin to fear. But not quite. Just a shudder. It licks him and goes away. Its moistness remains.

The young woman opens her legs wide, places her head between them, and vomits. She's crying and vomiting at the same time. She knows, knows well, that they're going to separate because they've seen this corpse together. Two and a half years of patience, waiting and perseverance down the drain. Down the drain!

She's crying and vomiting: two and a half years of effort down the drain! He doesn't even come and stroke her head. He doesn't even hold her hand. All of the togetherness that was built so carefully is gone because they've seen a corpse together.

She feels the urge to give the corpse a few kicks for interfering with their lives. Swift, hard kicks to its head. Couldn't he have died at some other time, in some other forest!

They run, breathless, as far as the car. Badi, surprised that they're not pleased with what he found, follows them. Slightly sensitive and hurt, he climbs into the back of the car. He also fears being abandoned.

They speed out of the forest in their *Volvo*. A little later, in the traffic of the main road, they begin to feel safe again.

The young man passes over his cell phone and says, 'Call the police, will you. Whatever happens don't give your name. You don't want to get involved in giving statements or anything.'

'You call,' says the young woman. 'You can call when you get to the agency.' She wipes the tears from her eyes with her sleeve. She doesn't have the strength to reach for the box of tissues. Finished! A two and a half year project finished, gone.

The young man thinks about the wound on the boy's throat. 'It was shaped like a boat: the centre was very deep. Something like a death boat.'

'Excuse me?' says the young woman. 'I'd like to see one on your throat' floats inside her like a boat and gets lost in her dark waters. 'Excuse me,' she says, making an effort to soften her voice, 'What did you say?'

Wounds caused by sharp instruments are generally in a straight line. There is much loss of blood, and the lips of the wound are uniform. The width of the wound varies according to the region. Where the skin is taut, the lips are far apart, and the wound is quite wide. Hence, wounds caused by sharp objects are wider than they are deep, crescent-shaped, deepest at the centre, tailing at both ends at a narrow angle, with uniform lips.

```
Sex: Male
Height: 176 cm.
Weight: 67 kilos
```

Wound characteristics from a forensic textbook:

1) Size and length of the wound: a cut section bounded by undamaged skin and visible to the naked eye.
2) Lips of the wound: the section of skin closest to and adjacent to the opening of the wound.
3) Width of the wound: the distance between the lips of the wound.
4) Angle of the wound: either of the two points at which both lips of the wound come together.
5) Tail of the wound: superficial scratches on the surface of the undamaged skin extending from either of the angles of the wound.
6) Depth of the wound: the inner section beneath the surface of the skin only visible when the lips of the wound are separated.

Of wounds caused by sharp instruments, those in the region of the throat are most hazardous. The lips of the wound are uniform, the beginning and end sections are superficial, the centre is deep. The wound can be in various segments of the throat. Sometimes on the trachea, sometimes between the larynx and the hyoid bone, and sometimes above the larynx.

Brown anorak : *Diesel*
Blue sweatshirt : *GAP*
Navy-blue T-shirt : *Guess*

Blue jeans : *Levi's Vintage*
Grey underpants : *Diesel*
Polka-dot socks : *Dr Martens*
Size 41 shoes : *Killer Loop*
Penis size : 14 cm

What the deceased was wearing and the size of his penis were not found to be relevant. For this reason they were not included in the forensic report given to the police.

Dream

· ·

Behiye would remember that first day, the first day they spent together, as if it was a dream.

The whole day was like a dream: the way you feel so happy, on top of the world, as if the world was a completely different place, but at the same time you feel – is this a dream, am I really living this, could all this be real, this whole new sense of being within you – I mean, could it be real? It is almost too nice –

It's not just too nice to be real. It's nice, but that's not all it is. It's not that simple. It's so many things. So many, many things. A feeling of softness, of order, of fluidity that isn't normally there. Nothing cuts her, twists her, weighs her down. The state of being absolutely filled with extreme happiness. No other feeling can enter her, no sliver, no scratch, no sputter.

Behiye will always remember that day as if it was a dream.

She knows this even while she's living it. All of this couldn't be real. This feeling of extreme delight that filled her, this state of happiness, couldn't be true.

Something she'd never lived before. Something she'd never known. The state of feeling that she couldn't help but be happy, that nothing in her real life could be real. As if some sort of veil had been stretched between her and the world. Everything she saw through that veil looked very beautiful. Strange. Beautiful.

They're walking, and Handan is right next to her.

Along the very edge of the sea. From time to time they stop and look into the sea. The moss that changes from dark green to light green as it sways in the water, the deeper shades of blue in the Bosphorus. The hard, curly brown seaweed. The silky, slippery green carpet on the stones. They look at the garbage. The various kinds of Bosphorus garbage. That's beautiful too.

Behiye shows Handan a washtub that's floating a little way off shore. A perfect red plastic washtub. It's travelling along like that all by itself. No, it doesn't make the sea ugly. It adds beauty to the sea. Garbage particular to the Bosphorus. This is a piece of Istanbul garbage. It makes the waters of the Bosphorus more beautiful. It Istanbulifies it. Today, everything beautifies everything. Today is like that.

A giant Russian ship is passing. Like a floating tower. It passes them swerving this way and that. All of the ships that pass them – even the most ugly and unwieldy of them – have something elegant and graceful about them. The passing ships wet them with waves of delight.

Over-fed seagulls come and go. They're screeching, then they're not screeching.

Handan's smell is like that too. Behiye smells it, then it escapes. The Handan smell comes and goes.

From time to time Behiye throws her arm around Handan's shoulder. At those moments the Handan smell leaps to her and fills her; spreads through her soul. Behiye has become whole. Handan came and Behiye is complete. She's become complete. WHOLE.

If she's not constantly smiling, it's because her nose is covered with freckles; if she's not constantly smiling, it's because she also wants to cry. To cry from happiness. She wants to cry her eyes out because she's united with Handan, because she's found Handan.

But she doesn't cry after all. Why should she cry? She's filled with smiles. Smiling carries her along.

They sit in the furthest of the restaurants right in front of the little mosque. They sit and eat dumplings at one of the round formica tables outside.

Handan – that hungry child – eats a large portion of dumplings. She drinks Cola. Behiye is not at all hungry. Behiye doesn't get hungry at all, and because of this she feels wonderful about herself. She only eats three or four of the dumplings on her plate. That's as much as she needs to eat. She doesn't even need that much, doesn't even want that much. Being with Handan, she's going to become very thin. Like a ruler. A knife. She'll become a completely new Behiye. How wonderful!

They've got into a taxi and are on their way to Handan's. As if they're doing something very natural. Without even discussing it first –

Not that they didn't discuss it, but they discussed very little. Perhaps Behiye said, 'Can I come to your house today?' It might not have been those exact words, but she said something like that.

'Of course you can come,' said Handan, like that. She said it exactly like that. With emphasis.

Like: what are you asking for, of course you'll come, of course you have to come, after all that's how we are, we're Handan and Behiye, don't you understand, for ever.

Everything became so incredibly fluid.

Behiye can't believe herself, her life, the fluidity her life has gained, the softness, the slipperiness. How difficult her life used to be, how little she'd been capable of…

Not 'capable', nor success, nor succeeding, seizing opportunity, ascending etc., etc; but what a nothing she'd been, how alone, abandoned, abandoned by life, how neglected, how invisible she'd been…

Behiye doesn't believe it. Had she been alive? Had she belonged here? Where is here anyway? Whose world is this?

It's not Behiye's world. This isn't her world. So whose world is it? Who lives here that the world belongs to? Who does it belong to, this world that spat Behiye out, that wouldn't accept her?

But with Handan, Behiye belongs somewhere.

She belongs to Handan. And Handan to her.

Behiye can't believe the slipperiness, the softness, that her life has taken on. 'Of course you can come,' she'd said. She'd said it exactly like that. Exactly.

Later, when she remembered that day, that first day, when she cut that day to pieces in the morgue of her memory, when she was trying to find consolation, redemption, some way to escape, much, much later, in amazement, Behiye would be surprised at how she could remember every single word Handan had said.

Later she would remember how, squeezed into the taxi, breathless with happiness, so happy she felt she would explode, as they climbed the hill, the taxi driver looked at Handan's breasts through the rear-view mirror like a hungry and impudent wolf – how he looked at her breasts like a disgusting animal that would never exist. Those little breasts rising and falling under her baby-blue T-shirt.

Later, Behiye will be surprised at herself for not beating that taxi driver right then and there, for not thrashing him severely, for not poking his eyes out with her two fingers. She'll be surprised.

But she was so happy that day. It was as if her happiness was a terrrific rain-coat – a yellow rain-coat – that made everything bad, everything that upset her, everything that disturbed her soul, every trouble, everything unpleasant slip to the ground. Nothing holds. She'll be surprised later at the way, because of that rain-coat of happiness – yellow – she could not record how, on their very first meeting, Leman treated her like shit. She recorded it without realising she was doing so.

She was so full of herself: of Handan, of happiness, of belonging to Handan. Yellow. Cow. Cow. Mooo.

They enter the house. They enter Handan's house. A slightly

strange house. Old furniture and new furniture, beautiful things and ugly things, expensive things and cheap things; definitely a complicated house; confused house. Clearly strange. Mixed-up house.

It doesn't look like any house Behiye has ever seen. But Behiye knows with certainty that it's not like any house anyone has ever seen. Messy and orderly, poor and rich, pleasant and unpleasant, an absurd house that was neither one thing nor another. Child house. Handan house.

As she remembers the Handan House, she trembles inwardly. She loved the house completely, without reservations or conditions. She wanted to belong to the house. This house ought to be the Handan and Behiye house. Behiye wants this. She can't stop herself from wanting this. She can't control this maniacal desire. She cannot tell herself to 'Stop!'

Behiye is surprised at the imprudence, her own imprudence. But there's nothing to be done. After meeting Handan, there was nothing to be done concerning life, concerning Handan, concerning her life with Handan. She can only keep going the way she's going. That's all. She knows this. She feels everything within her. She knows it as soon as she feels it. With Handan, life will flow; Behiye will be like a piece of garbage, she'll travel along like that red washtub they saw from the Hisar Road, she'll end up somewhere. There was no telling where. Sea garbage.

Suddenly, she thinks of something. She wants to cook lemon kofte for dinner. After all, she'd promised.

Handan leaps up and claps her hands. Behiye's eyes fill with tears. She's found a baby who'll clap her hands at the thought of having lemon kofte for dinner. Hungry baby. The world's most beautiful baby. Given to her. Come to her.

Handan goes into her room and puts on grey sweatpants with a white T-shirt. The T-shirt has *Bebe* written on it in rhinestones. She has furry pink slippers on her feet; shaped like cats. She runs into the living room and turns on *MTV*. She turns the volume up high; after all, she's listening to music from Number One, from *MTV*. Her favourites are *Britney Spears, Kylie Minogue, Robbie Williams, N'SYNC*. She counts them off to Behiye in one breath. She also likes *Geri Halliwell*. In her new state, that is. So thin.

'You like the most popular ones.' She smiles. She doesn't tell Handan which groups she likes. 'Shall I go buy ground meat? If there's none in the house.'

'There's never anything in our house,' says Handan. She orders a kilo of ground meat from the butcher by telephone. They don't call the butcher very often. He says he doesn't have anyone to make deliveries. She calls another place and begs someone named Cetin to run over to the butcher's.

Cetin and the ground meat arrive half an hour later.

They go into the kitchen together. They find a little rice in the back of one of the cupboards.

Lemons? No, they never have lemons in the house.

'I'll run down and get some,' says Handan. Behiye doesn't want to stay in this strange house without Handan.

'No,' she says. 'We'll make them without lemon. It doesn't matter. What can we do?'

When she opened the refrigerator she saw that when Handan said there was nothing, she really meant there was nothing. There isn't even an egg in the refrigerator. There is nothing but three boxes of *Toblerone*, a bottle of ketchup, three whisky bottles full of water, and half a pack of margarine. Really.

Handan puts on her sports shoes and is ready to go 'shop for ingredients'. That's what Behiye said.

'Let's go shop for ingredients,' she said. Handan laughed so much, grabbing her tummy. So much.

They left the house to buy parsley, black pepper, salt, lemons, onions, margarine, eggs, rice and bread (Behiye made a list).

On the way, Handan kept laughing and saying 'shopping

for ingredients'. Like a baby who was left breathless from being tickled.

'You're so strange,' she says. 'The words you use, the way you stand, the way you express yourself. Are you from this planet, Behiye?'

'Once you told me I was "peculiar". No, girl. I'll tell you my secret: I'm an alien. I was sent here to research and investigate.'

'My alien!' says Handan. She puts her arm around Behiye's waist and pulls her close. She plants a big kiss on her cheek. A resounding kiss, a real kiss.

Handan kissed her. Loved her. Handan loves her. She gave her a real kiss. Not like Çiğdem's superficial, perfunctory goodbye kisses.

Handan has a heart-warming genuineness about her. Heart-warming. The way children can be. Whoever her favourite singers are: so what if it's a list of the world's biggest jerks. She's the most beautiful, cleanest, most genuine thing on the face of the earth. She came to me. My Feeling You'll Be Rescued. You came to me. To love me. To watch over me. To rescue me.

They return with the 'ingredients'. Behiye goes into the kitchen and starts making lemon kofte.

From time to time Handan comes in and tells her something. She goes into the living room and reads her silly girls' magazines. Sitting sideways in the armchair with her legs hanging over the arm.

When everything is ready, while she's waiting to make the finishing touches, Behiye asks in an annoyed tone, 'Why do you read those magazines? They're stupid. They're written for retarded people. They're intended to keep girls back: at home, in bed, in the pool, on the trapeze, at work. So they'll be inflatable girls who won't think themselves capable of anything else.'

'Whaat? Behiye, why do you say things like that? They keep a person occupied; so what? They're not for retarded people. Everyone reads them. It passes the time.'

'I don't think you should read them. Mass-produced, wrongheaded, user's guides. I'll bring you books from home. Good books. Things that won't shrivel your soul. Things that are worth reading.'

'Don't be upset with meeee. My smart, super intelligent super friend. All right, bring me books, I'll read them too. I mean, if I can understand them, if I can read them – they can be boring – but I'll try to read them.'

As Handan sweetly compromises, Behiye comes to her senses. Why am I talking to her like this? To this soft baby cat girl? She didn't get upset with me. She didn't get upset. Her feelings weren't hurt. Thank God. Thank God. What an ox you are, an ox, a boor, what an unreasonable tree-trunk you are. Tree. Trunk. Trunk Behiye.

'Let's eat,' she says, trying to make up for things. Lemon kofte to compensate for being a tree-trunk.

'All right. I'll set the table right away,' says Handan. With the sweetness that flows from good-natured people.

The door of the flat opens. Behiye is looking at a woman in the corridor throwing her keys into her bag. A woman with yellow highlights in her short hair, bright blue eyes, a small, upturned nose, and a small, full-lipped mouth.

For a moment, a wave of fear washes through her. How beautiful, she says to herself. A person can be frightened by such a beautiful woman, by such undaunted beauty. It inspires fear and a desire to flee. To flee in order not to melt to the floor. A woman that beautiful must be bad, must be trouble. She could kill you. Right where you stand. She has that type of beauty. That type. That kind of beauty.

Frozen in place, Behiye looks at the woman.

'My baby!' says Handan, jumping up. 'My blue rabbit, my mother baby has come home. Look, mother. Look what Behiye has cooked for us. Lemon kofte! Behiye, come here. Look, this is my mother: Leman. Mother, this is Behiye. My very best friend. Really. Behiye has become my bestest friend.'

First time at Handan's

. . . .

'What's that smell?'

A cold voice. Barbed. A voice that bites a person as soon as it touches them. Intended to shake Behiye out of her dream: a voice of broken glass. Behiye is startled. Mrs Leman looks Behiye in the face with her unsettling blue eyes when she utters her first sentence. As if saying, 'Who are you, my dear? Are you this smell; where did you come from? You're all we needed.'

No! She's not going to shake Behiye out of her dream. She's not going to wake up to this world. With her nettle voice, she is not going to bring Behiye back to this world which punched her, constricted her, pushed her away. She's not going to be able to freeze her with her icy eyes. Not yet. Behiye is so happy in the cocoon of her dream, so complete; she'll only think of Leman as a crawling snake. A harmless, poisonless, insufficient, pitiful little snake. She tries to frighten her: Leman the inadequate snake. Yet.

'Lemon kofte, I say, mother. Behiye has cooked lemon kofte for our dinner. Because it's my favourite food. Come, let's sit down and eat.'

'I'm full, my baby. I am finished for today. I paid off most of my credit card debts.'

'Are there any debts left?'

'Some. But don't worry your pretty head about them. Your Leman will work things out.'

Her voice isn't as piercing when she's speaking to her daughter. When she looks at Handan the iciness of her eyes flies away. She takes off her high-heeled shoes and puts on a pair of high-heeled slippers. The tops of the slippers are of clear plastic. They show off the beauty of her feet.

Everything about this woman is beautiful. Everything. Her

hands, her shoulders, her back, her feet. She has that kind of beauty: a person can't help but look at her, but it's a kind of beauty you can't admire with peace of mind. Behiye has seen actresses with this kind of beauty. But this is the first time she's encountered it in real life.

Leman changes her clothes while they eat. Handan is crazy for the lemon kofte. Behiye can barely swallow two or three kofte. She's just not hungry. She's become a superior person: one who doesn't get hungry. That's all. Leman comes to the kitchen while she's serving Handan her second plate. She puts water on for her coffee. She's wearing a white T-shirt and blue sweatpants. She's removed all of her make-up. In this state she looks younger and more beautiful. But with clear plastic slippers on her feet. Under the sweatpants. Behiye thinks she needs them as a symbol of her womanhood. That kind of woman always has to send out some kind of signal.

'I don't know how you can eat so much and still stay so thin, Handan. You take after your father. He could eat and eat and not gain an ounce.' When she'd wiped away her ugly make-up with cotton she'd also wiped away the voice. Behiye feels more comfortable when she hears the new voice.

'Mother, why don't you eat just a little. Behiye is such a good cook. It's the best lemon kofte I've tasted in my life. Try some, my little blue rabbit. You can't live on coffee alone.'

Leman smiles and says, 'But I'm alive, aren't I?'

She can't be that bad after all, thinks Behiye. Such a sweet baby girl's mother can't be so terrible. She feels a bit ashamed for thinking her a snake. And she's still in her dream. Still in the dream. No snake, no sorcerer, no belly-dancer, no broken glass can enter this cocoon.

Mrs Leman's cell phone rings inside. She leaves the water for the coffee on the fire and goes to her bedroom. She talks on the phone for at least forty minutes. Muttering in her broken voice. From time to time, Behiye listens to her voice. Surprised at the range of climates her voice has.

Handan and Behiye tidy up the kitchen, giggling. They sit in front on the television and zap through the Friday night programmes. There's a lot of nonsense on television; a fruitful evening.

In the kitchen, Mrs Leman mutters a song while she makes her nescafé. She joins them, carrying her coffee and a pack of cigarettes, as if she was a completely different woman. As if someone had filled her with happiness, light and energy, in her bedroom.

Her voice is like that too; her cold voice has been softened and become slightly more high-pitched by happiness. There's a strange light shining in her eyes. Her eyes have become so beautiful that a person feels like stealing their light. She's ashamed to take a long look.

'Mr Şevket called from Moscow,' she says once she's well settled into the armchair.

'Who's Mr Şevket? Is he the latest one?'

'Handaaan. Don't do that to your Leman. Is that any way to talk? You know him. The gentleman Nevin introduced me to. The one who went to Moscow on business.'

'Mother, Behiye is going to stay with us tonight. Her house is very far away. We want her to stay with us, isn't that so?'

'If Muki comes where will she sleep?' asks Leman. But her words don't come out of her full-lipped little mouth in the annoyed tone she intended. As if it's been wrapped in a happy colour. A colour that would shine through any paint that covers it.

'If that lady comes, I can sleep on the floor in Handan's room,' says Behiye. Not in her own voice, but in a voice borrowed from a wretch: trembling, frightened, quivery.

'Are you going to sleep on the floor under Handan's bed like a dog?' asks Leman, with her icy eyes fastened on to Behiye's. Her voice is frightening, the way it was before.

Later, Behiye will be surprised at how she swallowed this comment, at how she accepted it. This poisonous comment will come back to her again and again. It will cause her temples to throb with anger. Like a dog. Like a dog. Later, she won't believe that she didn't smack Leman in the mouth for saying that.

'Yes. I can sleep there on the floor. I can sleep anywhere. If you don't mind, that is.'

'Mother, Muki is coming tomorrow morning. She told me on the telephone today. And we want Behiye to stay with us. Behiye, you can stay here whenever you want. How are you going to get home at this time of night?'

'We can give her the taxi money, my daughter.'

'Mother! Look, Mother, this is the first time I've wanted anyone to stay over. The first time in my life, Mother. Do you understand, Mother? Behiye is going to stay with us.'

Behiye can't believe this angry Handan that's emerged from Handan. Especially for her. She brought out another Handan for her: warrior Handan. Rescuing her, protecting her, guarding her from snake Leman.

Behiye wants to cry with happiness. Her baby girl rescuing, protecting, guarding her so heroically. She wants to cry.

She's prepared to rescue me; to protect me, to guard me. And I have to protect her. I have to protect and guard her from enemies, snakes, taxi drivers, disgusting women and frightening men. Tomorrow I have to find an instrument with which to protect her. A protection instrument. Some kind of weapon. Something that will protect Handan from all kinds of ugliness. Tomorrow I'll find something. A protection instrument. Something will definitely turn up in our enchanted world.

Behiye trusts the magical world they've entered. That whatever they wish for will happen. That they're armoured with happiness, love and completeness. With their yellow oilskin, they won't be wet by filthy, evil or foul waters. Evil won't infect them. It will flow off them. As if from an oilskin, on to the ground.

Leman goes into the kitchen to make another coffee. For some time she tries to find a radio station. In the end she decides on a Turkish station and turns the volume all the way up.

Growing accustomed is more difficult than love
Growing accustomed is like a bleeding wound.

Behiye remembers this tune from somewhere, this tune she's
sure was turned on simply to disturb them. Where did she hear
this tune; where, where?

The blind people's music! She heard it in Taksim, when the blind
people were playing the electric piano. That broken music that makes
people feel hot. Of course. The blind people were playing it. They
were suffocating the avenue with their loudspeakers: blind music.

'Don't let her get to you,' says Handan, taking her hand. 'She'll
get used to you in two days. Two days at the most; she'll end up
loving you more than she does me, you'll see. Never mind, at the
moment she's just jealous. She's like a child: she never grew up.
My child mother. Behiye, you can live with us.'

Behiye's nose becomes covered with freckles. With a million
freckles. She said it again, from her heart. They've become
Handan and Behiye. Forever. As long as they're together nothing
can go wrong. She feels like kissing Leman for being so rude, for
making Handan protect her.

They stay up until three o'clock watching television and talking.
Leman wanders like a cat from the kitchen to the bedroom to the
living room. Handan gives Behiye pyjamas with a rabbit design.
They're the biggest pyjamas she has. What can we do about the
rabbit design?

They make up the pull-out bed in the living room for Behiye.
Handan tucks Behiye in.

'May I kiss you on the cheeks?' she asks.

'You may kiss me. You may kiss me whenever you like, Handan.'

They kiss each other lovingly. She holds Behiye's hand again. 'I
don't really know you but I'm so happy I found you. I don't know
how to say it, but it's as if I've found something that was missing
and now I'm complete.'

'You feel completed?' says Behiye, almost screaming. 'Did you say you feel completed, Handan? Handan, you're the best thing that's ever happened to me. You're the only good thing in my life. You'll be rescued – look: It's as if I wouldn't have been able to live without you. Not as if, I would have died.'

Handan puts her index finger on Behiye's lips. 'Shhh,' she says. 'Shhh. Don't say it. Don't ever say things like that. Sweet dreams my beloved friend.'

Behiye wakes early in the morning. All night, thoughts galloped back and forth through her head. There was so much going on in her head that she didn't really get any sleep.

The doorbell rings, and she jumps out of her bed. She runs to the door, happy to escape from having been in bed. She opens the door. She sees an old woman who's all skin and bones. She has the same cold blue eyes as Leman. She has that frightful look of old women who, out of stubbornness, cover their lined faces with make-up. She looks more like a mummy witch than a witch. Or the skeleton of a witch.

'Muki,' Behiye thinks to herself. Just as Leman is called 'baby blue rabbit', 'Muki' seems an appropriate name for this old witch's skeleton by Handan.

As she takes off her overcoat, the mummy witch says, 'Who are you, my child? Wherever did Leman find you?'

Her false teeth spit a lot as she says this.

Behiye feels as if she'd like to grab something hard and heavy and hit this woman over and over the head with it. She doesn't want her to come in, to be included in this narrow and confused house, to soil and crowd it. She feels she wants to 'clean out' this skeleton so that she herself won't be driven out of her cocoon.

Handan runs to the door saying, 'Muki, my Muki has come.' She smothers the frightful creature with kisses. The witch skeleton kisses Handan on her beautiful cheeks. She stains Handan's baby cheeks with the blood red of her frightful lipstick.

'My Muki, look, this is Behiye. My best friend. She's so intelligent, she got into Bosphorus University this year. Last night she cooked lemon kofte for me. So your baby wouldn't be left hungry. When you're not here I'm always hungry.'

'Does she know how to cook lemon kofte?'

'Of course, my Muki. You want to lick your fingers. Behiye and I bought all kinds of things yesterday. We even bought parsley, if you can believe it. Let's order tomatoes from the greengrocers so you can make *menemen** for me. I'm as hungry as a wolf, Muki. The other day you went off while I was sleeping.'

'You know that your Muki has to work in those rich houses.' As the witch skeleton says this, she pronounces the word 'rich' with disgust; in spite of herself, in spite of everything, Behiye likes Muki for this.

She wonders what work this witch does. Who would want her in the house? She's like a walking bad omen. Like an evil talisman. No one in their right mind would want to have her around.

She turns to Handan and says, 'If you like, we could go and buy tomatoes, green peppers, fresh bread and so forth.'

'Shopping for "ingredients" again, you mean,' says Handan giggling. 'All right, I'll take a shower. I'll be ready in half an hour.'

Half an hour? Half an hour alone with this witch? Leman could get up during that time, too. She'll think of new things to do to Behiye. She can't believe Handan doesn't understand this. Nor can she believe her bond of love with these two creatures.

Without saying anything, she starts gathering up the sheets, blanket and pillow from the pull-out bed.

Wearing her little white nurse's slippers, Muki goes into the living room. ' Did she sleep in my bed?'

Behiye bites her lips to keep from shouting something rude. She bites so hard that her lips bleed a little.

Handan comes running out of her room with her cell phone: 'Behiye, there's a call for you. Çiğdem.'

'Where have you been? Your mother is going crazy with worry.

---

* Scrambled eggs done with tomatoes and green peppers.

If I hadn't remembered you might be with Handan the police would be looking for you now.'

'All right, Çiğdem. I'm coming home now. Tell my mother.'

'Come quick. I don't want to get involved. The poor woman is crazy with worry. She was beside herself when she learned you weren't with us from my mother.'

'What happened?' asks Handan. ' Didn't you tell your mother where you'd be?'

'I did. It was just a misunderstanding. I'd better go home now.'

'Go talk to your mother. Get your pyjamas and toothbrush. Come stay with us again tonight. Why not, we had so much fun. We could go to the cinema, to Akmerkez. Couldn't we, Behiye, huh? Couldn't we?'

'All right. I'll come towards evening. I'll come after I talk to my mother.' She stands there. 'I'll bring my CD player when I come. I'll bring some CDs.'

She can't believe she said this, but she did. As she goes out the door and puts on her boots, Handan kisses her goodbye. 'Don't be late Behiye. After all, this is Saturday night.'

'Yes. Saturday Night Fever.'

Handan starts laughing. 'You're so funny, Behiye. I have so much fun with you.'

From inside they hear Muki's voice. 'Is she still here?'

Behiye bites her lips again.

'Don't take them seriously,' says Handan. 'You'll see, they'll both be crazy for you. Anyway, I'm crazy for you, isn't that enough?'

'More than enough.' She closes the door. She skips down the stairs three by three. She is outside.

She was disgusted by this house. As disgusted as she was by her own house. But if she didn't come back in the evening, if she didn't see Handan again – Behiye would die. This new Behiye would die. She knows this. Handan gives the new Behiye life. That's all.

Lancet

· ·

When she leaves Handan's house, Behiye crosses the street and walks towards Levent. In any event, she could walk as far as her house in Çemberlitaş. She feels she could walk for hours, as she used to do in the old days when she was depressed. Until she couldn't take another step, until she collapsed on the pavement...

She doesn't feel the distress she used to feel. She feels the New Behiye distress. New distress. Much livelier, full of blood and life, and in the shape of a circle. Not a distress concerning the whole of her life; only concerning being apart from Handan. Not wanting to be in Handan's house but not wanting to leave it either, fear of Muki and Leman's world, not being able to endure it. A knife-like, sinking distress.

It will pass when she sees Handan. It will be over.

Behiye is certain of this. The moment she sees Handan again they'll be wrapped in the yellow oilskin of happiness, and all will be well; she'll be in her dream again, she'll be accepted back into the cocoon – she's certain.

But she feels a definite dependence on Handan. And now she's having a crisis of deprivation. She's surprised at herself. But that's how it is. Handan dependency. Yes, that's what it's called. The name of New Behiye's distress.

She was only able to walk a short distance. When she got to the Dove Stop – that's what the sign said: Dove Stop – Behiye jumped on the Eminönü bus. What Çiğdem had said, her mother crazy with worry. She should get home as soon as possible. Possible. Or. They'll start. Searching. Ching.

Behiye cooks in the sun in the seat next to the window. A little too hot for end of September sun. Too roasting.

She wants to shout out To The End Of September Sun that it should know its limits. Normally, if yesterday was normal, she would have said this, would have made this comment to Handan. They would have giggled together. Or Handan would have gone into one of her childlike laughing fits. She would have laughed until she had to hold her tummy. Then she would have sighed the way babies do: she would have sighed from laughing so much.

But it's not normal now. Or rather now it is normal. Tears stream out of her eyes towards her chin. Towards her nose. Her nose becomes stuffed up. She dries her cheeks with the sleeve of the sweatshirt hanging around her neck. Then she wipes her nose.

'He who laughs a great deal cries a great deal.' One of those folk sayings that comes to you when you don't intend it to, that you remember without wanting to, that you didn't even know you remembered, one of those stupid sayings that you don't even want to know, and here it comes falling on to her lap. That's how she feels. As if it fell on to her lap.

The certainty of the saying despite what nonsense the saying is. The self-assurance of the folk saying. She feels like laughing. But suddenly she can't make the transition to the state of laughing. There's a sort of helplessness in this ebb and tide. She feels it as pressure.

She starts crying again, without wanting to want to cry.

She dries her eyes again. Then she shields her eyes from the sun with her fingers. But the sun, even if it is late September sun, doesn't pay attention. Insistent in its power and in its sunniness. It sticks its fingers in her eyes. It burns her cheeks.

At Eminönü – last stop: graveyard (another saying) – she jumps off the sunny bus. This time the saying, last stop graveyard, has stuck in her head. There's no escape: from song lyrics, film titles, folk nonsense, clichés, no escape from the wisdom of the masses. Even the craziest, loneliest, most alienated people are under this big black umbrella with everyone else.

She finds herself climbing up through the crowded and eventful streets of Tahtakale. Tahtakale always makes her feel well, is always good for her. There's no bad in all that crowdedness and turmoil. Despite the seeming chaos, Tahtakale runs like clockwork. It's a place that doesn't cramp a person's soul. Doesn't make you a fool. It's a great place. Great. Great. Great because it's the opposite of great. Or something like that.

Suddenly, she thinks of Handan's comments about how strange she is. Not in order to hurt her, but just in her conversation. She's tired of herself too. She's sick to death of her black T-shirts, her hoods, her black jeans, her enormous boots.

The Produce Building should be somewhere just around here. Behiye finds it. She wants to buy a lovely new jacket. She's too impatient to look through the shops on all three floors. In the first shop she enters, she finds a wonderful blue and green checked tweed jacket. After some fierce bargaining she buys the jacket for twelve million. It's hers for twelve million. Just the jacket she needed. At just the moment she needed it most. What more could she want?

She balls up the purple sweatshirt that she'd just blown her nose and wiped her eyes with, and stuffs it somewhere in the shop. She puts on her wonderful new tweed jacket. The jacket smells slightly of mothballs. But not too much.

She decides that her hair is longer than it should be. It's not long really, in fact it's quite short. But she feels that the late September sun, her hair and Behiye have all gone beyond their proper limits. But Behiye is embarrassed to go into the first barber shop, a men's barber shop, and ask for a military style haircut. She'll do it herself at home. There's no need to put on that kind of show right now.

Climbing the steep streets of Tahtakale, she arrives at a market place near where Mercan is. She knows that there's a place called the Polish Market where they sell all kinds of strange nonsense. But she can't believe what she sees waiting for her right on the stall at the entrance to the market. A lancet! She's found a lancet! A protection instrument! That she wished for last night. Right there in front of her.

Behiye doesn't know how the word 'lancet' got stuck in her head. It's one of those little, pencil-like knives that surgeons use when they perform operations. A lancet. Somehow or other the word got stuck to the flypaper of Behiye's mind.

The vendor agrees to sell it for seven lucky million. He wraps it carefully in newspaper so she won't cut herself, puts it in a small black plastic bag, and presents it to her. How easy it is to get your hands on a protection instrument! As if by magic!

From the thirty million her mother left on the kitchen table that last morning. An example of how a lancet can make a sick person well.

Her mother usually only leaves her three or five million. She left that much more either because of the fight the night before or because she was starting university. Her mother is strange that way.

Behiye can't stand it, and throws the newspaper and the black plastic bag in the garbage. She holds the lancet by its handle in her pocket. It's so light, so elegant; so beautiful. She takes it out of her pocket and looks at it. No one will understand what it is.

It's just like one of those mechanical pencils. It's as light as a pencil, as pleasurable to hold. The razor-like point, the cutting edge, is just like the point of a pencil. You can cut a person's throat with it as if you were writing. It would be unbelievably easy. Just by drawing a thin line, as if you were writing, you can cause someone to cross the line between life and death. Magic pencil. Death pencil.

She looks at the blade in admiration. Behiye loves her lancet. This little blade that gives her so much power. She looks and looks. Then she decides to put it back in her pocket. But then she thinks the blade might cut the pocket of her new jacket. So she buys a newspaper and wraps up her lancet again. Her lancet: Magic pencil.

Behiye's head is spinning. From hunger. No! From happiness. She's not at all hungry. She doesn't get hungry any more. What should she do?

She's getting closer to home. Closer to home.

Today is Saturday. What if shit Tufan is home? Saturday is the day he goes to rich areas with his idiot friends. On the weekends, they go to rich neighbourhoods, in the hope of 'hunting', and because they wish they belonged there, and because it makes them feel good.

The weather is nice. Tufan won't be at home. He'll have gone to a rich neighbourhood to try and climb above himself.

For a moment she thinks about walking as far as her mother's shop in Aksaray. Should she talk to her face-to-face? The next moment, she changes her mind. It's better to arrange things without seeing her. Without facing her nonsense. She can't face her mother's nonsensical behaviour. She can't tolerate Mother's Crying. She has no room left for Mother Pressure. In any event, her plate is full. She carries it all with her every step of the way.

Her father is at work. It's better to pack up her things and then talk to her mother by telephone. That's the best thing to do. Arrange things on the telephone. That's the best thing. The cleanest thing. Clean telephone.

The moment she enters the house, she feels enveloped by distress. Here you are, it says; here's your Old Behiye Distress. You've been longing for it, so take it.

She feels her heart rise to her mouth. She feels it beating in her mouth. Hurry. Hurry. Hurry. Hurry.

A strange and completely unreasonable state of agitation. As if she was in a hurry to get someplace on time. As if she's terribly late for something very very important. She has to go; but she can't go. As if they've locked her in. Imprisoned her. The annoying way her heart always beats in that house: hurry. Hurry up, Behiye. Hurry.

The feeling of panic increases when she sees the disarray the house is in. It distresses her. She feels constricted to the point that she fears her heart will stop. Behiye can't get rid of the feeling. The house smothers her. It narrows her, shrivels her, shrinks her. She can't get rid of it. Where would it go?

Slow down. Slow down. Slow. Slow.

First she tidies up the living room. She goes and makes her mother's and father's beds. As she scrubs the bath she feels better. As she's cleaning the toilet she suddenly wants to vomit. She sticks her head into the toilet and vomits a little. But there's not much in her stomach to vomit out. To vomit a little like that doesn't feel so bad.

She brushes her teeth for a long time. She gargles. She goes to the kitchen and drinks water.

Her mother has left the kitchen in a shitty mess. It's clear that she's gone through her usual routine. The shards of a broken glass lie unswept on the floor.

First she clears the table. Then she carefully sweeps the floor. She washes the dishes. Then she scrubs the kitchen's stone floor. She likes the coldness of the stone. It always does Behiye good to scrub the stone floor. It helps her forget that terrible feeling of panic within her. It slows down her heart. It brings it gently back into place.

After everything is done, after she's dried the floor carefully, she makes herself some tea. She slices some bread. She takes cheese and olives out of the fridge. She slices a tomato and a cucumber. She sits down and eats. It's not much, but it's the most she's been able to eat in days. She drinks her tea with pleasure. Grateful for the consolation the tea brings her. She thinks of her mother.

Perhaps the most peaceful, most self-possessed moments of her mother's life occurred while she was drinking tea. Tea is such a break. Tea is being totally by yourself. Drinking tea is more restful than anything. Tea Harbour. Tea Country.

She feels sorrow. She feels sorrow for her mother.

She hasn't left any money anywhere. She hasn't left money in order that Behiye will have to see her. In any event, there's a place in the closet, behind the sweaters, where her mother hides money. She goes into the bedroom and reaches into the hiding place. Her mother has saved three hundred and seventy million in an envelope. She takes the money and puts it in her back pocket. Mother Money.

She goes into her partitioned room, which has no posters, no toys, no decorations, which looks like a cell in a monastery. On the wall, there's nothing but a cross she bought from a counter under the old and famous plane tree in Beyazit. She likes it both for its own sake and because it drives Tufan crazy. It strengthened her impression that it was a monk's cell. She takes the cross down from its place. She wraps it in a pillowcase and puts it at the back of the top drawer of the closet. She's afraid Tufan might damage it. The thought just occurred to her.

She has a backpack like a potato sack. A big, shapeless thing. She fills it with all of her underwear and socks. She takes three or four T-shirts at random.

On top of these she places the CD player her mother gave her two years ago for her birthday. It looks like a pot with whistles; but it's better than making do with the television at Handan's. She takes her CDs of The Cure, Limp Bizkit, Linkin Park and Blink-182. She takes a number of books down from the shelves on the wall.

She does all of this quickly, without thinking. Her mother won't be back before five or six. But she's beginning to fear that she'll be caught. Just as these thoughts begin to mount in her mind, the telephone rings. Oh, no!

She answers. It's her mother.

She starts crying immediately. 'Where have you been, Behiye? Why did you say you were at Çiğdem's? You weren't there when I called. Why did you lie, my daughter; who were you with? Whose house can a young girl stay in? I was very worried, my child. Your father and I were out of our minds with worry until Çiğdem found you.'

'All right, Mother.'

'What do you mean, all right? Don't do this, Behiye. Don't do this to your mother.' Her mother is going to suffocate from crying. She's having trouble breathing.

'Look, Mother, I'm at home now and I'm going. I've taken some of my things; I borrowed a little money from you. I've taken my CD player and so forth – please don't worry about me. I met a girl from Çiğdem's course. Her name: Handan. I'm going to help her with her studies this year. She lives alone with her mother. I mean, there's room for me. They also live very close to Bosphorus University. Is that all right, Mother; are you listening to me?'

'What are you doing moving in with someone you've just met? Don't you have your own house, Behiye?'

'No, Mother. I don't have my own house. It's never been my house. Do you understand?' Behiye is shouting at the top of her voice.

'My daughter, my child; why are you saying this? Didn't we look after you? Did you grow up on the streets, Behiye?'

'Mother, I have to go now. I'll call you next week or so. Maybe I'll come by – later.'

'What is this "I'll come by"? Am I such a bad mother; don't you have a home? Behiye? Behiye?'

Behiye hangs up the telephone. Then she takes it off the hook.

She can't stop the tears falling from her eyes. She goes into Tufan's room. That shit definitely has some money hidden somewhere. She repeats this to herself as if she's been hypnotised. This shit definitely has money. This shit has hidden money.

She turns Tufan's room upside-down. Just as if the police had raided and made one of their malicious searches. In a sock under the bed she finds all of 150 euros. How that jackal Tufan had managed to save up his pennies. He'd never contributed so much as a penny to the house in all his life.

Just as she's leaving the room, she takes the picture of Tufan soldier commando and flings it to the ground. The glass in the frame smashes to pieces.

She throws the potato sack on her back and leaves the house. She's leaving the house clean and in perfect order. Only Tufan's room looks as if it's been raided.

She calls Çiğdem from the grocery store across the street. Çiğdem is alone at home. Her mother and father have gone to *Metro* for their monthly shopping trip. They'll be gone at least three or four hours. 'I'm dropping by,' says Behiye.

'Where have you been, girl?' neighs Çiğdem. 'I was going to start posting pictures of you on trees.'

Çiğdem and Behiye

. . . .

'Ooh, Lady Behiye, what an honour. Who would imagine you'd stoop to visit us. You've brought eternal honour to our humble home.'

In her boots, Behiye is marching into the living room whose plaster work and wallpaper are so badly matched that a person's eyes get no rest. When Çiğdem's mother is at home she makes everyone wear those undersized, decorated, high-heeled slippers. In any event Behiye would never go into the living room, but would rush to the kitchen or to Çiğdem's room at the back of the house.

But today she throws her potato sack on to the coat rack and marches into the living room. She throws herself into one of the armchairs, with roses carved into the wood and upholstered with claret and white striped cloth, that Aunt Sevil thought were so first class, so noble and chic.

A frightening living room this: with three giant chandeliers, coffee tables and end tables, a heavily carved dining table with twelve chairs, crystal ashtrays, vases, white satin pillows embroidered with gold, it was truly a temple to provincial bad taste. But Uncle Yavuz is partners with his older brother in a hardware shop in Persembe Pazar; they make good money, and Aunt Sevil is constantly trying to dress up the house in a 'demiclassic style' as if she suffered from a chronic decorating sickness.

'Aunt Sevil did such a shitty job decorating the house that it's a joke. This living room is so crazy it could even be considered hip, Çiğdem. I mean, without intending to she's created a work of art.'

'Forget about Aunt Sevil's stupid decorations. You tell your mother you're staying here but you don't let me know? I could have answered the phone and taken care of things, and nothing would have happened.'

'It doesn't matter now, Çiğdem. I'm very thirsty. Get me something to drink.'

'You've really gone round the bend, Behiye. Do you know how Aunt Yildiz cried when she found out you weren't here? Come, let's go to the kitchen.'

'Have you ever seen Aunt Yildiz *not* crying, Çiğdemella. She's always crying, always making a mess, always breaking things, always burning herself. I've had enough.'

'What do you mean, you've had enough?'

'This is what it means: it means that I'm moving to Handan's today. For good.'

As she opens a soda and passes it, Çiğdemella asks, 'What are you talking about, Behiye? What do you mean for good? Does Handan's family want you? From what I've heard from the kids at the course who went to Etiler Lise, Handan's mother is a you-know-what; she's considered a you-know-what.'

'What? What is Handan's mother, Miss Long Ears? What is she: is she a whore? Is that the word you couldn't come out with? Don't make me shit in your big mouth now.'

Çiğdem's eyes turn into big blue marbles. A big lump appears in her throat. In a loud, angry voice she says, 'Why are you talking to me this way, Behiye? How quickly you forget, Behiye: I've been your closest friend since you were six years old. That's what I heard, and I thought I should tell you. You should have just hit me. You looked as if you were ready to do it.'

Çiğdem puts her head on the table and starts crying her eyes out. As she cries, her blue shirt moves back and forth. Behiye watches the moving shirt in horror. How am I going to stop this shirt from moving, she thinks. If she said 'Stop!' three times, stop! stop! stop! would the shirt stop? Would Çiğdem cut out her crying?

She finds her hand on Çiğdem's shoulder. 'My Çiğdem,' she says, 'don't cry, my friend. I'm sorry, I'm very sorry. My mother, my house and Tufan have really got on my nerves. I went too far. I'm sorry my true, childhood friend.'

Çiğdem raises her head and wipes her long eyelashes with the back of her hand. There are tears on her fat red cheeks. Behiye reaches out and wipes them off. To get rid of them. So they won't stay there glistening like that.

'You never used to talk to me like that,' sighs Çiğdem. 'You never, never, never used to talk to me like that.' She begins to hiccup.

'Booo!' shouts Behiye. 'See how the fright got rid of your hiccups.'

'All right, you've always been a little crazy, Behiye. But I swear that lately you've really gone out of your mind. God, look at the jacket you're wearing. I've never seen anything like it. You couldn't have stolen it from Uncle Salim because even he wouldn't wear something like that. All you need now is a beret and a dirty beard. I mean, what were you thinking?'

Behiye realises how much every word out of Çiğdem's mouth twists her heart. Later, she realises that it's been this way for years. For years Çiğdem's words, figures of speech, her tree-trunk sayings, have been painful for Behiye. They hurt her. They wound her. They scratch at her shell. They always upset her. Always.

She begins to feel cool towards the jacket and the lancet that she'd loved so much, that she'd thought so beautiful. With those comments, her relationship with the jacket had been ruined.

She takes off the jacket. She folds it carefully and places it on top of her potato sack.

'Look, Çiğdem, listen carefully,' she says, collapsing in the chair right across from her. She looks into Çiğdem's completely meaningless lake-blue eyes. 'This is very important. Please listen carefully. I've left my house. Tufan could go rabid on me. I did a couple of things in his room that will make him angry.'

'What kind of mischief have you got up to, Behiye? He loathes you already. He's turning into a vampire, a werewolf the moment he sees you. You never stop. Will you ever stop? You do and say everything to drive him crazy. You'll never do a thing to get along with someone, Behiye. You have no use for diplomacy. Human diplomacy.'

'To hell with your idiotic sayings, wherever you got them, and listen to me carefully. Look, I'm serious, very, very serious. If you give Handan's number to anyone, anyone at all, you'll never see my face again as long as you live, Çiğdem. I'll never look you in the face again. Seriously, I won't. It's that important. Do you understand me?'

'I'm not retarded. Of course I won't give it to anyone. But your mother knows I have the number. What am I going to tell her?'

'You'll tell her they've changed their number. And that Handan is no longer taking the course. That's what you'll say. Just like that. All right?'

'All right, Lady Behiye. I'll do whatever you want. Hasn't your slave Çiğdem always done exactly what you said for years? Haven't you always had the last word in this relationship, in this friendship? Hasn't it been that way for years?'

'Is that how it's always been?' Behiye asks in surprise. She looks into her Çiğdem-blue eyes, which are still wet under her brown bangs. A fat doll's face. Made in China. Çiğdem should have this tattooed on her forehead. To hide what's passing through her mind, she asks again, 'Is that how it's been?'

'Yes ma'am, that's how it's been. Whatever you say goes, it's always, always been like that. You've constantly put me down. Even my mother says so.'

'Oh, and what did your mother order?'

'You mock everything, Behiye. You're always mocking me, making fun of me. I'm fed up with your cleverness.'

'You put me down too, if you really want to know. You broke my heart with your boorishness. Do you have any idea of what I've been through, of my inner life, of what I've read, of what I've listened to? Have you ever wondered: where is she going, who is she, who she became. Have you ever asked yourself? Have you asked yourself, huh, Çiğdem?'

'Behiyeee. All of this talk is very upsetting. It's too much for me. I'm not used to it. With your famous saying: I'm a happy family child. You say it as if you're cursing. I'm empty-headed, that's all.

'All right. I'm sorry. I swear. I went too far. But Handan isn't taking the course any more; she never answers the phone. All right? Tell them: you wrote the number in a notebook, then you lost it. You lost the notebook. For instance, wherever you wrote it, throw that notebook away. That's the cleanest way.'

'I've even memorised it. Handan's cell phone number is very easy. It's also in my own cell phone.'

'All right, Çiğdem. As long as no one from my house gets hold of it. Or else I'll never forgive you.'

'I'll Never Forgive You: good old Turkish movie! On this channel, this week, this evening. You've gone out of your head over this Handan. What is this, Behiye; do they even want you in their house? It's as if you'd fallen in love. What is this Handan business about? I don't get it.'

'Don't start talking nonsense again. Come, let's go to Taksim and buy some new things for me. These boots are cooking my feet in this September sun.'

'I've got tired of talking about those. All summer we weren't able to solve the problem of your boots.'

They jump in a taxi and fly to Taksim. They go to a change office in which Çiğdem's uncle's son is a partner. They leave the potato sack there.

They go and buy Behiye a light blue windbreaker, oversized blue jeans and four T-shirts. None of them are black.

Behiye puts on the white T-shirt she bought last, and tosses the black one she's been wearing into the garbage.

Then they go and find a pair of Adidas. These are the calmest sports shoes. Çiğdem is crazy about a pair of red Pumas.

'Why don't you buy these, girl. They're sweet. And they're also very much in fashion.'

'That's why I won't buy them. Do you want to turn me into a fashion puppet? Like those stupid girls in the ads.'

'You've become very stylish, Behiye. No, no: you've become trendy. I swear that's what they say.'

'I'll show you trendy.' She starts running after Çiğdem.

They push and shove each other as far as Galatasaray. Behiye is hitting Çiğdem over the head with her packages. Here and there people with nothing to do stop and watch them. Çiğdem, the horse of the year. Childhood horse. Forever neighing. Without end.

'Should we find a barber around here; should I cut my hair very short, Çiğdem?'

'No, don't. It's already very short. Look at what beautiful red hair you have. Who has such beautiful hair in Turkey? Your face has got thinner lately. You should grow your hair a little. It suits you so well, Behiye. One notices how beautiful you are. This white and blue makes you look great, I swear.'

'That's the first time you've ever told me you like my hair, Çiğdem. Until today you've never said anything like that to me.'

'I used to tell you in primary school. Later, I don't know, you frighten a person, Behiye. At least you frightened me. I don't know what to do or say for fear of crossing you.'

'How frightened you are, my little pipe. How sensitive you are.'

'Don't make fun of me. Not like that.' Çiğdem sighs. They're both aware that something strange has happened today. That they've opened up. That they've opened many cans one by one, cans that had never been opened because they didn't want to bother, because they were afraid, daunted.

They sit in a café and drink tea. Çiğdem eats a huge sandwich, and on top of that a slice of chocolate cake.

'Let's get my potato sack before the change office closes,' says Behiye. For some reason, her eyes fill with tears as she says this. 'Look, Çiğdem: you don't have Handan's number; all right?'

'Yes, I've understood, my girl,' says Çiğdem, throwing her last forkful of cake into her mouth. 'This ends where you said it ends: I don't have the number. Handan has dropped out of the course.'

They take the sack and come out the mouth of Istiklal. 'I'm going to cross the street and jump into a taxi,' says Behiye.

'Lady Behiye is very rich today.'

'I took all of the money Tufan hid in his room, Çiğdem.'

'Mother! That psychopath will tear you to pieces. You already drive the guy crazy. He's completely out of his head with all that commando stuff. You're in deep shit, Behiye. This is all you needed.'

'Don't worry. He can't find me. I trust you, Çiğdem. The most Çiğdem of Çiğdems. Our Çiğdem!' She kisses Çiğdem lovingly on the cheeks. She gives her a tight embrace and smells her head.

Çiğdem has a smell like everyone else. Çiğdem smell: a mixture of shampoo, perfume and cleanness. It's not like the Handan Smell. There's no resemblance. There couldn't be.

'Everyone has the same smell.'

'What did you say, Behiye?'

'I didn't say anything. It's nothing. Until we see each other again look after all the parts.'

'Behiye, you'll call me, won't you? I'll see you again, won't I? You'll call, won't you, before too long?'

'I will, before long.' Behiye jumps into the first taxi standing in front of them. Through the window she sees Çiğdem, looking like a fat peanut in her tight little pants, waving at her. She isn't able to keep the tears coming out of her eyes. She doesn't know if she'll see Çiğdem again, if she'll ever hear that neighing voice again. She can not help but the pain of separation settles into her heart like an insolent snake. Snake. Nake. Cake.

Saturday night

· ·

Handan appears on the landing, clapping her hands, just as Behiye was ringing the bell at the door to the apartment building.

'Where have you been, Behiye? I've been waiting with my heart in my mouth for hours. I was so frightened. Well, you've come!'

Her cat eyes seem to have absorbed the colour of the green T-shirt she's wearing. They shine like pebbles that have been thrown into the sea. She's smiling at Behiye, showing her dimples. She was so bored waiting, she painted her fingernails in pearl colour. Right away, she holds out her hands and shows her nails. 'I painted them well this time. Look, I didn't put too much on, Behiye.'

'Is your mother home?' Behiye reaches in and flings out the question that's been troubling her soul. In a troubled, ill-tempered, broken voice.

'No, no. She went to the hairdresser's. From there she'll go to Sister Nevin's. You know, this latest man she's set her mind on: Mr Necdet, or whatever his name was, the man who called her from Moscow. They'll talk about him now until morning. I call these their man sessions. They're always talking about some man or other. Don't think it's ever useful, Behiye. Really. They talk and talk but they don't really say anything.'

Handan talks breathlessly, as if she's been waiting all day to say these things. The world's loneliest baby, thinks Behiye. The world's hungriest baby. Her heart shivers. She fills herself with the love she feels for Handan. First her house emptied her out, and then Çiğdem did. What she lived today finished her. All that's left are shards and shells. They're piercing.

'How nice you look in that T-shirt. And I love your blue, blue windbreaker. Come, let's put your things in my room. My closet is crammed, though. But we'll make some room. While I was waiting for you, Behiye: just a little while ago, half an hour ago, I mean – you won't be angry with me? I did a very shameful thing. I was like a child, I couldn't stop myself.'

'What did you do?' asks Behiye, her heart beating with a kind of fear she'd never known existed.

'Well, I was very hungry. I couldn't stand it. I ate all the lemon kofte. There's none left for you. But you won't be left hungry. We can go and eat at Akmerkez. Not that I have any money. But some friends of mine called earlier. I mean, they might call again. They'll treat us.'

'What a silly baby girl you are.' Behiye starts laughing. 'She finished the lemon kofte. As if I cared!' She goes and kisses her left cheek. She holds her face and draws in her smell. Handan smell. Do me good. Take me away from here. What is this place, anyway? This place doesn't work. I can't exist in this place. Narrowwww.

'Look, I brought my pot with whistles. Can I put my CDs here?' She points to the big glass coffee table in the living room. There are five or six silly magazines on the bottom shelf, that's all.

'No. My mother rests her feet on that. I don't know, she'll get annoyed. Let's put it in my room, we can bring it out to the living room when we want to play it.'

They squeeze Behiye's T-shirts into Handan's closet. They put her underwear and socks into a bag and stuff it into the bottom drawer. They have to struggle to shut the drawer. There's no room for anyone's things in Handan's room.

Behiye doesn't allow herself to feel cramped. Her soul waits for her to cover herself with the yellow oilcloth. With Handan now, she'll be free of her inner distress. Yellow oilcloth. Come cover me.

'I'm going to hang my jacket on one of your hangers, Handan. Let's throw out something you never wear.'

'Since childhood I've never been able to throw out any of my clothes. Even if I know I'll never wear it; they all hold good or bad memories for me. It's a habit; I can't throw things out.'

'Throw out a couple of things that hold bad memories. I have to hang my jacket up.'

Handan's lower lip falls. With difficulty she frees a hanger and hands it to Behiye. She tries to squeeze the clothes she took from the hanger back into the closet again. The closet spits them out like an animal that's eaten its fill. There's no room.

'Handan, what's this? Your closet can't take any more clothes. Let's buy a packet of huge garbage bags and fill them with clothes you don't wear. Why should you keep all these?'

'All right, Behiye.' The baby girl is put out. Her eyes fill with tears. Behiye has made three women cry today. Her mother, Çiğdem, Handan. She's fed up with crying. Her own, and theirs. Oilskin of happiness: yellow. Where are you? Come cover me. Come quick.

'Look at me. Don't be upset. You see the state your closet is in. If there's no room for a few of my things, I can leave.'

'No! Don't go, Behiye. This is the first time in my life I've had such a close friend. I'm very alone in this world. Don't even think of leaving. All right, I'll throw out some thousand-year-old things. They're unnecessary. You're right, my dear. Don't be angry with me; don't you go. All right, Behiye?'

'All right.' They're sitting on Handan's bed. Behiye puts her arm around her. Handan rests her head softly on her shoulder.

Their eyes fill with tears at the same moment. They're crying like two lonely and desperate cartoon characters just above water on their raft. There's nothing to be done about it. There's nothing else but to cry about their desperation and powerlessness.

They'll go wherever the current takes them. They have no one but each other. They have no power in this vast ocean. They don't even have a pair of oars. It grieves them to know that this is how it is. What can they do? What recourse do they have but to let the currents take them where they will? None. None. That's all.

Suddenly, Behiye thinks of the jacket hanging in the over-stuffed closet. The lancet in the jacket pocket. The lancet is an oar. The oar of the boat. An instrument that can change the way things are going. A protection instrument. A magical instrument capable of drawing lines.

When I put on that jacket, I'll have power. My jacket has a talisman. There's a magic pencil in the pocket. Whatever happens, it can draw the line between life and death. It can do whatever it wants with its blade. Write whatever it wants on a person. Oar pencil.

The possibility of power suddenly makes Behiye feel better. Her sails fill with wind. 'Shall I play The Cure for you?' she says. 'I'm going to put everything on the coffee table in the living room. Your mother can go crazy if she wants. There's lots of room on the coffee table for her to rest her feet. Later we can empty out the closet. We'll make room, Handan. In life you have to make room. All right, my baby cat girl?'

'All right, Behiye,' she says sweetly. 'Your joy is as strange as your sorrow. Whatever mood you're in, I get the same mood right away. I've noticed that. However you are, I too suddenly...'

'Contagious, you mean.'

'Yes, yes. That's the word I was looking for. That's it; it passes from you to me.'

They leave and go to Akmerkez.

Handan is a true child of Akmerkez. Behiye sees this the

moment they pass through the door. She starts breathing and swimming happily, flipping her tail, like a goldfish in her bowl. She knows all its shores and corners by heart. All its possibilities. As well its impossibilities. Handan doesn't have any money. She knows the price and the quality of everything, each and every label, that Akmerkez will never present to her. What a frightful thing to have memorised! What a heavy load!

They go up to the top floor, where the cinemas and fast-food places are. Handan wants a doughnut. She eats two doughnuts sprinkled with pistachio nuts and drinks a coffee. Behiye watches her; and drinks water. Handan is so beautiful. Little by little, she feels filled. It feels good.

Because it's nice outside, it's not very crowded. They sit and watch the passers-by.

'Rich people make me sick to my stomach, but they also give me a strange desire to laugh,' says Behiye. 'That's how it is at first. But if I spend time looking at them, if I really contemplate them, I feel like making them disappear. Cleaning them off one by one. Cleaning is such a nice word, isn't it?'

'Why are you talking like that? As if you wouldn't want to be rich, as if you wouldn't want to be able to buy anything you wanted. If you ask me, you say these things because you envy them.'

'I don't envy them; I don't have that kind of feeling at all. Ha, I've thought of it: where's the famous enemy of the rich, Muki? Or aren't we going to be graced with her joyful presence this evening?'

'First of all, my Muki isn't any kind of enemy of the rich. At her age, being an attendant and a cleaning woman is hard for her. She was just a little bit cross with you because you slept in her place. She has some relatives in Pendik or someplace; some distant neighbourhood. She's gone to stay there. I begged her to stay with us, but she went.'

'That's too bad,' says Behiye. Just as she's about to make a joke about Muki's charm, Handan's phone rings.

'Buraaak! Is Erim there too? We're here, on the top floor. No, no, a girlfriend of mine you don't know. All right, we'll come down. Right away, I said. Fine. All right. Bye.'

Handan's cheeks become very red. Her eyes shine, her lips get thicker, her teeth longer, and so forth. Or so it seems to Behiye. 'What happened?' she asks in a dry voice. 'Is someone on the ground floor going to reveal the secrets of Atlantis to us?'

'Oh, Behiye! Burak and his friend have gone into the *Home Store*. Let's go and hang out with them a bit. And look, this is Saturday night. Maybe they'll take us to some bars or something.'

Boys! How could these unavoidable creatures not flock around Handan? Around someone so beautiful, such a beautiful baby: a hundred, ten thousand of them.

And what about their cocoon? That protective and fortunate cocoon of happiness that was just for the two of them? Is Behiye going to have to endure other people in order to be with Handan? Is she constantly going to have to endure more and more people? Behiye doesn't want to have to be patient. To be patient, to wait, to make an effort; like everything else you have to do in this world. To pick things apart, to pluck things, to be plucked, to dig up, building site – excavation. She doesn't want excavation. She just doesn't want it.

'You go, Handan. I don't have the energy to socialize with anyone at this time of the evening. I'll wander around here a little.'

'Don't be silly, Behiye. Look, I've thought of something: you go buy those trash bags you wanted at *Makro*. Then come get me, and we'll go home together. I only want to be with you; that's all. Don't you understand?'

'Fine. However you want. I'll come get you within half an hour.'

As they go down one floor together on the escalator, side by side, Behiye feels that they've re-entered their magic. Handan has only her in her life, nothing else. That's how it is. Handan doesn't have anything else. Just as Behiye has nothing but Handan, it's the same way for Handan. That's all. It's that simple and COMPLETE.

Behiye goes up and down the aisles of Makro, doing some heavy shopping. She wants to fill up the hungry child house for Sunday and the days after that. When they open the refrigerator, she wants them to see it completely full.

She buys a number of things for breakfast. She buys eggs, and packages and packages of pasta. Potatoes, onions, a bottle of olive oil, and other things. She also buys a package of jumbo size trash bags. She diverts herself there for at least an hour.

As she goes into the place called *Home Store* with all of her grocery bags, the idiots look at her with irritation. From somewhere in the back, Handan waves to her joyfully.

Behiye nods her head to say 'come on', and goes out the door. Two or three minutes later Handan comes out breathless.

'How much stuff you bought, Behiye! That's more food than enters our house in a year. You didn't meet the boys. Burak is my friend from school. Erim is awfully nice. You'd have really liked him if you'd met him; you didn't even look.'

'Never mind. Let's go home and put these things away. You're sure you don't want to stay? Give me the key if you want, and you can go hang out with them, Handan. I can amuse myself in your house.'

'I'm fine with you. Come, let's go home. Give me one of those bags.'

'I'll carry them,' says Behiye. 'Baby girls never carry bags. Carrying bags is for donkey girls. Not for cat girls.'

Handan giggles. 'You're the funniest,' she says. 'You're the funniest when you're not ill-tempered. I don't enjoy myself with anyone else the way I do with you. I was ready to explode with those boys. You came and rescued me, Behiye.'

They return home and fill the refrigerator and the kitchen shelves. Handan's first task is to take off her blue jeans and put on her grey sweatpants. Handan has a habit of wearing different clothes at home. Behiye doesn't. Whatever she puts on in the morning, she's wearing when she goes to sleep at night.

Handan finds Linkin Park very heavy. She wrinkles her face and her eyes like a child as she drinks her coffee. Behiye puts on The Cure's *Bloodflowers* CD. They listen to it as they watch the idiocy on television.

Behiye sings along with The Cure, the ninth song on the CD. She shouts. At the top of her voice. She shouts at the top of her voice.

They watch television until two o'clock in the morning, zapping among the channels. They watch and talk. About everything under the sun. About. Under.

'Shall we go to sleep now, Handan? I'm done. I'm very tired.'

She wants to be asleep before Leman returns. They make Behiye's bed: They complete the transformation of the pull-out bed.

'Good night, Behiye.' Once again Handan gives her a real kiss that makes her tremble within. With her teeth freshly brushed, and wearing underwear and an oversized T-shirt, Behiye feels very well in the bed. She feels as snug as a pearl in its shell. Handan turns out the light and goes to her room.

Before she falls asleep, some of the lyrics from *Bloodflowers* wander through Behiye's mind.

Later, the lyrics get tired too. Behiye thinks of a labyrinth of shaped greenery. Garden labyrinth. Labyrinth garden. Behiye doesn't know who the gardener is.

Did she prune the greenery this way herself? Who holds the shears? Her mind is very tired after all. Little by little, it turns off. With The Cure's lyrics, the garden and the gardener going around in her head, she sinks to the bottom of the well of sleep.

Pool

. . . .

Behiye wakes from a deep and perfect sleep. She wakes around ten, completely rested and renewed. She didn't hear Leman come in. Nothing interrupted her sleep. Nothing interrupted its wholeness.

As she splashes her face with water, a scene appears in her mind like a bead from the necklace of her dreams. She was in a pool. She was swimming with Handan in a beautiful blue pool. Handan was wearing a pink swimsuit. A long-sleeved pink swimsuit: like the ones ballet students wear. Behiye's swimsuit was black, with long sleeves and a straight collar. The two of them were making wonderful synchronised movements in the pool. More like ice-skating than water ballet; such smooth, gliding graceful movements. Everything was very beautiful. It was very sunny. It was bright, bright blue. Both of them were breathless with happiness. They were enveloped in an excess of happiness that left them breathless.

That's as much as Behiye remembers. As with all dreams, something bad has to happen later. Things that stab the wholeness of that perfect happiness. Something like that must have happened. But Behiye can't recall. As she keeps splashing water on her face, the extraordinary happiness of her dream of the pool is with her. That's all.

She gets dressed and gathers up her bed. The moment she

goes into the kitchen, Leman appears half-asleep at the door like a cat. She's wearing a very transparent nightgown. Underneath, she's wearing nothing but very small white panties. Her pert breasts move aggressively under the transparency.

Behiye feels besieged by this obscene assault. Behiye acts like it's very normal to see Leman half-naked in the kitchen, and she's not the least bit concerned or put out; she's trying to act as if it doesn't interest her, and she doesn't care. But her eyes, all by themselves, without asking permission, fall on to Leman's breasts, her stomach, her legs, the little lace panties that barely cover her pubic hair. They look. They're drawn as if by magnetism to the beauty, the shamelessness, the exhibitionism, of Leman's body. At the places that were necessary to look at, one by one. They look straight.

'Eh, you're an early-bird, Behiye. You're making breakfast for your little Handan, are you?'

Her voice crackles; there are cracks in it that a person could disappear into. As soon as she hears the voice, Behiye understands why she's wandering around half-naked. She drank all night; she drank and talked about her latest boyfriend.

Then, just as she was getting ready for bed, a provocative late-night phone call. From Moscow, Mr Şevket or whatever his name was, from him. This was her costume for an erotic conversation. An outfit to get herself into the mood for that provocative game. The almost non-existent nightgown and the panties were accessories. Leman is too. In that state she's also a sex accessory. Leman is a sex object that glows when it uses itself. That's all.

The moment she thinks these things, Behiye feels more relaxed. She lets out her breath like an over-inflated balloon.

Then the phrase 'your little Handan' slides in to the square like a hopscotch stone. The mad jealousy in that comment. Leman's loss of control. A style of loss of control that was frightening and nauseating. She averts her eyes from Leman and all her brazenness. As she's making tea she gives her enraged answer.

'Yes, I'm making breakfast for Handan and myself. If you like, why don't you get dressed and join us; eat something with us.'

Leman hits the ball while it's still in the air: 'Are you saying I have to dress appropriately for a good family breakfast, Behiye?' She makes crackling laughing sounds. She puts out her cigarette in the dirty ashtray and goes back to her room. Taking her dry laughter with her.

Perhaps she'll sleep. She'll sleep for two or three hours; before Handan wakes she'll have time to come back to herself. Behiye feels good about herself. She feels like an expert player, or something. She and Leman have to be in a game of balls, slides and top-notch power. She thinks of this. Pleased at how sharp her mind is this morning. This. These.

When the breakfast is just about ready, Handan wakes up. After washing her face and brushing her teeth quickly, she takes her place in front of her plate and her nicely brewed tea.

She claps her hands again as an omelette is being put on her plate. My baby girl claps when I give her food, thinks Behiye, loving Handan again as if for the first time. The moment Handan came in and sat down in her chair, she felt as if the kitchen had been cleaned and purified. As if the window had been opened and a summer breeze had filled the room. Clearing out evil spirits, smells, influences and Lemans. Leaving only the goodness of their breakfast; clean, pure, child spirits.

They eat breakfast joyfully. Handan eats perhaps a thousand pieces of toast. She drinks two thousand teas. 'The smell of toast! The smell of tea! How wonderful!' she says all of a sudden. 'These are the smells of home. You came and made our house a home; You've done us good, you've done our house good, Behiye. Has my mother woken yet? She always wakes early.'

'She woke. Then she went back to bed. Once we've tidied up, let's take a look at your closet. We'll throw out some unnecessary things and make some room. We talked about this yesterday evening, remember?'

'All right, my Behiye,' says Handan.

My Behiye? Behiye isn't used to such tenderness, such sweetness, to being addressed affectionately, and she finds it wonderful, strangely wonderful.

'I'm going to go into sugar shock soon.'

'What kind of shock?'

'Sugar shock. You're so sweet, you're such a doll, Handan. I'm like a biscuit that's been dipped in hot milk. I'm completely softened by happiness.'

'Behiye, where do you get these phrases? You're something else, really. Let me make my bed and then we can take care of the closet.'

Behiye clears up the kitchen and turns on the dishwasher. Leman comes and puts on water for coffee. She turns on the radio and lights a cigarette. She's wearing a blue bathrobe with the belt tied very tightly. It's clear that she's planning to take a bath after her morning session of nescafé, cigarettes and music.

'Has my mother rabbit woken up?' says Handan in a sing-song voice as she comes into the kitchen. She kisses and hugs her mother. Then she sits on her lap and starts telling her what she's been doing.

Behiye goes into Handan's room and opens the warped door of the pink painted closet. She doesn't know where to begin. She stands and looks. Handan returns from her session with her mother.

'Since we moved here from our house in Bomonti, I mean since I was eight years old, it's been eight years, in eight years I haven't thrown anything out, I couldn't bear to, Behiye.'

They take out a number of shrunken, faded things, things she'd only worn once and hated. More. More. They fill three blue, jumbo-sized *Koroplast* trash bags.

Handan has squeezed the oldest things into the very back. They find her childhood things. Both of them are touched: child Handan's *Stone Age* T-shirt, blue jeans with lace-work, pink polka-dot tights, a red anorak with *Tom and Jerry* on the back. Handan takes a bright blue jacket out of the very back. SYDNEY is written in white letters over the heart. She hugs the jacket in her arms. She collapses on her bed.

'Look, this jacket is from our house in Bomonti. I've had it since I was seven. I never wear it for fear my mother will take it from me. I've always kept it hidden in the depths of the closet.'

'Who brought it to you from Sydney?' Behiye noticed how broken the cat girl's voice was; it twisted her heart.

'Harun brought it: my father.'

'Did you see your father when you were a child? I didn't know he lived in Australia.'

'He came to get me,' says Handan. 'To the house in Bomonti. With a lot of presents: stuffed animals, paint sets, shoes, bags, swimsuits, Barbie dolls – this and that. To try to win me over with a bag full of things. To bring me to Australia. For good.'

'What happened?'

'My mother wouldn't let me go. She threw a fit, fainted, she fought, shouted, insulted, everything she could do. He should have thought about this before he left her, she said. She had nothing to live for but me. She said things like that. She never let him see me again. Saying she was afraid he'd kidnap me. So I stayed here: as Leman's daughter…I remained fatherless. Here with Leman. Just with her.'

At first, a few small tears ran down her cheeks. Then Handan couldn't hold herself back, and started crying her eyes out. She sighs as her crying increases. She stops crying suddenly, the way babies do. She breathes, then starts again. She cries like a baby; from her heart, from the depths of her being. She is pure crying. Crying baby.

Behiye feels stopped up. She doesn't know what to do. She feels as if she's been punched in the stomach, she feels stopped up.

'Don't be upset, Handan. My baby cat girl, don't upset yourself. I'm certain you'll find your father again. You'll be reunited with him. It's not that difficult; you can find out where he lives.'

'My mother tore up his address and phone number years ago. And we also moved. I don't know anyone who knows my father.

How am I going to find my father? I'm not going to be able to find him. I'll never be able to find him.'

'Terribly easy,' says Behiye. 'Send an e-mail to the Australian Consulate. You can find out if you give his name and surname. It's that easy, I'm sure. You'll see.'

'I've upset you with my troubles this morning, Behiye. But I wouldn't throw this jacket out for the whole world. This is the only thing left from what he brought. My mother gave everything else away. Even one of the Barbies, no matter how much I begged; she wouldn't let me keep it.'

'You know, this jacket isn't so small. Even if it's a bit short, it will suit you. Why don't you wear it today, Handan.'

Handan puts the jacket on over her white T-shirt. Below, she's wearing blue jeans and her grey-white shoes. They leave the house with the trash bags on their backs. As they go out the door, she calls, 'See you later, mother!' She doesn't want to have to account for cleaning out her closet or for wearing the jacket with SYDNEY written on it.

They leave the trash bags next to the container not far from the building. Someone might see it and want something. There's a lovely September sun out. The end of summer; but not the end of the sun. It warms you without being impudent or biting. Rather, it caresses you.

They start walking towards Hisarustu. People are showing off their brand new cars in the Sunday traffic. They don't care about anything. Neither the comments shouted from the passing cars nor the sound of the horns. Handan and Behiye walk for hours, one with her arm around the other's shoulder, the other with her arm around the other's waist, talking to each other about their lost childhood, laughing, and crying sweetly.

They descend the steep hill to Hisar. From Hisar they walk as far as Yeniköy. The way they were talking, they couldn't get enough of walking. They didn't feel at all tired. Or if they did, they didn't register it.

They drink tea at a coffee-house right on the sea. Handan eats fried potatoes and a hamburger. Behiye drinks tea. From time to time she looks at the writing on the jacket. SYDNEY. SYDNEY.

'That's the seventh continent. Handan, it's a whole new world. The newest world. Lots of land and few people. And look how it is here. It's so over-crowded here. Everyone's on top of each other. Sometimes I feel like I'm going to suffocate. Not just sometimes. Until I found you, constantly. I always felt like I was going to suffocate, die, explode. What if we got up and went there; found your father. Started a new life there. A new life on the new continent. What do you say, Handan; wouldn't it be fantastic?'

'It would, Behiye. It would be awfully nice, we'd be free of this place. But wouldn't it be a shame for Muki and Leman? My mother would be destroyed if I left her.'

'She's kept you quite a few years. She's kept you imprisoned in her own world. Isn't sixteen years enough? Sixteen years with you, isn't it enough?'

Handan hangs her head. The thought of abandoning Leman hurts her deeply.

Behiye reaches out and lifts her chin. 'We'll be well there, Handan. You'll see how well we'll be there.'

'Passport, visa, plane ticket; we don't have any of these things. We don't have any money. It's not that easy to just go off to Australia.'

'First we'll find your father,' says Behiye. 'He can take care of everything. Everything will solve itself. We'll be well there.'

They've turned and started walking back. Talking about the likelihood of Australia, the new continent, and a new life. They talk constantly as they walk. As they're passing the lower gate of Bosphorus University, Behiye remembers that there's a swimming pool there. The pool idea drops right in front of her as if it had fallen from a pear tree.

'Come, let's go to the pool. I saw it the last time I was here. There's an enormous pool, right here through the gate.'

'It's eleven at night. The pool will be closed, Behiye. We don't even have swimsuits with us. They'll never give us permission.'

'Who needs permission,' says Behiye laughing. 'They can take their permission and stick it I don't know where.'

Handan giggles. 'You're so crazy, Behiye. How are we going to do it?'

Behiye shows her identity card at the gate and they enter. Saying they're two 'new' girls staying at the dormitory. Everything is taken care of.

The gate-man looks at Handan's breasts while he listens to their excuses. He lets them both in. All the gates to the pool are locked. Up above, Behiye finds a gap between the university grounds and a neighbouring apartment building. They creep into the pool area.

Behiye takes off her clothes quickly. She jumps into the pool in her underwear. She dives in and out like a dolphin. Behiye and the water are beautiful together. As if she belongs there. Pool girl.

Handan also jumps into the pool in her underwear. They swim up and down. They push each other under water. They dive in and out. Two baby dolphins who've found each other in a sea of happiness: Unable to get their fill of playing, of the water; of being enveloped by the water, of the water's beauty.

Two baby dolphins. Unfettered by circuses and parks and pirates. They haven't been captured, won't be captured; two free, happy, loving and beloved spirits. They look so beautiful playing in the pool. Playing as babies do, with no sense of time or place.

Later, Handan and Behiye will relive those moments at the pool in the cinema of their minds. So much like babies, so pure, free and happy. Beautiful gifts so rarely bestowed by life.

When they climb out their teeth chatter; their limbs are blue-white, their skin puckered from the cold. They're freezing. They're freezing; but they're laughing and they're very happy. They even find a towel that someone has forgotten. They dry themselves as best they can. They stick their wet underwear in the back pockets of their blue jeans. On the avenue they jump into a taxi and go home. To dry their hair, put on dry clothes, drink hot tea, warm up, put on woollen socks.

While Handan is taking off her blue jeans, the telephone rings. Behiye can't hear anything over the sound of the hairdryer. Handan hands her the phone from the bathroom door. 'Çiğdem. She's been calling you for hours.'

'Girl, I've called you about four hundred and forty-two times in the last two hours. As far as I know, a cell phone is something to be carried around. A phone that sits at home is called a home phone by common people.'

'What's the problem, Çiğdem?'

'That maniac Tufan dropped by on us late at night. Don't worry, he didn't get your number out of us. But he found out from your mother that Handan is in the same course as me. He's rabid about his money disappearing. I swear he was foaming at the mouth.'

'Thanks, Çiğdem. You're such a friend, my friend. I guess I'm in deep shit.'

'What are you going to do, Behiye? I think you should give the maniac his money back. So he won't go to the police or something, God forbid.'

'My mother won't let anything like that happen. I'll think it over. We'll talk later. Thanks, Çiğdem. You're my best and oldest friend. Bye.'

She hangs up the phone before Çiğdem can dive into a new sentence.

She remembers the end of the pool dream. A man appeared at the pool gate. A man appeared and ruined everything. He came to harm Handan and Behiye. Serious harm. He couldn't, but he ruined the happiness of the pool. They were chased out of that happiness. What else could happen? He couldn't harm them, but the pool dream was finished. Everything was ruined. Destroyed. That was the end of the dream.

Evil eye

· ·

'Do you have an alarm clock, Handan? We have to get up early tomorrow.' Behiye has brewed tea and is putting the glasses on the table.

'I have an alarm clock in my room. What happened, Behiye; have you decided to start school?'

The baby cat girl has dried her hair and has entered the kitchen in her pink cat slippers. Behiye plants her eyes on Handan. In order to look at what it was that dragged her into this whirlpool. In order to derive new pleasure from seeing Handan, and to be surprised that this pleasure has not diminished. To feel good again, to feel complete within herself. To know once again the yellow oilcloth that will wrap itself tightly around them and protect them from all provocations, dangers and stains.

She looks at Handan as if she's praying. At the beauty of Handan, newly emerged from the bath. At The Feeling You'll Be Rescued. At the feeling that I'll protect you too. No! Her love for Handan doesn't diminish with time. This love is increasing, growing deeper. It completes and is completed. This love is a miracle. A miracle. House. Whose house? Behiye's Handan house.

Behiye is at home for the first time. In her own home. She's never had a home before.

She's pouring tea for Handan. As she's filling the other glass, she cracks it. It splits in two down the middle: as if it had been cut in two by an invisible diamond cutter. The glass is so evenly and perfectly split that Behiye is dumbfounded. As she looks, she spills hot tea on her hand. She has burned her hand badly. In an instant it turns red and swollen.

'Behiyee! What have you done to your hand! Behiye, dear, does it hurt? Does it burn, Behiye? Tell me if it's burning.'

A very red and blood-curdling pain leaps from Behiye's hand and runs to her heart. A physical pain, just like an emotional pain, is thrust into the heart just like the arrows in paintings.

Behiye shudders from the violence of the pain. She's taut as a bow. She wants to thrust the arrow somewhere. She wants to bury the pain in the ground like an arrow.

Handan turns on the tap and holds Behiye's hand under cold water.

Behiye didn't think of it. She was so absorbed in the pain that she didn't think of water or anything. Handan runs into the bathroom and starts opening and closing drawers. She comes running back with an ointment: *Bepanthene*. Blue.

She takes her hand from the water and dries it without causing pain. Then she applies the ointment slowly. The pain comes in waves. It starts coming and going. Later it lessens. It's no longer a violent pain, no longer an arrow pain. The pain shrank; it lessened. The pain is local now. Just an echo of the first pain.

'There must be an evil eye on us, really,' says Handan. 'Just look at how the glass broke right down the middle.'

'An evil eye?' Behiye repeats it, as if it's a magic word that came from the secret pots of an enchanted cave, as if it's being whispered helpfully to her by fairies and demons: 'Evil eye. Evil eye.'

'Behiye, are you all right, my dear? Has the pain passed? You really burned yourself badly.'

'I'm fine, I'm fine. Pain is such a peculiar thing. At first it's so like the other pain, emotional pain, the way it goes into your heart like an arrow. One passes right away. Cold water and ointment break its strength. The other lasts much longer. It grows, it increases. It swallows a person. You don't know when it will stop. Perhaps that's why my mother...'

'Your mother?'

'Yes, yes. Perhaps that's why Yildiz is constantly doing what she does, in order to be able to bear the other, inner pain. Yildiz: my mother. The seamstress.'

'I know. You told me.'

'Pour me some tea, Handan. We have to get up early tomorrow and go to your course. You have to talk to the director. You have to cry about your grandmother, money for her operation, tell him whatever you want. But you have to get the tuition money back. You can't go there.'

She puts tea, very weak tea, in front of Behiye. 'Why can't I go there? If I don't, how will I get into university?' Her voice is broken. She's going to cry now.

'What are you going to study here? What can we study here, what can we become here? It's too congested here. It's full up, it's finished. Do you think there's any room for us here? We'll study in Australia. We'll do well there, Handan. There's no evil eye there, there's no rebuke there; there's no pushing and shoving.'

'Where did you get the idea of getting the course money back? Will they even give it to me?'

'They'll give it to you. As soon as they see you, anyone will give you whatever you want. You don't know it yet, but that's how it is. Handan, I have this disgusting brother I told you about, and before I left the house I took his money. I mean I stole it. He went to Çiğdem's this evening. He'll come and find you at the course if you continue going there. He'll find you, and he'll find me; he'll follow our scent like a bloodhound. Early tomorrow morning we have to go and erase your registration. And get your money back. It's not small potatoes. With that money, and 1,500 euros on top of it – the seventh continent is within our reach. What will we be able to do here, Handan? It's bad here. Evil eye land. That's all.'

'You never told me you'd stolen money. You never told me we were going to be in trouble, Behiye.'

'If Tufan wasn't such a disgusting specimen we wouldn't be in trouble. And we're not really in trouble. He has the intelligence of a lentil, he can't get the better of me. And tomorrow first thing we'll change your cell phone number. How will that retard ever be able to find us? That is, if we erase everything?'

'Behiye, I don't like any of this. For one thing, I want to go to the course. And I don't want to change my phone number either. How will anyone get hold of me?'

'What shit does the course have to offer? What shit does this place have to offer? You don't like any of this, but what is there to like about our situation? If you won't do these two things for me, if it's too much for you to ask for the course money back, then I'll go away. It's that simple. That simple.'

'But my phone number, Behiye…'

'You can make a list and give it to me. I'll send each one a message, I'll let your admirers know your new number. Whose calls are so important to you, anyway? Those two idiotic puppies you met at Akmerkez?'

'Yes, them, for instance. The boy who was with Burak, I mean. Erim. I've liked him for some time. He asked for my number yesterday evening. I want him to call; I want to see him. Why shouldn't I? Aren't I a beautiful young girl?'

Handan begins to cry. Like a spoiled child. Her lower lip is sticking out. These are 'I'm upset with you' tears, her 'I'm crying because I'm upset with you' face.

She can't bear it. 'You're a young and beautiful girl,' says Behiye. Cringing at the stupidity of the phrase. Something she wouldn't come up with if she thought for forty years. Young girl: get out of here!

'With me, we make two young girls. Or rather we don't. I want to think of myself as an old girl. An ugly old girl plus a beautiful young girl, that makes three quarters of a girl.'

Handan starts laughing. She's no longer pouting. 'Behiyee. Behiyee. You're such a maniac. You're so weird. Really, you're something else.'

'Handan, if I'm trying to turn you into something you aren't, if I'm pushing you – and you can't take it, I mean. Handan, I'll leave. I'll leave right away. Perhaps it's better that way.'

Handan runs up and hugs her from behind. She rests her beautiful head on Behiye's shoulder. Behiye catches the Handan smell. Every molecule of her being is filled with Handan. Handan do me good. Don't let me leave your side.

'Don't leave, Behiye. I'm very sorry for being such a goat. Forgive me. I'll call Burak and give him my new number. He'll give it to Erim. I'll get the course money back, I'll do whatever you say. But please don't leave my life. I just can't go on without Behiye. I'm a new person when I'm with you. I can't explain, but I become something when I'm with you. I become stronger. I grow. I become something better, really. I can't explain, but what can I do?'

She takes Handan by the wrist and draws her close. Handan is sitting on her lap now on one of those narrow kitchen stools. Behiye is stroking her hair. It's good for both of them. They scrape off the weariness of their squabbling.

The telephone rings. Handan runs to answer it.

'Yes, Behiye is staying here, mother. Yes, my blue rabbit; however you wish. Kiss Sister Nevin for me. All right. Fine; don't you worry. No, our Muki didn't call. I'll call her right away. Fine, all right. I kiss your rabbit cheeks. Bye bye.'

'My mother won't be here tonight.'

Behiye puts *Blink-182* on the CD player. She turns up the volume. Handan goes into her mother's bedroom. To take off her nail polish. With acetone.

A-ce-tone. Had Behiye ever heard this word before? She'd heard it. She must have heard it. Çiğdem paints her nails in 'young girl colours'. She just never got into those rituals herself; that's all.

Handan has called her Muki and is murmuring to her on the telephone. Behiye turns Blink-182 down. Muki is a housekeeper or something in some very rich person's house. That's what Handan said. Witch housekeeper. Muki who fills in her wrinkles with powder: witch skeleton with make-up. Filling in the crow's feet on her lips with pink lipstick…Handan's voice comes and goes. Her sweet voice talking lovingly to Muki. Handan's Snow White voice. Talking so sweetly to the witch who's sent her into the forest.

'Don't upset yourself, my Muki. There's not long left. We'll get you out of there. How we've missed our Muki. No, it's not like that. She's a good girl. She feeds me. Your Handan baby. And I love her too. Believe me, Muki, she's very good for me.'

Everyone becomes a baby, everyone babies each other in Handan's world. Handan's baby world: Everyone is loved, kissed, forgiven, everyone is quickly embraced.

Please Take Me Home starts playing. Behiye is bewildered by the way the song fits. She abandons Handan's baby voice. She listens to Blink-182 with her heart's ear. Heart ear. Her heart has pain, and an ear. Her heart has many compartments. And an unquenchable distress. Heart distress. Ress. Dist. Dirty snake heart distress.

Handan comes into the living room. She wrinkles her face. She can't help it. Right now she wants to listen to Kylie Minogue's *Can't Get You Out of My Head*. She wants that, not this.

Handan flees to the bathroom. Behiye can't turn the music off. Her hand won't obey her. She doesn't feel like it.

Handan has returned to the living room. 'Aren't you tired, Behiye? Why don't we go to bed?'

Behiye turned off the CD player. They made up the pull-out bed. Behiye hates the pull-out bed. The temporary nature of the bed. That it can't be hers. That it can't be anyone's. The pull-out bed doesn't belong to anyone. Not even to Muki.

Handan covers her nicely. Again she sends her off to sleep with a hug and a kiss. But she falls into such a strange web of dreams; she's caught in a state between sleep and wakefulness, and she doesn't know what to do. She can't get up and turn on the music again. She can't turn on the light. She can't go to the kitchen. She doesn't have the strength. She's in the grip of sleep.

In the midst of being sleepy but not able to fall asleep, she sees Tufan planted in front of her, dressed in his Tufan soldier commando outfit. Behiye's heart rises to her throat.

He's found me. He's found us. Found. FOUND.

Tufan pulls out his Rambo knife. He lunges at Behiye's flank. She tosses and turns in the bed, warding off the Rambo attacks. She thinks she's warding them off.

'I've cut you, you bitch,' says Tufan.

Behiye puts her hand to her groin. Her hand is bloody. Tufan has stabbed her in several places. She hadn't noticed. You don't notice knife wounds at first.

Later she hears a rapping sound. Rap. Rap.

Leman has come home. She's unlocking the door with her key. She flings her shoes into the corridor. She bumps into things. She goes to the bathroom and pees.

Behiye listens to the Leman Noises. Tufan was just a nightmare. He hasn't stabbed her. He didn't come into the house.

Leman goes to her bedroom, leaving the bathroom light on. She knocks something over in her room. A stool or something. She gets into bed and goes to sleep with the wheezing of cigarette-congested lungs.

Behiye goes to the kitchen and drinks a glass of water.

She goes to the bathroom and pees. She turns off the bathroom light.

Through the half-open door, she watches Leman sleeping in her underwear. She contemplates Leman's beauty. Leman has stretched out one of her arms as if in a plea for help. Her hand is open. As if to say, hold me, pull me up. With her body.

A terrible pain plants itself in Behiye's heart. Leman rescued her from Tufan's Rambo knife. Who's going to rescue Leman? Who's going to protect and look out for Leman, and Handan? From Tufan. From men. From the evil ones. From their attacks. Who?

She thinks of the lancet.

She feels cool, clean water flowing through her. It cleans out the silt within her. But Behiye still can't be completely calm. She can't settle down.

She's afraid of what's going to happen to her.

She's afraid of what's going to happen to them.

She turns to the right. To the left. Whichever way she turns, her heart beats wildly. Behiye's heart won't let her sleep. It's as if she's asleep, but she's not completely asleep.

When the alarm rings at half past seven, she leaps up out of the deep. In her dream she was with Leman. They were doing something together. She can't quite remember what. She doesn't want to remember.

Course money

∙ ∙

Behiye runs to the bathroom, washes her hands and face, and brushes her teeth. She wants to make Handan a quick breakfast. At least a couple of pieces of toast with butter and jam, a soft-boiled egg, and a glass of milk. The moment she opens her eyes, she feels the need to feed her baby.

There's no time for any of this, though. They need to be at the course director's door before he arrives. Before Tufan arrives. Before Tufan arrives, they need to deal with the registration, get the money, and jump aboard Noah's Arc. She smiles grimly as she thinks this.

She goes and wakes Handan. 'Come on, baby baby. It's time for the cat girls of Istanbul to wake up.'

Handan feigns reluctance. She turns her back and tries to catch a little more sleep. Behiye take a T-shirt from the drawer that was assigned to her. What an orange T-shirt! With her red hair, she'll look as if she's dressed as an orange for Domestic Goods Week. She puts it back. She takes out the one at the bottom: Olive green. This will do. She puts on the T-shirt.

'Come on, Handan. Go wash your face. You have to catch the director at the door as he arrives.'

'All right, my Behiye.' Handan goes off to the bathroom like a sleepy baby.

Behiye takes her jacket from the hanger. She feels in the pocket. Good, it's still there.

She puts on the blue jeans she's left folded on the armchair in the living room.

She goes and taps on the bathroom door. 'Come on, don't dally. Let's get this over as quickly as we can.'

Handan emerges from her room wearing a short-sleeved white shirt and low-waisted beige trousers. She's tied her hair into a ponytail at the very top of her head. Her barrette, two yellow furry cat heads.

When she puts on her Sydney jacket, she's ready.

Who could resist her, thinks Behiye. She melts as she looks at Handan. Why don't I take her into my cave. Protect her from wolves, jackals and birds of prey. Like a bear. I have to kidnap her. In order to protect and look after her. In order to feed her. So she won't be eaten by wolves and birds, so she can get through the winter. Just like a bear. Red Bear Behiye: protect your baby girl. Protect her!

They cross the avenue and jump into a taxi. Fifteen minutes later they're at the school door. Inside, there's no one but two cleaning men. They're mopping the floor. That's all.

'What time does the director arrive in the morning?'

'The director is an early riser. He'll be here within half an hour.'

'Within half an hour?'

'You woke me up this early for nothing, Behiye. Now we're going to wait.'

They sit on the stools in the corridor and begin to wait. What if Tufan acts as urgently as they did. What if Tufan…

Handan rests her head on Behiye's shoulder. Birds of prey peck at Behiye's heart. They peck at her liver, her heart, her intestines, biting off pieces and flying away with them. They tear Behiye to pieces. She's torn to pieces by worry and anxiety. She doesn't want to be collared by Tufan. She doesn't want herself and Handan to fall into Tufan's hands. She doesn't want to be belittled. Hasn't life belittled her enough already? Hadn't life torn her to small pieces? Hadn't it disregarded her completely? Hadn't it counted her for nothing? Hadn't it examined her? Hadn't it flunked her in all its exams?

She holds the lancet tightly in her hand.

She fantasises about lunging at Tufan's throat with the lancet. At his throat. At the middle of his throat. At his larynx. At his arteries. Once the image is established in her head, she feels calmer. It's as if she's found consolation. But just a little. Her heart is still going thud thud. Thud. Thud.

'Handan! Handan, please wake up!'

'Excuse me?' With her green cat's eyes wide open she looks at Behiye. Behiye wants to draw Handan into her. To draw her into her and escape. She wants to run away. To flee running.

'Handan.'

'Yes my Behiye?'

'I'm not going to be able to stand waiting here. I just can't wait here. The man will come in a little while. You won't miss him, you'll see him going into his office. You'll see him, won't you?'

'I won't miss him. I'll see him, Behiye.'

'Follow him into his office. Cry and so forth; tell him something pitiful. Get your course money back. How much money was it?'

'One billion seven hundred and thirty-four lira, Behiye.'

'All right, get back as much as you can. But more important than that – the registration forms. Get them back from him. You wrote your address and telephone number on a bunch of forms, didn't you?'

'Yes, yes, I did, when I was registering.'

'You definitely have to get them back. We have to tear them up and throw them away. Those forms are more important than the money, Handan. Tufan can't find us without them.'

'I understand, Behiye. Don't you worry.'

'I'm going to sit in the patisserie across the way. The one across the street that we went to with Çiğdem when we first met: *Hakan*

Pastanesi. Come get me there when you've finished. And if Tufan sees you he doesn't know you. If you get to the director's office first, we've made it, Handan.'

'All right, my Behiye. I'll take care of everything. Go on, you go and have your breakfast. I'll come in a little while.'

Behiye doesn't believe the childlike confidence in Handan's voice. How sure Handan is that everything will flow just the way she wants it to. Behiye is just the opposite. Behiye is used to everything going completely wrong. Accustomed. Rehearsed. Committed.

She runs out of the school and crosses the street. She doesn't wait at the lights. A car's brakes screech because of her. The driver shouts after her.

She gives the man the finger. She hopes he knows what the gesture means.

She goes into the *Hakan Pastanesi* and collapses on a white iron chair at one of the white iron tables. They've tied a foam-rubber pillow to the chair so people's asses won't hurt. White iron. Summer iron. Wrought iron. What a silly name. Behiye knows this, from somewhere. Her memory is like flypaper. It's enough for her to see a word once. Sometimes she's fed up with her treasury of words. Treasury. Fucking word. It's nonsense. Like a repertoire. Cerebellum. Medulla oblongata. Long. Gata.

She remembers Rezzan Hanim, her literature teacher in her last class. Annoying bitch. All year she gave her fours, or threes. 'My child, you write such negative things. Your view of life is negative. Scattered and irrelevant: where's the beginning, the end, the clarity? You have no sense of order, my child. All right, you're talented. But it doesn't work, it doesn't work. In life you have to be positive. You have to be affirmative, positive, full of love. Do you understand, Behiye, my child?'

Rezzan Hanim, with an ass as big as a teacher's desk, elephant legs, and her pitiful hair, dyed blond and showing pitch black at the roots. With blue lenses in her eyes: she gave herself dead eyes.

She'd look at you like a corpse with those blue-lensed eyes. With her fish-net stockings, décolleté blouses, her sweat smelling. Her collars always decorated with fur or lace or bows or whatnot. With her plump, mottled flesh showing. Nightmare literature teacher. She had it in for Behiye.

She doesn't say anything to anyone else when she hands out the papers. Until that day Behiye had always got top marks for her compositions. Only Rezzan Hanim sees her as being worthy of these marks. She talks away at her. Puts her down. She polluted Behiye's space. Her ships dump their garbage in Behiye's waters and then flee.

Behiye wants to kill Rezzan Hanim. Let her die. Let her be run over by a car, let her be poisoned, let her be burned, let her drown – let her disappear. The whole year was like that.

Now, Handan is with the course director. She threw her baby in front of the director without any shyness or embarrassment. The director would plant his eyes on Handan's breasts and lick his lips. His eyes would spin all around. Perhaps he would even grope the cat girl. Take her on his lap and molest her. All because of Behiye! Because of her disgusting selfishness.

After all, I'm using Handan too. I'm using my baby cat girl as a means to get something. I've disrupted her life and made her do the dirty work. I'm throwing her in front of men. I'm disgusting. I'm dis-gus-ting. Disgussssting.

Why can't I take care of my own business? Why can't I manage Tufan? Why am I eating shit instead of slicing him right across the throat? Would he be able to harm us then? Would he be able to track us down? My God, what have I done? I'm disgusting. I've used my Handan.

She leaves so abruptly that her chair falls over. The chair hits the ground. Iron. Made a lot of noise when it fell over. She runs out of the patisserie. She runs into the middle of the avenue.

Suddenly she sees Handan coming down the school steps. Handan bouncing down the steps. Then she sees Tufan walking towards the school from the opposite pavement. As Handan walks toward the lights, Tufan begins to climb the stairs.

He doesn't recognise Handan. He doesn't know her.

Handan sees Behiye. She waves the papers in her hand with delight. She jumps up and down as she waits for the green light. Behiye stands looking from the island in the middle of the avenue: now at Tufan at the school door. Now at Handan running towards Behiye.

Holding hands, they run to the other side.

'Quick, let's go to Taksim,' says Behiye. 'Let's not stay here. Come on.'

They jump into a minibus right near them.

'What happened?'

'I did everything, Behiye. I got every penny of the money, and the forms. The man felt very sorry for me. He'd have started crying in a minute.'

'What did you tell the man? Did you tell him your grandmother needed an operation, or something like that?'

'Nooo. I said…'

'What did you say?'

'I said, well. I said I had a friend. I said, Behiye, well, I said. I said my friend's brother was very bad, and that he mustn't ever find us. Please give me the forms, and the money. I said I couldn't come to the course, and that my friend would help me study. I said that in any event we were leaving this place. I said there was no future for us here.'

'Handan, you told the man everything exactly as it is.'

'I couldn't lie, Behiye. I don't even know how to tell a lie.'

'Handan, do you mean to say you've never, never, told a lie in your life?'

'Honest to God I never have, Behiye. Cross my heart, I never have. I thought about it while I was waiting for the director. I decided I wasn't going to tell him any lies. I couldn't think of a lie, anyway. And I don't know how to tell lies. Because of my mother.

We're not really a family. I never learned how to tell lies. I never had any reason to lie to Leman. Nor to Muki. My mother can lie if she has to. But I've never lied to anyone. I mean, isn't it the same as stealing, Behiye? You have to be accustomed to telling lies. Otherwise it doesn't work. You can't do it.'

Handan speaks breathlessly, as if asking for forgiveness.

Behiye can't stand it, and takes hold of her hands. She begins kissing those beautiful, elegant fingers. Her bird-wings. My truthful girl. My beauty baby.

My truthful baby. She doesn't even know how to lie or cheat. She hasn't been raped by the world. She's not from around here. She's not from here. She came to me.

As they climb up through Gümüşsuyu they begin tearing up the forms. They tear them into tiny pieces. Many tiny pieces. They throw them on each other's heads like confetti. They laugh as they run up the hill.

Istiklal, still with the deserted air it has in the early morning. It is so gentle, so beautiful when it was empty.

Only one of the music and book shops is playing music. Tarkan is singing *Lamb Lamb* to the avenue.

> *Difficult! Your absence is so difficult – I'm not accustomed*
> *Strike, strike this brainless head*
> *Strike it against the wall, against stones – do me a favour*
> *Then forgive me, embrace me*

Right away, Handan begins to sing along with Tarkan. The avenue, *Lamb Lamb*, Handan; they're all so beautiful.

A small boy waits on the corner with his scale. Behiye weighs herself. She's lost four kilos. How many days has it been? She counts on her fingers: Wednesday, Thursday, Friday, Saturday, Sunday.

'I've lost four kilos in five days. Imagine that, Handan. Since Wednesday. Since I had The Feeling You'll Be Rescued.'

'What did you say, Behiye?'

They put their arms around each other's waists as they walk. When you enter the flower market, there's a coffee-house on the top floor of an apartment building. Behiye brings Handan there.

Handan eats an enormous sandwich and drinks orange juice. From time to time she licks the moustache left by the orange juice. Behiye drinks tea. They can see a little bit of sky between the building at the corner and Galatasaray Lise. There's a partial view of the Bosphorus and Istanbul in the distance. Behiye drinks tea and looks at this little bit of sky, little bit of Bosphorus, of Istanbul. More at Handan, and less at Istanbul, and hot tea. She feels so very well. Well enough to pass through the eye of a needle. Enough to pass through the eye of her happiness. That much.

Monday October 1st

· ·

They leave. While they're still in the lift, she feels a pain plant itself in her heart like an arrow. Monday October 1st, Monday October 1st. The date echoes in her head.

The date is not at all important. Since they got the course money back, nothing can happen. But Behiye can't get Monday October 1st out of her head.

Perhaps in order to remind herself how little time had passed. In order to remind herself how much had happened in so short a time. In order to be surprised at how eventful it had been. In order to surprise herself. Short time. Short. Time. Shorttt.

She holds her breath. She couldn't drive Monday October 1st out of her mind. She didn't want to. It came into her thoughts all on its own. It came like a harmless thing, and remained in her system.

Behiye is distressed. She's distressed. Her heart is beating. I have to be in time, I have to be in time, I have to be quick, quick. Why? Where, Behiye? She asks herself, and struggles to calm down. Handan is talking away beside her. She doesn't listen to Handan. But she pretends she's listening. At the appropriate places she says things like, 'Uh, huh,' and 'Is that so?' The kind of things people say when they're listening. She feels so turned upside down that it's impossible to listen to Handan. There, at that moment, it is impossible to be with Handan.

She feels cramped, distressed, turned around. She feels like a propeller stuck in place. She can't do anything. Like a useless propeller. She can only spin. A useless spinning. Useless propeller. Get out of me! Go! Leave me.

Handan buys a half kilo of strawberries in the flower market, at one of those wonderful greengrocer's. Very fat strawberries; very red, very aromatic, very beautiful. Impossibly beautiful. Too firm, too perfect. Hormone strawberries. Strawberries with hormones. Fake! Fake strawberries.

Now 'fake' is stuck in her mind. Is what she has lived with Handan real? Is she real; am I myself real? Who is the real Behiye? Where is the real Behiye; is there such a person? Will she be able to appear one day; will she appear?

Handan holds a strawberry by its stem and offers it to her. 'Please eat it, please eat at least one, Behiye.'

She takes the strawberry and tosses it in her mouth. She turns and looks at Handan. At least one. After all, Handan is part of her life. Why does she allow herself to be like her old self? She is beside her. She's a different Behiye. Behiye as she is with Handan. Why does she forget this? Why doesn't she stop herself; why don't her thoughts leave Behiye in peace?

'Let's get you a new phone number.'

'All right, Behiye.'

They buy Handan a new cell phone chip: a new number. Handan doesn't display any ill-temper in the *Turkcell* shop. Handan is so good-natured that Behiye feels herself melt.

As they go out onto the avenue, she puts her arm around Handan's waist. 'You're so sweet,' she says. 'You're such a baby.'

Handan blushes. She closes her eyes, and her long cat eyelashes rest on her cheeks. When my cat girl is embarrassed she closes her eyes, thinks Behiye, trembling within. But she doesn't say what she feels. She keeps it to herself. After all, Handan is embarrassed.

'Shall we go to a film at eleven-thirty, Handan?'

'Fine. All right.'

'Look, shall we go to this Chinese film? Or rather Hong Kong film. The director is very good. It's called *In The Mood For Love*.'

Handan doesn't want to go to that film. 'The Chinese aren't very good-looking, Behiye.'

'What does it have to do with the film if the people in it aren't good-looking? And the Chinese are very good-looking.'

'No, they're not. They all look alike. And if the people in a film are good-looking a person is more emotional, and wants to live what they're living, Behiye.'

'Then I shouldn't be in your film, Handan. No one gets emotional when they see me.'

'You're beautiful. You're my one and only.' Handan plants a number of childlike kisses on her face. This time Behiye blushes from head to toe. But with all of her freckles, it's not as apparent when Behiye blushes.

They go to the film. It's a love story that takes place in Hong Kong in the sixties. But it's a story about pure, unadulterated love. Behiye loves it. Handan starts to make sounds of complaint after the first half. She keeps looking at her watch. She tries to make out the numbers in the dark.

'How long this Hong Kong film is,' she says during the intermission. 'Nothing happens, Behiye. Nothing at all has happened yet in the film.'

'Does it have to be like those idiotic American films where there are five thousand events every five minutes? That's the way the film is. That's why it's good. Real life is like that. Years go by without anything happening in anyone's life. Life is a heavy, crippled thing that moves slowly.'

'I'm very bored, Behiye,' says Handan, opening her cat eyes wide. 'I'll wait for you somewhere around here. And I can send my friends my new number. Otherwise no one will be able to reach me if they call me. My mother will start to worry too.'

Behiye is annoyed that all Handan can think about is missing a telephone call.

But she doesn't tell this to Handan. She doesn't want to be irritable and then regret it later. She doesn't want to be the way she is with everyone else, doesn't want to be the way she always is with her mother. Her mother! She shivers at the thought. Her mother is the last thing she wants to remember: The way her mother is, the way she is with her mother.

No matter how much she likes the film, she doesn't want to part from Handan. She's afraid she'll become depressed again. Before Handan: the way she was then. The way she was in the morning. It's after Handan now, and she doesn't want to be the way she was before. She fears that.

They leave the cinema.

Behiye thinks of converting the course money into dollars. They buy 1000 dollars. The rest of the money will get them by for some time. Behiye still has some of her mother's money.

They get into a taxi and go back to Handan's. Handan wants to take taxis all the time. Behiye doesn't want to be interfering all the time. Do this, do that! Change your number, convert the money into dollars. It distresses her to be always telling Handan what to do. It distresses her to be like that. But she can't help it. That's how it is.

Leman is home. The radio in the kitchen is blasting out *Kral FM*. Wherever Leman is, you can't escape these songs. There's no escape from these fucking love songs. The kitchen is very smoky. Leman, forever in a cloud of cigarette smoke and love songs, is swaying. She spends hours that way. She's not aware of the passage of time; she's constantly swaying.

Handan runs off to her room saying she wants to send her messages. Behiye goes off by herself to the shops in Levent. She buys fruit and vegetables. She calms down while she's picking them out. She begins to feel better. She remembers how good it is to have found Handan, to be with Handan.

Embracing The Feeling You'll Be Rescued, she enjoys picking out the tomatoes, cucumbers, squash and apples. It soothes her to look over the spring onions and dill, lettuce and turnips. Soothe: what a beautiful word. Lettuce is like that. Soothing lettuce. Behiye laughs.

'Always laugh at life like that, my beautiful child,' says the greengrocer, handing her the bags with his wet hands.

'Thank you, Uncle.'

Uncle Lettuce? It's like a happy neighbourhood scene from a television programme. Purslane Behiye and Uncle Lettuce. Like a picture in a children's book.

Never mind. It made her feel good.

She doesn't want to be constantly scratching herself. She doesn't want to be constantly falling into the caves of her inner self. She wants to feel soothed: Uncle Lettuce or purslane.

On her way home she buys half a kilo of lamb from the butcher's. Again, Handan greets her, clapping her hands with joy.

She's happy I'm home. She's jumping for joy. My beautiful baby cat girl. My new life. My new book.

Behiye's eyes fill with tears as Handan takes the plastic bags from her. 'I'll cook you something wonderful,' she says. 'Meat with potatoes, tomato pilaff, squash pastries. I learned the recipe for the squash pastries from a cooking programme on television. Believe me, they're very good.'

'You'll never believe it! You'll never believe what happened, Behiye!'

'What happened, Handan?' She turns and looks at her. They're in the kitchen.

'Burak called as soon as he got my new number. Erim has been calling since morning. He gave him my new number at once, of course. Erim called right away. He asked if I wanted to go out tomorrow night. And do you know where? For dinner at

TGIF's in Etiler. I've always wanted to go there. What a classy boy, don't you think?'

'Then you can go tomorrow evening.' Behiye's eyes become very narrow as she looks at Handan.

I'm not enough for her, after all. I'm not enough. There will always be others. There will always be people after her. They'll want to capture her. They'll want to throw her somewhere. Like hunters. Just like hunting.

Behiye's heart twists. She feels very hurt. She feels like such a fool. She thought she was happy because she'd come home. She thought she'd be happy every time she came home. But Behiye isn't enough for her. She isn't enough.

'Behiye! Don't do that with your eyes. I get frightened when you're angry and your eyes disappear like that. But you're coming too. And so is Burak. If you're not coming I won't go. How could I go without you? It wouldn't be any fun. I'd be bored without you.'

'No! Don't be silly. I'd rather die than go out with those stupid puppies. What would I want with them? Go by yourself.'

'Why are you talking like this, Behiye? Why are you being like this? A young girl likes to go out sometimes. Why are you doing this! Why are you so angry?' Handan begins crying in the middle of her sentence. She rests her head on the table.

Behiye is mortified.

Handan runs crying to her room. Lying on her bed and crying is surely much more young girlish, Behiye can't help thinking.

She cooks. Before she starts, she gives the oven a good cleaning. As the squash pastries cook, she's amazed that this family's oven actually works.

Family? They're a family too, after all.

Leman comes in. She's wearing a denim shirt that matches the colour of her eyes. She puts high-heeled beige slippers on her feet.

'Oh, I see you're preparing another banquet for us, Behiye.'

Behiye doesn't answer. After all, they're a family too. Even if it's the smallest possible family. Mother and daughter.

Handan is not Snow White. She's not all alone in the forest. She has her nanny, she has her witch mother; there are princes who want her.

And what is Behiye? All seven dwarfs in one. She's the seven dwarfs who want to be close to the princess. But it doesn't hurt her. It pleases her to see even Leman in all her beauty. It does her good.

'I fell asleep,' says Handan, coming in. She starts setting the table. They've become a family. It's as if this petty squabbling is normal, part of family life. A new little family: Handan, Behiye, Leman.

They sit at the table. Handan talks away cheerfully to Leman.

Leman eats very little. Yet it's the first time Behiye has seen Leman eat anything. Her cell phone rings. She takes her phone and runs to her bedroom.

'Why, Behiye. I wouldn't go anywhere without you. Don't you understand, I only accepted the invitation because you're here. Otherwise I'd never have gone on my own. Honestly, I thought you'd want to go too.'

'Didn't you go out with those boys before you knew me? Go to dinner or whatnot again. I can sit here and read a book or something.'

'I didn't go out with them. Just for coffee, to sit a little. I never really went out with anyone, Behiye. Why don't you believe me?'

'I believe you.' Handan's eyes have filled with tears again. Handan has a way of softening people; Behiye doesn't have the heart to be upset with her. She doesn't know how she could have upset her, how she could have made her cry; she's surprised at herself.

'You'll come with me, won't you? You won't break my heart, will you? I love you very much, Behiye. Why don't you understand?'

'I understand. Fine, all right.'

'That means we're going. Hurray! Hip hip hurray!' Handan jumps up and sits on Behiye's lap. She throws her arms around her neck. 'My dear friend,' she keeps saying. 'My dear, dear friend.'

Leman comes into the kitchen to find them embracing. She

raises one eyebrow, as if to say, 'aren't you going a bit far?' But only briefly. Leman glows with happiness. With delight.

'Do you know what happened, my beautiful daughter?'

'What happened?'

'Mr Şevket is back from Moscow. He's meeting your mother tomorrow evening. He's bought your mother a diamond and sapphire ring. And for days I've been destroyed thinking I had no chance with the man. Look at your Leman now. The man went and bought me a diamond and sapphire ring.'

'Why were you upset, my mother rabbit?' says Handan, running to her lap. 'Don't you know how beautiful you are my blue baby mother?'

Brother, what's going on here, thinks Behiye. Will you look at Leman. She measures her life and her happiness according to what men think of her.

Her life is like a taxi meter that she turns on for men.

But Handan isn't like that.

Behiye comes first for Handan. Behiye comes first, and last. The others are like salt and pepper.

For Behiye Handan comes first. And last. There's only Handan. Only her.

Enough of this Monday, thinks Behiye. This Monday October 1st. Let it be over and done with. Other places and other things are waiting for us.

Handan and I. Just the two of us.

A new life is waiting for us there. A new continent.

Behiye feels this. And because she feels this, she wants Monday to be over and done with.

She wants it to bugger off. To go wherever finished days go. The garbage heap of days.

Behiye wants to be rid of it: Monday October 1st.

Shore

• •

He nagged.

Early in the morning he nagged. 'Let's go, Father. Let's go down to the shore, Father. Please, Father. Please, let's go.'

He doesn't want to leave the house on Sunday mornings. He doesn't want to leave the house on Sundays. Let there be one day of the week when he doesn't have to face the outside world.

He's tired of facing the world. Life has worn him out, left him disgusted.

He doesn't want to face the thing called 'home' either. He wants to lie on the sofa all day in his sweatpants. He wants to read all his newspapers and supplements. To cut his fingernails. To eat whatever he feels like eating. To relax, and so forth. That simple. That's how he wants to waste his Sundays. He doesn't want to face the home situation either. Why not? Is that asking too much?

He doesn't want anything. He looks, and doesn't believe what he sees. All right, he's not going to be *Frank Lloyd Wright*. But even though he's a reasonably good architect, there's nothing he can do in this country. He's only done apprentice work. Nothing but apprentice work. Because of this, he doesn't even want to hear the word 'architect'. The world makes him feel ashamed. He's been an apprentice, not an architect.

Let his wife take the boy; let them go to his mother-in-law's or *Bauhaus* or wherever they want to go. So he can sit at home like a potato. To read his newspaper, doze off, watch television, read his newspapers some more. That's all. He doesn't expect anything more from his Sundays. And Sundays shouldn't expect anything from him, either.

If life expects nothing else of him.

If he doesn't expect anything else of this life.

But the boy is waiting. On Sundays the boy waits like a hungry wolf to ask things of his father, to hold on to his father, to rub on to his father, for any kind of contact with his father.

He knows this. This too is a source of pain.

Boy? The boy has one name: Ozancan.

Even the boy's name is a disaster. Ozan-Can. Couldn't he have just had one? Isn't one name enough for a boy, for this boy? For any boy?

It didn't work out that way. He wanted his son to be named Can. His wife insisted on Ozan. Later, she decided that the name Ozancan was wonderful. So many times he said, 'Forget about Can then. Let it just be Ozan.' But no! Ozancan was the name his wife wanted most in the world.

Ozancan. His obese ten-year-old son. Like his name, everything about him makes his father feel ashamed. In spite of being so fat, his legs are skinny. He cries easily. He cries constantly. One breaks his heart; it breaks at once, and tears start to run down his fat red cheeks. He cries, and doesn't try to hide his tears.

He cries openly, without shame.

He sits all day in his room, in front of his computer, eating *Cheetos*, *Pringles*, *Amigo* and *Lays* – always stuffing himself – always sitting.

He doesn't go out into the street to play hide-and-seek. He

doesn't play cowboys, or king-of-the-castle, or any game that involves pushing and shoving. He doesn't play. But then there's no street. Children don't play in the street any more.

He started nagging the moment he opened his eyes. 'Come on, Father, let's go to the shore. I want to collect pebbles. I'm going to paint them and put them in my grandmother's aquarium. Come on, let's go. Please.'

He's going to go down to the shore. He's going to collect pebbles. He's going to close himself in his room and paint. Later, with his mother, he'll bring them to his grandmother. Painted pebbles to decorate his grandmother's new aquarium!

Where does he come up with such nonsense.

What kind of boy is this child!

He's ashamed of everything the boy is. He's ashamed to be ashamed of his son.

He and his wife work their asses off to pay Ozancan's school fees. But he's certain that the other parents are secretly ashamed of their children as well. In those frightful performances they put on at school, he observes this. Children are not loved and appreciated the way they used to be. These children, whom they spend so little time with, whom they've neglected, abandoned in a way, are the children of guilt. At their parents, the strangers in the house, they create the feeling of 'what the heck are we ever going to do with these?'

Perhaps he's trying to lighten his guilt by attributing his feelings to others. He doesn't know.

His son has been begging him since he sat down to breakfast, since he opened his eyes.

He put him off. He made excuses. He distracted him. Then he was disappointed to see that the supplement was missing from his *Radikal* newspaper. That meant an hour and a half of not knowing what to do. And his son is pleading. Nagging.

While his wife does the laundry, the father and son go out. Five or ten minutes from their house, near the park, there's a vacant lot. From there they can reach the shore; and Ozancan can collect pebbles. On the way back, he can get the *Radikal* supplement from the grocery store. That way, in about forty minutes he can be rid of his son. Then the rest of his Sunday will be free of interference.

'Zip up your jacket, Ozancan darling,' says his mother. 'Don't let the morning cold in.'

'All right, Mother dear.'

'Put on your beret; and your scarf, please. Come back quickly, don't linger there; you'll catch cold.'

'We're not going to the North Pole today,' he says.

There's no answer; his son puts on his scarf. It's been years since she's laughed at his jokes. Now his comments only annoy her.

Ozancan talks the whole way, without pausing for a moment. Near the park he lights a cigarette. 'You go on ahead; go down to the shore. I'll finish my cigarette and catch up with you.'

He feels bad for not listening to his son's stories, for pretending to listen. Of course he doesn't need to smoke a cigarette by himself out in the open. But he just wants to have a five-minute break from his son. For fifteen minutes together, a five-minute break.

He walks through the park deep in thought. As he approaches the vacant lot he hears a scream of 'Father!'

For the rest of his life he'll never forget the urgency of this piercing scream. He understands this the moment the scream reaches his ears. For the rest of his life, he'll never forgive himself for letting his son go on towards the shore by himself. He knows this at once.

'Father! Father! Father!' His son's voice is not very loud. Like one of those nightmares when you try to scream but no sound emerges.

He's standing next to a young man laid out on the stones; calling to him. He's frozen with terror. He's come across a frightful accident. His fat arms are spread. He can't take his eyes off the corpse. Poor boy! Poor, lonely, beloved son. Poor Ozancan.

He goes and embraces his son at once. He holds his face between his hands.

'Look at me, look at me, son.'

Tears are rolling down Ozancan's firm, red apple cheeks. In a trembling voice, he struggles to speak. 'He's dead. He's dead. He's dead, father.'

He pulls his son towards him by the shoulders. He hugs him tightly. 'Come on, son,' he says. 'Let's get away from here.'

He leads his son up out of the lot. 'I didn't see it, Ozancan,' he says. 'You didn't see it either.'

'But I did see it,' he says. 'I saw it. He's dead. They killed him. Father. I saw a corpse.'

He's crying his eyes out now. They collapse on one of the park benches. He doesn't take his arm off his son's shoulder. He takes his son's head and presses it against his chest. He strokes his face and his eyes, as if he could erase what he'd seen. As if he could cause his son not to have seen a corpse, not to have seen someone whose throat had been cut.

'My dear son,' he says. 'My dear son. I love you so very, very much.'

'Dad, dad.' They hug each other. Now both of them are crying.

'Hug me, daddie,' says Ozancan. 'I've seen a body. They killed the young man.'

'Wounds caused by sharp objects' are those caused by objects which have a sharp surface and cut the tissue by the abrasion or penetration by the sharp surface. Some examples of sharp objects are razors, glass, tin-plate and lancets. As the sharp surface is narrow, it is not necessary to apply much force in order to damage the tissue.

```
Sex : Male
Height : 181 cm
Weight : 76 kilos
```

Autopsy report provided by the Forensic Institute, Morgue Department:

EXTERNAL EXAMINATION

The corpse is that of a brown-haired, circumcised male aged 20-25, beyond the stage of rigor mortis, with lividity apparent on the head, hands, forearms, feet and legs. A wound was observed in the side region of the neck, 11 cm in length, caused by a sharp object, stretching from below the left earlobe and extending to the right across the laryngeal cartilage. Apart from this, no other external findings were observed.

INTERNAL EXAMINATION

The head was opened. The underskin of the scalp was pale, and the temporal muscles were undamaged. The skull was opened. The bones of the skull were undamaged. The brain was found to be swollen and edemic. Apart from paleness, no particularities were observed in the brain segments. The bones at the base of the skull were undamaged.

The chest was opened. The left carotid artery and jugular vein were observed to be almost completely severed. No particular damage to the neck organs was observed. The plastron was lifted. No bleeding of any type was found in the chest cavity.

The lungs and heart were removed. There were no particularities in the lung segments.

The heart was weighed at 420 g. No particularities were found in the segments.

The abdomen was opened. No particularities apart from paleness were found in the abdominal organs. The stomach contents were found to be liquid.

Histopathologic examination established autolysis in all of the organs. Systematic toxicology examination established a blood alcohol level of 96 mg/dl. No other toxic substances were found.

Conclusion:
In the autopsy conducted:
1 Apart from 96 mg of alcohol, no toxic substance was encountered.
2 The report concludes that death was caused by loss of blood caused by the severing of the arteries on the left side of the throat.

Hooded jacket : *Dolce & Gabbana*
Grey sweater : *Armani Exchange*
Patterned shirt : *Paul Smith*
Black trousers : *Girbaud*
White underpants : *Calvin Klein*
Black socks : *Burlington*
Size 44 shoes : *Prada Sport*
Penis size : 11cm

The brand names of the clothes and the penis size were not included in the autopsy report, and are listed here separately.

Alcohol clouded week

. . . .

That week, the one that began with Monday October 1st being thrown on the garbage heap, was to unfold in a strange way.

Haphazardly. Though not with a great clatter.

As if life were fat, twisted, slippery, and Handan and Behiye had climbed to the top of this slipperiness, had looked down and not looked down, and had let themselves slide. The week passes as if they were skiing down this slipperiness: it passes very quickly, in a slippery manner, and very strangely.

They are sliding towards so much beyond their usual life, towards times so full of unexpected things, that they can no longer tell the difference between the expected and the unexpected, normal and abnormal, nonsense and the regular. From the moment they went out the door, everything became possible.

They let themselves be carried along by the current of this nonsensical life. They give themselves completely to this joyful sliding. But it was fun; a lot of fun.

From the moment, on Tuesday evening, when Behiye agreed to go to the restaurant called *Thank God It's Friday*'s, she knew that she was going to slide away from her accustomed life.

How had Behiye existed until that day? The suffocation of school, home, family, Çiğdem, books and music. The distress of life. Keeping it all inside, and feeling as if she was going to explode into a thousand pieces. Peopleless. Seldom seeing anyone, or going out, or talking. Without her own milieu. Milieuless Behiye.

People are social creatures, Behiye.

Now, when she repeats this sentence, she laughs aloud to herself.

She truly had been a social creature. She really had been a social nothingness. She erased the Behiye she had known and become accustomed to. When she let herself slide down that slope, she left behind the other Behiye – the true Behiye: if indeed there ever was a true Behiye. At the bottom of the slippery steps. Let her stay there for ever, chewing her fingernails. Let her fall apart from distress. In her brand new and constantly attenuating shell, Behiye became social Behiye.

The social Behiye discovered a powerful helper as she began her slide: alcohol. Behiye's guardian angel. Duty nurse. Courageous pilot.

Wine, let's say. Later beer: Great beer. Vodka if it was necessary, whisky in an emergency. Whatever presented itself to her. And this medicine, this cape, presented itself to her wherever she went. From the moment Behiye wrapped herself in alcohol, she left behind that defensive, touchy, angry, offended persona. She blooms: she becomes fun girl. She's able to send everyone into fits of laughter; she can make the strangest comments at the least expected moment. She's also ready to go anywhere at any time. The place to be could be anywhere. That is to say, congenial things are happening: New Start Behiye.

As soon as that car stopped in front of the building, as soon as she got in with Handan, it was as if Behiye had passed through a door into another realm. Balm.

The car – it was a *Mitsubishi Lancer*. Later, Handan keeps repeating this: '*Mitsubishi Lancer, Mitsubishi Lancer*. Erim has a *Mitsubishi Lancer*.' Behiye had no idea about the make of the car, about the make of any car. But everything important has a brand name apparently. And brand names are extremely important. Welcome to the world of brand names, Behiye. Where have you been sleeping all these years? In which castle, which tower?

The moment she gets into the car – the *Mitsubishi Lancer* – the moment she sees the two boys – Burak and Erim – Behiye will understand that she urgently needs to find something. She has to find something that will make it possible for her to be with them. To be with them without being with them. Urgently.

Later they're going to go to *TGIF*'s, which is only four minutes away from the Petrol Complex. In the *Mitsubishi Lancer*.

Behiye will call it *Thank Allah a Thousand Times it's Friday*. Everyone will laugh. They'll laugh a great deal. But all of this will be on account of the red wine they ordered to go with the steak. Behiye will throw herself upon the wine bottles. No one else will drink as much as the new and funny and social Behiye.

That's how they'll slide down the slippery slope. She and Handan. She couldn't have lived that week if she'd been thinking sensibly, if she'd been on her feet. She couldn't have got through it.

She doesn't need alcohol in order to get through the week.

The week gets through her.

They go to a number of places. At night, a number of places. They go regularly to that out of this world place, Baghdad Avenue. Erim's cousins live there. There are young people who like street racing. They play *Play Station* at a number of houses. They play endless games. They play games with names like *Tabu*, and then they play computer games. It is as if they belong to some sort of endless infants' school. They get by with at most fifty words.

The boys names were Cenk, Yaman, Tunç, Bilek, Yiğit. The girls were called Melisa, Ceylan, Biricik, Tuğba and Eda. If Behiye were to meet any of them again, she wouldn't recognise them.

Boys with gel, girls with highlights in their hair. They all looked terribly alike. They wear the same clothes, speak in the same tone of voice, use the same meaningless expressions.

'They're really Chinese,' she says to Handan.

'How do you mean, Behiye?'

'They all resemble one another. Inflatable girls, inflatable boys.'

From time to time, when she happened to be next to Handan, when she was able to get next to her, she whispered comments like this into her ear. From time to time.

But most of the time they're in the car, going from here to there. Handan sits in front with Erim.

Behiye, in the back seat.

Behiye the girl in the back seat.

Sometimes Burak or someone else is sitting beside her. Boys who wear aftershave, who smell of money. But most of them want to be driving their own *Audi S3*s or their *Mazda MX5*s. Behiye sits alone in the back seat. She watches from there.

They wander aimlessly, in a languid cloud. As if they're in a different slice of time. Time passes quickly, slips by. There's no concept of day or night, early or late. At four in the morning, one phone call will take them from a kebab stand in Hisarustu to a house in Caddebostan. In a state of aimless motion.

Alcohol clouded week. Later, Behiye will remember it as the week clouded by alcohol. She'll remember the boys, places, houses, cafés, bars, restaurants and cars as if it was a massed woollen ball from which it was impossible to escape.

The woollen ball has several strands. But it can't have several strands, it should have one strand. A massed woollen ball with many strands. It's impossible to see an accurate picture: like a puzzle that has more pieces than necessary.

Of what happened later, she'll only remember the last event of the last evening. The sobering event: frame by frame by frame. Later, she'll remember that event with shame and anger. That alone.

As they raced around here and there in the *Mitsubishi Lancer*, acting as if Istanbul and the night were nothing more than a playground for rich puppies, they found themselves in this square.

At the beginning of the wide avenue that leads down to

Kadiköy. At the conjunction of six roads. She's not quite sure what the neighbourhood is called. She knows it was at the beginning of the road that leads down to Kadiköy Square and the ferry station: a massive bronze statue of a bull. Bronze bull. From the pool in the centre, spraying fountains wet the surrounding area. The pool is its pool. It does what it wants, wets whatever it wishes to wet.

As the car roars along she sees the bull. 'Stop! Will you stop, Erim. Stop right here.'

'What is it, Behiye? What happened?' asks Handan, turning around and leaning back.

'Standing bull. Come on, let's go into the bull's pool. I'm very hot. Look how lovely the water is. Come on, Handan!'

Behiye leaps out of the car and throws herself into the bull's water. She dives and emerges. She creates an ocean out of the little pool.

Like a fish that's found its way back to the water. An aquatic creature; belonging to the water, happy in the water, able to exist only in water.

Handan watches, clapping her hands and giggling. But she doesn't jump into the bull's pool with her. She leaves her there alone in the beauty of that nonsense.

If there was anything inappropriate, unfitting, untimely, she was doing it on her own. Handan has given her that role, and has taken on the starring role for herself, the role of the sensible girl sitting in the front seat with her boyfriend. It hurts Behiye terribly that in their togetherness with Handan she's now playing a secondary role. Later, she'll think about this a great deal.

As she dives in and out of the water in the middle of the night, they enjoy themselves watching her as a couple. They're together, they're one, and Behiye is outside. Outside.

As she gets out of the pool and leaves the bull's water behind, Handan kisses her. She embraces her warmly. But she didn't go into the pool with her. She didn't jump.

Along the way, Erim is on his cell phone, chuckling, telling

Burak and Yaman about Behiye's latest crazy antics. Behiye's jumping into the pool and embracing the water has turned into a stale act. Erim is presenting his girlfriend's best friend's antics for sale. He's marketing with pride.

Shivering, sobered by the water, Behiye is very upset with Handan for having sold out their togetherness for that lout Erim, for dragging her around everywhere like a stick or a blanket or a boat, like something useful. Her heart is twisting.

Behiye has sobered up. She wants to strangle Erim from behind, show him what it means to have sold her out to those louts. But she doesn't do anything. She doesn't say anything. She simply records the fact that a huge wave of resentment is building within her. She registers it.

When they get home she takes a shower and dries herself. She puts on her pyjamas and prepares the pull-out bed. Handan comes out of the bathroom and comes to give her a good night kiss as if it were a religious ritual.

'Sweet dreams, Behiye. I'm dead tired.' She leans over Behiye. To give her a kiss.

She pushes Handan away with both hands. Violently.

Handan is bewildered. Her beautiful cat eyes open wide: 'Behiyee!'

'You sold me out, Handan. You sold me out to the first loutish boy you came across.'

'Where do you come up with these things? What did I do?'

'For me there's only you. Only *you*. Everything I do is in order to be with you. In order to be with you…'

'Don't go mad, Behiye. Please don't go mad. We're enjoying ourselves together after all; what's wrong? What happened? For me there's nothing more important than you. There's only you. Don't you understand; don't you see, Behiye?'

She hugs Behiye. Behiye hugs her too, with longing. She takes in her smell. She loses herself in the Handan smell. They're both crying. They're back on that raft. They're all alone; they have no strength, no will. They're drifting wherever the sea carries them. But at least they're together. They're Handan and Behiye. Isn't that enough?

'Let's call the Australian Consulate tomorrow. Remember, we were going to get out of here. We forgot the point of everything.'

'Don't be sad, Behiye. Everything will work out. You'll see, I have a plan, too. We'll get out of this hole together. We'll be free of this life.'

Handan is mothering her now. Their roles are changing; it's the first time they've spoken this way. It's the first time, but Behiye isn't aware. She's aware, but not completely. She'll understand later. Much later.

'I love you so much. I'd do anything for you, Handan.'

'Shhh. You have a good sleep now. My baby. My Behiye.'

How long it's been since they hugged each other. Since they've cried together. It feels good. It makes Behiye feel as if some things haven't diminished. It feels sweet.

They fall asleep in each other's arms on the pull-out bed. Sleep has carried them off to its home. To sleep home. The best place for two little girls to go. The safest place.

Requested songs

· ·

The song has a sweet, slightly immoral melody. A song that begins to flirt the moment it starts. Merry. Jocular. Sensitive.

That's to say, it's played with a whistle. Even before the words start, the melody is played with a whistle.

Is Selami Şahin whistling himself? Or did he hire a whistler: someone who whistles very well?

Selami Şahin whistles himself at the beginning and the middle of this immortal tune. He himself is the whistler. It couldn't be anyone else. That's how it seems to Behiye. *Selami Şahin* wouldn't countenance allowing anyone else to whistle these wonderful whistle parts: She's certain of this.

(Whistlewhistlewhistle)
I don't know what will become of us
Perhaps our love will be endless, perhaps it will be left half
Every day you change, you console me
You're like a puzzle, I haven't been able to solve you.

I'm losing my mind over you, I don't know what to do
You are a part of my life, I can't get rid of you
(Whistlewhistlewhistle)

Some days you quarrel, some days you make peace
Some days you long to lose yourself
Every day you change, you console me
You're like a puzzle, I haven't been able to solve you.

I'm losing my mind over you – of course, later it goes back to that verse. After all, that's the song's title. What she's lived at Handan's house: going to bed late at night, towards morning, waking in the morning, or rather in the afternoon, at strange hours, in that house you're under Leman Smoke.

Leman's radio in the kitchen is on most of the time, tuned to *Kral FM*. When the radio isn't enough, she resorts to Selami Şahin's tape, *My Songs and I – Nostalgia*.

This is the background music of the house. They're constantly, but constantly, listening to *I'm Losing My Mind Over You, Growing Accustomed Is More Difficult Than Love, Don't Leave I Need You, You're Like The Seasons*; or at least Behiye hears them.

The music is terribly oppressive and constricting, but you get used to it in time. *Selami Şahin*'s songs are an important element of the house. She's also getting used to Leman, because with Leman's songs one becomes Leman Smoked. Like always sitting in a cloud of cigarette smoke, swaying to her love songs.

Throughout the alcohol clouded week, Leman went out every single night. Her latest 'boyfriend', Mr Şevket, is very much on her mind; on the nights when Mr Şevket has to stay home with his wife, she goes to Sister Nevin's. There's a group of women who openly live as mistresses, whose profession is to 'have affairs'. Code name: The Sisters Nevin. They give each other advice and solidarity, and drink a great deal.

Behiye can't believe she's becoming used to all this talk, all this coming and going, all these fucking love songs, that, to tell the truth, she actually likes the super-carefree-but-super-in-love mood of *I'm Losing My Mind Over You*.

And wherever Leman goes, she requests *Selami Şahin*'s songs, writing the titles on napkins, visiting cards sent with roses, and various pieces of paper. But the song she requests most often is *I'm Losing My Mind Over You*.

Wherever she goes she requests the songs for herself. Leman, who measures her existence by the desire and lust she provokes in others, wants those lyrics to be for her. She wants to feel that those songs are only and truly written for her, she creates exactly these feelings in men.

Leman In Requested Songs Land. Like that.

Tuesday begins with *I'm Losing My Mind Over You* being broadcast from the kitchen. Leman with a light Salem between her fingers, a nescafé in front of her, acting as if she's hearing the song for the first time, as if she believes she's surprised at how much the song suits her, somewhere between the lyrics and the melody. Undulating within the song.

Behiye makes tea. And some *menemen*. For Handan. Behiye still lives without eating anything. Even the blue jeans she bought with Çiğdem are beginning to fall off her.

While Handan is eating her eggs and cheese toast, she soaks half a packet of beans in a plastic bowl. She wants to cook beans and pilaff for Handan's dinner. Cooking for Handan is an important sign that their lives are going well, that they are well, happy and at peace.

Today, for instance, she wants to do things like go shopping in Levent, cook dinner and find the telephone number and internet address of the Australian Consulate.

Health list, she says to herself. Now, she's afraid not to have a list of the day's tasks. That she won't be able to tick off the useful things she's done. That some crazy life will enslave them. That someone – who are they – will push them from behind and cause them to roll down that shameless slope. Of an alcohol clouded week. She feels in her bones that she couldn't endure another week like that. She goes brrr.

Leman wants to eat some toast too. There's an old model toaster, and Behiye makes wonderful toast with tomatoes and cheese.

'It's delicious, Behiye dear,' says Leman. 'Should I drink some tea too, I wonder.'

It's the first time she's called her 'Behiye dear'. Just like Behiye has been taken prisoner by her silly universe, Leman becomes accustomed to Behiye. 'Growing accustomed' is such a strange situation. *Growing Accustomed Is More Difficult Than Love*, just as the master made clear. Like that.

Behiye pours herself a tea and sits down.

Handan's cell phone rings inside, in her room. Handan runs. She returns with the phone in her hand.

'I shut it off, my Behiye. I don't want anyone to call us today. I want today to be like the old days. We miss those times so much. Don't we?' She smiles as she says this, showing her dimples.

The 'old times' she's talking about were only seven or eight days ago. Indeed, it's been only thirteen days since she met Handan. Only?

It seems a thousand years to Behiye. It seems like it's been a thousand years, but at the same time it seems as if it's only been a day. But at that moment the only, the only thing she wants to do is embrace Handan. To lick her dimples. To bury her nose in her neck. She wants to take her in her arms and run off with her, in order to kiss her and love her. But she knows there's no chance of having her fill of Handan. Of Handan being enough to fill Behiye's Handan gap.

At this moment, at this hour, this day, because Handan felt exactly what was on her mind, and, hearing her, gave her what she wanted (for them to be alone together! to be alone with her), she experienced a Handan Pressure. She holds herself back, but her eyes fill with tears. The relationship between her eyes and her tears is free of any control. Since Handan came into her life.

After taking a bath and putting on what for her is light make-

up, Leman leaves the house to go to the hairdresser's and then
to Akmerkez just across the way. She's wearing a white shirt and
tight blue jeans. She looks immensely beautiful. Leman becomes
more beautiful as she gains power over Mr Şevket. The more she's
desired, the more at peace she feels. She frees her unique beauty,
which is blocked more than anything by nerves and sadness.

In any event, she goes hopping out of the house. For the first
time Behiye sees her wearing Handan's sports shoes instead
of her usual high-heels. She's surprised to see how much the
mother's way of walking resembles her daughter's. That meant
that Handan's bouncing walk was Leman's walk. Their bottoms
move so nicely behind them. Everyone would look at their
bottoms. But everyone, Behiye says to herself.

After they drink yet another tea, she clears the breakfast table
with Handan. Handan decides to wash her whites. In any event,
she's out of socks and underwear.

While Handan is taking a bath, Behiye calls information and
gets the telephone number for the Australian Consulate. 257 70
50. 257 70 50.

Later, for the rest of her life, she'll never forget The Consulate's
telephone number. She doesn't know why, she repeated it twice
and it embedded itself.

The recorded voice that answers the phone gives the internet
address. Behiye writes it on a piece of paper. She makes another
call to something that's part of something Australian, and gets
the address: Tepecik Road No. 58 Etiler.

That simple.

It's about fifteen–twenty minutes walk from Handan's house.
The address of their salvation is right under their noses!

She goes to Handan's room and checks on the 1,500 euros
and the 1,000 dollars that she's stuffed in the inside pocket of her
jacket. The money is there. Then she checks on the lancet. It's
also still there. All three are waiting as sweet as lambs for them in
the jacket. They're ready.

Behiye feels very well. As if she's found The Feeling You'll Be Rescued all over again. Then she sees someone in the full-length mirror in the closet.

Is this me? Is this you, Behiye?

She's got so thin, she's someone else. Her cheekbones have emerged. Her brown eyes have got bigger. Purple pools have appeared beneath them. Pools that make Behiye look older, more mature, more beautiful. Her red hair has become wavy. With her belly gone, her breasts are more apparent.

She's unable to say it, but Behiye has become beautiful. She looks like the foreign models in the magazines. She turns around and tries to look at her bottom. It's become smaller and more shapely. It's firm and beautiful. Behiye doesn't believe the New Behiye's beauty. For the first time in her life it pleases her to look at herself.

'Aren't you a beautiful girl, my Behiye,' says Handan, coming up and embracing her from behind.

Behiye looks at the two of them together in the mirror. She's so beautiful. They're both so beautiful: Handan with Behiye.

'There must be a photographer's in the Levent Market. Please, can we have our picture taken, Handan?'

'All right,' laughs Handan.

Behiye is a bit embarrassed. But they're so beautiful. Will they always stay this beautiful? Behiye wants what she sees in the mirror to be fixed for ever. Perhaps if they're photographed, they'll stay this way. The kind of magic that pictures have sometimes.

Handan knows a photographer's very near by. They go down to the lower floor – to the studio, to the studio? – and have a number of pictures taken. At least eight poses. That's enough, says the photographer. 'One more, one more,' they beg him.

Later they buy lamb from the butcher's.

They buy some fruit in the market. And tomatoes, cucumbers, lettuce, onions and lemons.

They return home hopping and skipping. Behiye wants to go to Tepecik Road to look at the Consulate. They can get forms or something. At any rate, they'll see it.

'Let's go to their website and find out what they want first.'

'You're right. Let's see if we can get citizens' addresses from their website. For your father.'

'For. My father.'

Handan is hurt. When she hears the word 'father', it's as if a bead necklace has been scattered inside her. Behiye feels it.

Towards evening, zapping through the television channels, they come across a Turkan Şoray film.

'I can't believe it!' shouts Handan. 'I haven't come across this in months. It's my mother's and my favourite Turkan Sultan film.'

Behiye doesn't believe it either as she watches the film. The film's theme song is *I'm Losing My Mind Over You*. The title of the film is probably *Mistress*.

Can Gurzap is a handsome, rich, married man; Turkan Şoray, in the role of the city's flashiest mistress, is in love with him. Neriman Koksal is in it too. As 'Sister Nevin'.

In any event, Handan knows all of the scenes, the dialogue and the music by heart. She's a child of old Turkish films. Handan grew up in front of the television. Leman got a television to serve as the cheapest and least troublesome baby-sitter. She left Handan alone like that. With the television. For her to grow up.

At the end of *Mistress* she starts to cry.

'What can I do; I can't take it. I can't sit through a Turkan Şoray film without crying.'

'How very upset my baby girl is.'

'Don't make fun of me Behiye. My mother always cries at the end of this film too.'

'Could we say this is because there might be autobiographical elements?'

'You're so low! You have no pity, no fear of hurting other people's feelings, Behiye.'

'I'm just joking, Handan. Please don't be angry. But I'm sorry. Aiiighg! Aiiighg! What an ass I am. But don't be angry.'

Behiye goes into the kitchen and starts cooking the beans. As she sautés the onions and adds the meat, she feels very happy with her life. If she's cooking for Handan, it means everything is going as it should. It means the Yellow Oilcloth is wrapped tightly around them. She wants to cook for Handan for the rest of her life. She wants to be with Handan. She knows that life is only possible with Handan.

That's how it is.

That's how. That's how.

She runs to the living room and embraces Handan.

'My Feeling You'll Be Rescued,' she says in a loud voice.

'What feeling? What feeling?'

'The feeling of everything. Handan, nothing will ever part us, will it?'

'Where did you come up with this, Behiye? Inside cooking beans for your baby?'

'My baby,' says Behiye. 'You're my baby. My Feeling You'll Be Rescued. My everything, my everything.'

'I'm as hungry as a wolf. Will the food be ready in half an hour, Behiye?'

'It won't,' says Behiye. 'I'll make you some toast right away. Baby girls can't stand to be left hungry.'

Handan laughs. 'You're crazy, honestly,' she says. 'I'm losing my mind over you.'

'I don't know what to do,' says Behiye. 'You're a part of my life I can't get rid of.'

At the same moment they both go into a fit of laughter. For minutes they laugh, with their eyes watering, bending over. They laugh.

Libra woman

• •

At about ten in the evening, with her arms full of packages, a breathless Leman, bouncing along in Handan's sports shoes, returns home. A Leman who's too beautiful to be real. As if she's been touched by a magic wand.

Her hair is much shorter. She's got rid of the highlights and dyed her hair completely blond. The morning's make-up is gone from her face. There's a strange light in her eyes; they shine like a blue pine forest after a rain. Happy Leman. Leman forest.

In this state, she has an ageless youth. It's the first time Behiye has seen her so lively, so full of electricity. She can't take her eyes off her. She wants to swallow her. It's strange, but she feels the same things for Leman that she feels for Handan. She doesn't believe herself. But that's how it is.

'My blue rabbit! My God, how beautiful you are with your short blond hair!' Handan runs to embrace her mother. Leman flings her packages and throws herself into an armchair.

'I'm finished today, Handan,' she says. 'But I had such a good time. Shopping does a person so much good. How long it's been since I've been able to buy myself a few things. Oh! I feel like myself again. New hair and everything; it's been months since I've felt this good, honestly.'

Handan sits on her lap. 'Let's see what my baby mother bought for herself? What lovely things did she buy herself? Show me, I'm so curious. Show me quickly, come on. Let us see too.'

Leman looks at the girl on her lap lovingly. Behiye can see the pride in her beautiful face, her pride in how beautiful her daughter has grown up to become.

Whatever kind of mother Leman is, at least she's a loving mother. She may not always have managed to fulfil her responsibilities to Handan. At times when she was preoccupied with her own problems, she may have completely neglected her daughter. She may have let her grow up alone in front of the television, to be fed, bathed, put to bed and have her fingernails clipped by aunt-like neighbours. But Behiye feels that having Handan as her daughter is the most important thing in her life. She feels from the way Leman looks at Handan how crazy she is for her, how she loves her with all her heart.

It was odd to see them sitting there, one on the other's lap, in that living room, on the threadbare armchair. Two layers of beauty and well-being. Suffocating, almost. Sufffocate Behiye.

Behiye feels how much she's taken to their waters. That she couldn't live anywhere but in their waters. A little fish breathing in the Handan-Leman waters. An anchovy, a mackerel. An ordinary fish. A stupid fish. Stupid fish Behiye. Just living in these waters.

'Don't hide them, I say. Are you going to hide them from us? Show them all, one by one.' Handan starts to tickle her mother.

'Oh stop, Handan! Stop, I say! Stop! I'm going to split open, honestly.' She struggles to beg through her laughter.

It also hurts to watch them. Two little girls who'd been left alone in a sand pool. The mother is a child, has remained a child, they look like they're just children. They both seem to be completely worldly and don't seem to be of this world. It's strange. She's never seen a mother and daughter like this. Not even in books or films. Now, here she is, right with them.

'Stop! All right, Handan. I'll show them to you.'

Leman has bought herself a pair of blue jeans, a shirt and a light blue sweater.

'I also bought this swimsuit. As soon as he has time Mr Şevket is going to take me to that famous hotel in Dubai. But I bought two things – you'll love them, Handan. I swear you'll love them.'

She opens two paper bags with the *Beymen* logo on them. From one, she takes a shoebox with the *Jil Sander* logo on it, and from the other a bag.

'Mother! This bag is *Moschino*!'

'How could you tell so quickly?'

'Mother, there's a big logo on it. As if *Jil Sander* shoes weren't enough, you got a *Moschino* bag too. I don't believe it. Where did you find that much money? I thought we didn't have two pennies to rub together?'

'Handan! Am I accountable to you? The other day Mr Şevket gave me a billion. And last night he gave me a *Beymen* gift certificate for two billion, as a birthday present. Tomorrow is your mother's birthday, baby. This man thinks a lot of your mother. He wants to make her happy. Is that a bad thing?'

'But Mother, you're always doing this. You can barely pay the interest on the credit cards every month. We're four months behind on the apartment payments. Mother, you're always doing this. We have no money at all put aside!'

'Handan, please, be quiet. Your Leman is turning thirty-five, doesn't she deserve a *Moschino*? It's not as if I went and bought *Gucci*. The two together cost one billion eight hundred and fifty million. With the rest I bought some perfume. I didn't pay any extra money.'

'You don't have any extra money to give! Be reasonable, Mother. You're like a child. Don't you ever think of anything but yourself?'

'Get a grip on yourself, Handan. You're being very rude. Is this any way to talk to your mother? Didn't this woman raise you by herself in Istanbul? Are you lacking anything, my daughter? Was there ever anything you wanted that I didn't buy you? Didn't I get you *Donna Karan* this summer?'

'Mother, you're always talking nonsense! Do we have money in the house for even our most basic needs? Every time I say anything I get the same nonsense. We have no order in our lives, do you understand? Am I supposed to be grateful you didn't buy *Gucci*?' Handan is breathless. Her voice is strained; it's clear she's making an effort not to cry.

'My darling baby, didn't I tell you the man gave me a gift certificate? What was I supposed to do? Go to *Beymen* and ask them to put it towards the apartment payments? The man was making a gesture to your Leman. Don't you understand that your mother is turning thirty-five? A chapter of my life is closing. And aren't I a Libra woman?'

'Oh, Mother. What does that have to do with anything?'

'Handan, your mother is a Libra woman. Libras are like that, what can I do?'

'Don't do anything. Just go on being a Libra.'

'My baby. Come to your mother's arms. You're still young, you don't understand. Tomorrow your mother will be thirty-five. I'm not a young woman any more, Handan. I'm no longer young and beautiful. I have to be very sensible, very balanced. Libras have a balance problem, you know that, my baby.'

Handan doesn't go to her mother's lap. She's perched herself on the arm of another armchair, and is sticking out her lower lip; holding herself back from crying, from shouting too much.

She's dying to cry, but she doesn't cry. She doesn't want to scold Leman too much, and at the same time she's ashamed about taking back the course money. Her first lie, her first secret. She lowers her eyes and struggles to keep from crying.

In order to take the tension out of this mother–daughter scene, Behiye runs to turn on the television. Thank God, *Britney Spears* is singing *Overprotected* on *MTV*. She doesn't understand why, but Handan is crazy for that girl. In Leman World, people are even crazy for *Selami Şahin*'s songs. But why Handan thinks so much of this stupid girl is one of the unsolvable mysteries of life for Behiye.

As *Britney* starts singing for them, writhing as if in agony in pants that start halfway down her ass, Behiye goes off by herself to the kitchen. She makes tea. But first she boils water and makes a nescafé for Leman.

She's still afraid to go back to the living room. All her life Behiye has been frightened of family fights. She doesn't know what to do. What she should say, what she should do – if she did a cartwheel, for instance, would it dissipate the atmosphere of the fight?

The nescafé is getting cold on the tiles. After making tea she gathers her courage and goes back to the living room. Handan has changed seats. She's on her mother's lap again. They're not angry with each other any more. They can't bear to upset each other. After they squabbled, they flow towards each other. Like two lovers. Just like that.

'Libra woman and her daughter have made peace.'

Handan giggles. She kisses her mother. Behiye hands Leman her coffee.

'How sweet you are, my Behiye. How thoughtful,' says Leman, with all the rancour gone from her voice. She takes Behiye by the hand and pulls her toward her. She kisses her right cheek.

'Girls, do you like my scent? *Gucci Rush*. Even if I didn't get the bag, this scent would have been enough.'

'All right, Mother. You win.' Handan laughs. The atmosphere in the room has changed.

'I'm making tea for us too, Handan.'

'All right, Behiye. I'll be right there.'

Behiye returns to the kitchen. What is this about? What is she doing in this house, moving in like this? Where did this unknown relative come from, this volunteer maid, this refugee?

This place doesn't belong to her and Handan. This is Leman's

· house. Libra House. She's just taking refuge in Libra House. Refugee Behiye.

We have to leave at once. From here. We have to get out altogether. We mustn't lose time fooling around. We have to go before anything happens. Before anything fills up.

Behiye feels pressed by an immediate sense of urgency. She feels as if she's neglected herself, as if she's going to miss out, as if it's already too late.

She feels a deep sense of impatience. A clock has started ticking within her, threatening her. Come on. Come on. Come on, Behiye.

All right! Enough! Stop!

She wants to put her hands around her throat and squeeze her larynx. To stop the clock. To shut it up.

Handan comes in. She immediately reads Behiye's distress.

'What's happened, my Behiye? Don't be upset. Honestly, I'm constantly thinking the same thing, too. But I'm certain we'll get out of this situation. We'll find a way. Definitely.'

She buries her nose in the nape of Handan's neck. Handan smell. It washes and cleans her soul. It opens her pores.

'What can she do, she's like a child. She never grew up, she's always been like this.'

'It's because of her sign: Libra woman.'

'Oh, don't ask. She'll be more balanced starting tomorrow. Turning thirty-five is very important to her. Tomorrow is a very important day.'

'Let's decorate the house. We'll make cakes and pastries and cookies. Since she doesn't grow up, let's have a child's birthday party for her. Leman Day. Won't it be nice?'

'It would be very sweet. Let's do it.'

Leman comes into the kitchen for more coffee. 'Mr Şevket has to be at home tomorrow night,' she says. 'Let's have a girls' party. Muki has tomorrow night off; she's staying with us. If we called Sister Nevin too...'

'It would be great, Mother. The birthday party of the century.'

'You don't say. You thought a *Moschino* was too much for your mother. Don't I warrant a bag and a pair of shoes at this age?'

'All right, Mother. I said I was sorry. May you be blessed with all the brand names in the world. Is anyone better or more beautiful than you? Is anyone more worthy than my blue rabbit?'

'Just wait and see how your Leman is going to pull herself together. Until today the scale was broken, it was all feelings, feelings, feelings. From now on I'm going to be all good judgement, you'll see. After I turn thirty-five, I'm not going to go running off after this one or that one. I'm closing the book of desire for good. I'm starting all over, that's all.'

'Ohhhhh, what a decisive girl, what a sensible girl my Leman has become.' She hugs her mother.

The New Libra Woman and her daughter shone in that run-down kitchen. Behiye can't take her eyes off them. They're the beautiful mother and daughter. They've come to Behiye. They're Leman, Handan and Behiye. That's how it is, after all. Behiye watches. She watches herself watching from the outside too. She watches.

Preparation work

· ·

As they're having breakfast Handan's phone rings: Erim. Of course!

'No, we can't get together today either. No, no, I'm fine. There's nothing. No, I said. It's my mother's birthday today.'

Handan gets up from the table and flees to her room. Presumably in order to be able to talk more comfortably to Erim. So she can talk without Behiye. Presumably.

How this distresses Behiye, how confused she becomes. She'd been gullible enough to think that because Handan had turned off her phone for a day, that because she'd agreed to turn it off for a day, they were free of Erim. That they were free for ever of those feeble-minded idiots who stank of the perfume of money. She thought they were free of their brand-name clothes, their brand-name bars and restaurants, their *Mitsubishi Lancer*s, their *Audi*s, *BMW*s and *Mazda*s. For ever. Gullible.

To erase those ugly, suffocating sights from the screen of their lives with the touch of a button, by pressing a button – to be able to get rid of them completely; she'd thought they'd be able to stay for ever far away from them and their world, wherever they come from, whatever they belong to.

It doesn't work that way, Behiye! What were you thinking? That idiot boy and his crew have entered Handan's space. They've stuck there like a stain. You thought that just because they disgust and revolt you they would disappear from view. There's no way they'll leave Handan and Handan's beauty in peace. Was Handan something one came across every day? Was she ordinary, run of the mill?

This idiot puppy has stuck to Handan, and won't leave before he's grown like a stain on Handan, before he's knocked her about, shaken her out, wounded her. Of course he won't leave Handan alone. What did you think, Behiye? That you would be rid of them so quickly, so easily?

In the kitchen, Behiye finds a bread knife in her hand. She doesn't know what she's going to do with the bread knife. She doesn't remember opening the drawer and taking the knife out. A knife in her hand and her arteries throbbing from irritation and anger; she finds herself struggling to stay on her feet. There, in the kitchen, there's no one but herself to stick a knife into. It's not as if it doesn't occur to her to stick the knife into herself. She feels something like that: as if I'd stuck that knife into my flank.

Her arms and legs drained from irritation, struggling to stay on her feet, there's a knife in her hand, a knife in her hand. Handan returns to the kitchen. Chirping. Like a bird. Handan is chirping.

'I told Erim I wouldn't be able to see him today. I said we could meet tomorrow if he really wanted to. He said, "Are you crazy, girl, how could I not want to see you."' Handan giggles. 'He keeps begging me to go to his summer house. What are we going to do in his summer house on a winter day? We can't go into the pool, can't do anything. Isn't that so, Behiye?'

'See him whenever you want. I'd rather die than go anywhere again with those idiot puppies.'

'What happened, Behiye? Why have you gone crazy again? We're just passing time. What's wrong with that? And Erim isn't a bad boy. Honestly, he's a good boy. Why are you mad at him now? Sometimes I don't understand you at all.'

'You'll see him, Handan. Come on, let's go shopping. Your mother will go to the hairdresser's or wherever when she wakes up. We'll be back by then.'

'I'll get ready right away, Behiye.'

She turns on the tap and washes the dishes one by one. She holds her fingers under the water and looks at them.

Handan has gone into the bathroom. To wash.

That means there's time. She bends down and begins scrubbing the kitchen tiles. With *Ammonia Cif*. The coldness of the stone does her good. She struggles to keep that ass Erim and his crew out of her mind. But it's not easy. It's as if she's reserved an artery in her forehead for them; it throbs and throbs and throbs.

She tries to scrub Erim, with his hair-gel and his small white face, off the tiles. It's tattooed 'imbecile' on Erim's forehead. She sees it in the tiles. Imbecile. Then the idiot Burak appears in the tiles, with his spiky blond hair. Fat idiot. The feeble-minded Burak with his fat, pink meat. There's a 'pigboy' tattoo on his forehead. On the other boy's forehead, the one with the *Audi*, it writes 'rich bastard'. They all have tattoos on their foreheads. Like a tag. Whatever they are, that's what's written. When she wipes the tiles, they're there one moment and gone the next. There one moment, gone the next, there one moment, gone the next.

'Why are you cleaning the tiles, Behiye? Didn't our Nazmiye clean them yesterday?'

'All right, excuse me. I just felt like doing it.'

She grabs her windbreaker, and they go out. It's a lovely warm autumn day. The weather relaxes Behiye a bit. That idiot crew recedes from her mind. For the moment. A bit.

In two paces they're at Akmerkez. Before they get there, Handan brings up the subject of gifts: 'What can I get for my mother, what can I get for my mother?'

After throwing around a few ideas, Handan buys her mother a tiny pair of gold earrings, from the jeweller's there, from *Sait Koc*, the place Leman loves so much.

'A pair of baby earrings for my baby. Imagine how sweet they'll look on her with her short hair. Imagine!'

'All right,' says Behiye. 'I'm imagining the baby earrings and I don't exist.'

'Don't make me laugh. You've become ill-tempered again, Behiye. But why? You were fine at breakfast. It's because Erim called. Isn't it? Just because he called, because I'm going to meet him?'

'I'm afraid that he's going to hurt you, Handan. I'm terribly afraid that he'll break your heart. All of them are such imbeciles. To sum it up in a sentence, they're selfish, mentally handicapped oxen.'

'What do you mean?'

'I mean to hell with all of them.'

'Behiye! But why? Why are you always doing this to me?'

Handan collapses on one of the metal benches and starts crying. Behiye wants to throw herself over the railing into the middle of the café on the bottom floor. To land with her head in the middle of someone's schnitzel. Breaking her neck. Right on the plate of schnitzel. One of her shoes flying off into some woman's *Gucci* bag. The woman picks her huge boot out of her *Gucci* bag. She picks it out so she can put the bag on her arm and go on about her business. So her bag won't go to waste. Behiye thinks these things as she stands in front of Handan.

'I'm sorry, Handan. I didn't know what I was doing. I'm very sorry. I'm just afraid that they'll hurt you. I'm very very frightened that they'll do something to you, that they'll do something to us. We're going to run away to Australia, aren't we? We're not going to stay here, we're not going to allow them to hurt us. Look, I got the Australian Embassy's internet address. I keep it with me. We're getting out of this place, aren't we, Handan? I'm frightened, I can't help it.'

She's on her knees in front of Handan as she talks. Handan is stroking her face with her hand. 'We're going, Behiye. Please don't worry. I'm thinking about it all the time too. Don't be afraid, my Behiye.'

They hug each other and go up to the top floor. Handan drinks a coffee, and Behiye drinks a tea. Handan eats a doughnut. In order to forget Behiye's behaviour. In order to forgive her. Behiye can carry on like that.

'I've found it, I've found it. I've found what I'm going to buy Leman,' says Behiye. Right away she goes to the nearby T-shirt printing place and tells them what she wants. She has them print:

LIBRA WOMAN
The mossst beautiful

on a small white T-shirt. This is her gift for Leman. Handan loves it.

Hand in hand, they go down to *Makro*. Behiye wants to make a cake with hazelnuts, tangerines and lady's fingers. 'It was the best cake I've ever eaten in my life. The shape wasn't so nice. But it was terribly delicious.' Then homemade cookies. Little sandwiches, this and that.

They shop for at least an hour. They also buy a few decorations: balloons, confetti, other nonsense. Paper plates with *Tweety* designs. A paper tablecloth with *Tweety* designs.

'Let's have a real child's birthday for Leman. She's growing up after all: she's turning thirty-five. Tonight, sensible Leman comes into being, and emotional Leman will be left behind. Da-da-daaan.'

'Oh, it will be so sweet, my Behiye. She'll love it. We've never had a child's birthday party for her like this. And it was your idea. You're the one who has all the wonderful ideas.'

'You don't say: Behiye, creator of wonderful ideas. Have I presented you with my visiting card?'

Their arms are so full of packages that they jump into a taxi right in front of Akmerkez. They tell the driver to make a U-turn. Then another U-turn in front of the place called Dove. Then to enter the complex and leave them right in front of the door.

The driver is a real bastard. He pays a lot of attention to the rear-view mirror, presumably in order to look at Handan's breasts.

He is like that the whole way. Whenever a traffic light turns green, there is always honking from behind. He can't take his eyes off Handan's breasts.

Behiye can feel the arteries in her forehead throbbing. 'Keep your eyes on the road,' she tells the driver once or twice.

The guy turns and gives Behiye a dirty look. Then he continues to dissect Handan in the mirror. This is how Behiye feels: as if he's cutting Handan to pieces; as if he's cut her into pieces consisting of her breasts, her behind, her stomach. He's cut Handan to pieces with his eyes. She feels as if Handan has been cut up and killed with the filthiness of his glances.

She wants to protect Handan. To rescue her from this disgusting creature's aggression. She wants Handan to remain in one piece. She wants her to remain Handan.

Handan! Handan!

The two arteries in her forehead are throbbing so wildly that she feels they might jump out of place.

When the taxi stops outside the building, Behiye is so irritated she's ready to fall into a heap on the ground. She feels as tense as a bow. Very tense. Ready to let loose.

The bastard jumps out and opens the door on Handan's side. While pretending to help her take the packages out, he manages to rub himself against Handan's breasts.

Behiye sees this.

'Don't you dare touch my friend, you faggot.'

'Your father is a faggot! How dare you call me a faggot. I'll make you eat your words!'

Behiye puts her hand in her pocket. She's wearing her fucking windbreaker. She didn't wear her jacket. She hasn't got her jacket on.

She sees the driver walking towards her.

'Behiye! Behiye!' Handan jumps in front of Behiye. 'Please leave. Just go. Quickly! Help! Heeelp!'

The driver is surprised at what he's got himself into. He jumps into his car and races off.

'Faggot! Faggot! All of your ancestors are faggots!' Behiye runs after the taxi like a madwoman.

She picks up a stone and throws it. It hits the licence plate, that's all.

Her legs are trembling. Fiercely. She wishes that shit hadn't run off. She wants to see blood. She wants to show the bastard how far she can go, even if it means killing him. She's blind with rage. That's how mad she's gone. That's how mad she's gone. She's gone mad.

'My Behiye, are you all right? Are you all right, my dear? Are you all right? You're not hurt, are you? I was so frightened. I was frightened he was going to hit you.'

'I wish you hadn't come between us, Handan. I wish he'd killed me. I wish I'd killed him too. I wish I'd hit him with my head like this.'

'Behiye, what's wrong with you? Why are you being like this? He didn't even really touch me. Men do dirty things like that sometimes; I'm revolted by it, of course; but I'm used to it.'

'They shouldn't touch you. They can't touch you. What do they think you are? Do they think that your body is a field for them to trample on? A field for them to soil – what, what, what? Who do they think they are?'

Behiye is unable to speak. There's a little garden in front of the building. They collapse on the grass. But it's good. She doesn't cry. She doesn't carry on. But it's good. She feels as if her brain has galloped away. A lot of thoughts. Thoughts fuelled by anger like a rancorous wick.

'No one will ever soil you again, Handan. No one will cut you to pieces. I'll kill any bastard who tries to touch you, who insults you. I'll cut the faggot to pieces. You'll see.'

'Behiye. Stop already. Enough already.' Handan hugs her from behind. They roll together on the grass. The grass embraces them. The smell of the earth and so forth. It swaddles them. It wraps them tightly. It struggles to do them good. To be good for them. A tiny bit.

Leman's birthday

• •

'Never mind, Behiye,' says Handan. 'Your nerves are a wreck. You're not in a state to prepare anything. We can go to *Pelit* later to get a cake and whatever else we need.'

They're in the kitchen. They're putting the things they bought on to the shelves and into the refrigerator.

'I just have a bad taste in my mouth, that's all. I'm fine. Don't you worry. What could repair an angry and offended soul better than preparing for a birthday party? Better than making hazelnut cookies and cake? Tell me what else could possibly restore me?'

Handan laughs. The thirty-five girl appears in the kitchen door, and then vanishes. She's going to Sister Nevin's for coffee. From there to the hairdresser's. From there to somewhere else and from there back here.

'See you in the evening, girls,' says Leman. 'Don't wear yourselves out.' She winks and leaves the house.

'I suppose she's understood we're preparing some surprises. Let her understand. It's better. She'll be happier all day. She'll be excited, she'll be waiting. Isn't that so?'

'Yes, yes,' says Behiye. She'd like Handan to leave the kitchen. So she can make the cookies and put them in the oven, so she can make the cake, so she can prepare the sandwiches. She wants to have the kitchen to herself. She knows that nothing else will make her feel better.

What can repair an angry and offended soul better than preparing pastries. What? What?

'All right, I'm going inside. It's clear you don't want me here. But please give me a shout if you need any help. I'll read one of your books. Or at least I'll try to read. Otherwise you'll think I'm a stupid girl and get bored with me.'

Behiye pulls Handan's head to her chest. She embraces her tightly. She buries her nose in the nape of her neck. She draws the Handan smell into her soul. The world's most beautiful, most Handan smell. The smell of another world. A new and different world. It's not the smell of a world to which Behiye doesn't belong, but of a completely different world, of a different continent.

www.immi.gov.au

She repeats this to herself as if it were a prayer. The internet address of the Australian Embassy. *www.immi.gov.au*. It's engraved in her memory. She hadn't been aware of this.

'All right. I'm going inside.'

'Handan.'

'Yes, dear?'

'I could never be bored with you. I'll never get bored. I feel, I don't know, as if you are, as if I belong to you for the rest of my life. The first time, I mean, the first time.'

'Behiye. My Behiye.'

Handan hugs and kisses Behiye. 'Believe me, I don't know what to say.'

'Don't say anything. Go on, go inside.'

'All right, my Behiye.'

Behiye prepares a tray of walnut and hazelnut cookies and puts them in the oven. Then she begins making the cake. She learned how to make the cake from a magazine she saw at

Çiğdem's house. That day they got up and made the cake right away. In Aunt Sevil's flawless kitchen. The cake has no shape. And it is not cooked. They prepare chocolate sauce, and put the hazelnuts, tangerines and lady's fingers on top. It's delicious.

Çiğdem says it looks like a cave cake, the way it comes out in a shapeless heap. But it's amazingly delicious. Çiğdem ate half of it. The cake was finished half an hour after they made it.

Çiğdem.

How many days it's been since she's heard her voice, seen her face. A childhood friend is like that. You can be unfaithful, you can hurt them, you can disappear, and you still feel them next to you. They stay there. Where they belong. For ever.

Behiye has prepared the cake. It's time for the sandwiches. She cuts sixty or seventy tiny slices of sandwich bread in two down the middle. On each one she spreads a little butter, mayonnaise and mustard. Then she places salami and cheese on them. She puts slices of cucumber on half of them and slices of tomato on the other half.

The cookies are ready now. The house smells of cookies and cake, like a witch's house in a fairy tale.

Handan can't bear it, and comes to look three or four times. With Moravia's *Woman of Rome* in her hand. She chose it because of the title. She chose it thinking, if it's about a woman I won't be very bored.

'Behiye, if I don't have a few cookies and sandwiches now I'm going to fall down and faint. Both from hunger and from envy. No one has ever prepared a birthday party like this for me. It was always Leman ordering a cake and some snacks by telephone at the last minute.'

'We'll do it for you too. Don't be envious of the thirty-five girl.'

'Promise me. You'll do all of this for my birthday next summer. Doesn't the cake look a little strange, Behiye?'

'It's a cave cake. That's what Çiğdem called it. But you'll see, you'll lick your fingers.'

She sticks five thin candles into the cake. And five sparklers. Then they decorate the kitchen with the things they bought. At Handan's, there's no table in the living room. In that house, almost everything takes place in the kitchen.

They put the paper *Tweety* tablecloth on the orange formica table. They put out the *Tweety* paper plates. Tea glasses, forks, knives, so forth.

They hang the streamers from the kitchen cupboards. They blow up balloons and fill the entry hall with them. Baby-blue and white balloons. By the front door. So that Leman will be surrounded by balloons the moment she walks in. On the front door they hang a huge card that says,

Happy Birthday

The house is looks very merry. It becomes a birthday house: the atmosphere is light and happy.

Handan goes and puts on a pink shirt and her favourite blue jeans. She does her hair in pigtails. She looks so lovely, so babyish like this.

Behiye puts on a white T-shirt. And, as always, the blue jeans she bought with Çiğdem, which hang halfway down her ass now. As she looks at herself in the closet mirror, she makes a decision to buy herself some new clothes. Things that will fit her. Her new body. In her New Behiye state.

As she thinks about the New Behiye state, she opens the closet again and looks in the jacket pocket. In the inner pocket, the dollars and euros are waiting for the day when they can run to their aid. So politely. In the outer pocket is the lancet. Also waiting politely. Waiting patiently for the day when it can run to their aid. That's how it seems to Behiye. As if the lancet is waiting there patiently, politely. The taxi driver's disgusting face enters her thoughts like a meteor.

It burns her.

He's left a mark in her. A crater has been formed.

If she'd been wearing the jacket, if she'd had the lancet with her, he wouldn't have left a mark like that. She would have scraped him off the face of the earth.

He wouldn't have got in; wouldn't have made a crater. She's twisted with regret and guilt.

Behiye cuts it out. She won't allow that faggot to ruin her day any more. Won't allow that creature to stain her day...

She goes inside.

Handan has left the book on the coffee table. She's watching *MTV*. The inescapable *Kylie Minogue* is singing her inescapable song.

'I love this woman so much. She looks like my mother.'

'Leman is more beautiful than her. More full, more, I don't know, more sexy.'

'Whaaat? My mother is sexy?'

'Be fair, Handan.'

Just at that moment the doorbell rings. Handan runs and presses the buzzer.

Muki the witch! Her hair is all done up, and she's painted her face and so forth. She comes in.

'How nicely you've decorated the house. Poor Leman will be so pleased. Good for you, my little Handan.'

'It's not me, Muki. It was all Behiye's idea. She's made cake and cookies and everything for our blue rabbit. And she has a new name for her. She calls her the thirty-five girl. Isn't that sweet?'

Handan giggles. A grin passes briefly across Muki's face. She looks Behiye up and down carefully, but without a hint of approval.

'I see you've become part of the household, Lady Behiye.'

Behiye holds herself back from saying – you mean I've occupied your bed, you witch skeleton. She flees to the kitchen. Muki looks like a puppet that's lost its clothes, its hair, its voice, its speech and its troupe. Like all of those worn-out puppets that have been thrown out of the theatre and into the garbage. Still trying to put on a show all by herself. She can't help it, Behiye feels sorry for Muki. She can't believe it, but that's how it is. The feeling of pity is so close to the feeling of tenderness. They mingle together.

Strange. But true.

A key turns in the lock. Leman has come in. She's among the balloons now.

'Handan! Behiye! What a lovely surprise! All these balloons!'

She starts picking up balloons and throwing them around. A woman delighted by balloons that have been blown up for her! Leman beauty. Watching Leman play with the balloons in the hall, Behiye feels as if she's about to burst with happiness. As if she's so inflated with happiness that her feet are about to lift off the ground.

'My baby mother, my blue rabbit. The most beautiful of all beauties.'

How Handan embraces her mother. Muki, planted in the doorway of the living room, is also watching the mother and daughter. Her eyes have moistened a little. Even Muki the witch's heart has been softened and melted a bit by this sweetness and beauty.

If Behiye doesn't hold herself back she'll go and hug Muki. All four of them will hold hands and do a birthday dance. She turns her back and returns to the kitchen. She lights the candles and sparklers on the cake, and turns out the lights.

'Birthday people. Come to the kitchen,' she shouts.

They come running.

Happy birthday Leman
Happy birthday Leman
Happy birthday, happy birthday
Happy birthday – Mother!

They sang at the top of their voices, with good spirits and enthusiasm. Then they embraced wholeheartedly.

Handan gave her mother her gift. Leman put on the baby earrings right away. Muki bought a frightful ashtray as a gift. The ugliest and most aggressive ashtray Behiye had ever seen in her life. Ceramic.

'Reminder of my mother. The one and only Muki. I'll use this for the rest of my life.' Leman's frosty laughter fills the kitchen. She hugs Handan and Muki and kisses them.

Behiye, feeling embarrassed and biting her lower lip, hands Leman her gift.

'I love it, I love it. You're the sweetest, my Behiye.'

She runs to her room and puts on the T-shirt. She looks so very beautiful in that short, tight, white T-shirt. She shines. She catches one's eye and one's desire. Birthday Leman.

The most desirable mother and daughter in the world. No one has ever called Behiye 'the sweetest' before. Thieves of desire. Pirates of the heart. This mother and daughter are like that. They have Behiye on puppet strings. From happiness. From delight. From flying. Fly Behiye. Fly, fly, fly bug. Fly wherever you can. Go on, fly.

Lie

· ·

They sit down to enjoy their cake, their cookies and their sandwiches. Behiye is constantly freshening their tea.

'Sister Nevin? Did we forget to wait for her?'

'No, it's all right. She might drop by at a late hour. She was going to be here with us. At the last moment Mr Ozcan called and said it was convenient.'

Sister Nevins' lives, which were arranged according to the whims of their men. Those women who went running with their tongues hanging out whenever the men said it was 'convenient'. Women who were ready and willing. A flock of heart-rending women. This is the golden rule of Sister Nevins to be willing to obey any command wholeheartedly, from the very depths of their beings, to be one hundred percent dependent. Behiye is burning up.

Handan! Just at that moment her telephone rings. She answers with the cheerful, flirtatious voice she uses to answer Erim's calls. She runs to her room. She's going to account for herself to him. In her baby voice she's going to try to tell him, to explain to him, why she hasn't been able to see him for two days. She's going to bring water from a thousand streams in order to please him.

Behiye is churning inside. She wants to snatch Handan away from Sister Nevins' rules. From Leman worlds. Let her not become like them. Not like them. It would be such a shame for Handan.

Before Handan returns, the house phone rings. Behiye fidgets in her seat. The house phone at Handan's doesn't ring very often. Everyone calls the mother and daughter on their cell phones.

Leman doesn't feel like getting up. 'Could you answer it please, Behiye?'

Behiye runs into the living room with her heart beating. Let it not be for her. Let it not be for her. She picks up the phone on the coffee table and answers in a faint voice. 'Hello,' she says.

A deep, man's voice says, 'May I speak with Ms Leman? Is she in?'

'Yes, one moment. I'll call her.'

Behiye runs to the kitchen.

'It's for you.'

'Oh, don't make me get up. Everyone knows my cell phone number, who could it be? Was it a man or a woman? It's got to be some ridiculous person.'

'It's a man.'

'Go ask who he is, Behiye.'

'Excuse me, could you tell me who's calling Ms Leman?' Behiye says to the receiver. Her face is red from the absurdity of what she's doing.

'Ayhan Atacan. I'm a friend of Ms Leman's.'

'One moment, Mr Ayhan.'

Leman runs into the living room. 'Is it Ayhan?'

Behiye nods her head. Leman collapses on to the sofa. She puts a hand over her heart. With the other hand she signals for the telephone. Behiye hands it to her.

Evidently it's a very important call. Ayhan isn't just anyone. Leman was pressing a hand over her heart so that it wouldn't leap out of her chest.

When she returns to the kitchen Behiye eats three slices of cake. Cave cake to calm her nerves.

She wants to disappear into the cake. To hide inside the cave cake. She doesn't quite know why, but she feels very embarrassed. Her cheeks are bright red. Both her cheeks and her soul.

'I'm meeting Erim tomorrow afternoon, Behiye. The phone rang, was it for my mother?'

'Yes, yes. Someone called Ayhan.'

'Ayhan?' Handan's cat eyes open wide.

'Is that good-for-nothing bastard calling again? Which hell did he emerge from?' shouts Muki, spraying spittle through her false teeth.

'Quiet, Muki. She'll hear us. She's talking to him inside. What can we do?'

'That snake slithered out of his bucket on Leman's happiest day. And things were going so well with her latest one, Mr Şevket or whatever his name was. The man really seems to be taken with her lately.'

'Shhh. She hung up. She's coming.'

Leman doesn't come to the kitchen. She runs straight to the bathroom. She turns on the bathroom tap. The three of them listen to the sound of the tap, and of the toilet flushing, with their ears perked.

'I'm sure she's crying. She's turned on the tap so we won't hear.'

'She cried for months over that centipede. Wasn't that enough! God damn that Ayhan. Damn him.'

'Don't curse him Muki. Ayhan was very much in love with Leman. It just didn't work out. After all, these married men have to make a choice in the end.'

How well Handan knows the mysterious circumstances of Leman World. How naturally she's understood the rules. Behiye listens in amazement. Her Handan! Baby cat girl! Perhaps Handan is more grown-up than she is. Perhaps, as Handan said, Behiye is her baby. Behiye doesn't understand these worlds at all. She doesn't have a clue about the rules of 'desire'. She knows absolutely zero about the subject. Zero Behiye.

After scrubbing her face well, Leman returns to the table.

'Well, you all know: he called. But let's not talk about him. He wanted to wish me a happy birthday, he couldn't bear it, and so forth. So on and so forth. That's all, that's all.'

'My blue rabbit's eyes are all puffy,' says Handan, climbing on to her lap.

'God damn that bastard. May he get boils all over his body,' says Muki as if she's whispering a prayer.

'Muki! What could the man do? He's working for his father-in-law, he has three little children, his wife is his aunt's daughter – he couldn't get out of that loop; he was trapped. Don't get me going, Muki. Wasn't there a bottle of *Absolut* around here somewhere? Don't you think we deserve a vodka?'

Leman climbs on to a stool and retrieves a bottle of vodka from the very top of one of the cupboards.

'Come on,' she says. 'Who wants vodka and orange?'

Behiye doesn't know how many kilos of oranges she squeezed or how many times they listened to the *Selami Şahin* song *Lie* over the next four or five hours.

They rewound the tape about thirty times. They listened to *Lie* at least a hundred times. Two bottles of *Absolut*, and on top of that six beers and a half bottle of *Tekirdag* raki. When they'd consumed all this, they even finished that frightful sweet yellow drink they had in the house, vermouth, they even finished the vermouth!

Muki, Handan, Behiye and Leman. All right, Leman drank a great deal. But within their limits they also drank a great deal. A great deal.

The song of the evening, as if it had been specially requested for Leman's birthday, was *Lie*. Even now, Behiye still knows the song by heart. The song that penetrated the garbage of her soul.

Lie lie lie, it's a lie that I don't love you
A lie I told in a moment of anger
It's a lie that I don't love you

Later, there was a verse that they all sang together at the tops of their voices.

Let them come and take whatever I have
Believe me, I'm ready to share
It's only you I cannot share

This is the most important verse. That is, of Selami Şahin singing.

Lie lie lie; it's a lie that I forgot you
A childlike joy is born in me
Whenever I see you

Yes, just as the master said. That's how it is.

At about two, the legendary Sister Nevin drops by the house. Behiye was so drunk when she came that she remembers her only as a very decorated, interfering creature with lots of very black hair and a chattering voice. A monster from outer space. She came to take over their ship.

At the insistence of the legendary Sister Nevin, they brought Muki, who was snoring away with her head on the table, to the pull-out bed in the living room. She remembers that.

Sister Nevin was probably also drinking with them too when they sank to the level of degrading themselves with that sweet yellow poison vermouth. In the end, as their leader she played the whistle. With her voice, that is.

Later, she remembers this while vomiting into the toilet. Lying on the cold tiles in the bathroom she remembers how, under the leadership of Sister Nevin's Space Committee, they struggled to drag her to Handan's bedroom. She remembers half of it, a quarter of it, a tenth of it. Rememberrr.

Around seven in the morning she wakes feeling as if skewers had been stuck into her temples. She has to pee. As soon as she stands up, she realises that this was nothing. She feels terribly nauseous. Her stomach is turning in her mouth. Get the fuck back where you belong, stomach! Get back where you belong!

Within ten seconds her ruined body was prostate before the toilet as she struggled to vomit. But she can't really vomit. You can't recover that quickly from last night's shame, Behiye. Go ahead, suffer. You're hung over. You fell into today from last night! Why did you have to drink so much? What was your problem? Can't you just drink as much as you can handle? Senseless child! Unconscious Behiye. Cons. Cious. Ous.

She looks into the living room, her temples throbbing at every step. Muki is snoring away on the pull-out bed. When she takes out her teeth she's just like a skeleton. Pitiful, worn-out puppet, poor excuse for a useless witch. She watches Muki with confused affection. Then she goes back to Handan's room. They put Behiye in the baby cat girl's bed. Presumably Handan slept with her mother.

She wants to go to Leman's door and look at the two of them. But she doesn't have the strength. As she drags herself to the bed, she drinks half a glass of water. It makes her stomach worse. She puts her head on the pillow and tries to sleep. If she could get a good sleep, her stomach might feel better.

The pillow presses the skewers into her head. Her stomach is turning, and she feels as if she was in a bad car going up a very steep hill. She feels as if she hasn't slept, as if she never fell asleep. But when she looks at the clock she sees that it's one. That meant she'd slept for six hours. She'd slept in spite of her headache and her upset stomach.

When she gets up to go to the bathroom, she's surprised to find that even though her stomach is a bit better, it's still upset. While washing her face and brushing her teeth, at how drained of strength she was. At how difficult every movement was. Hangover.

In the kitchen she finds Handan and Leman sitting across from each other drinking nescafé.

'Drink a little vodka and you'll be fine,' says Leman.

'Never,' shouts Behiye. 'I'm dying.'

'A hair of the dog, Behiye. There's no other cure for you.' Leman laughs.

'I'm going to cook pilaff and eat it. Mushy! Pilaff is best when it's mushy.'

'But how wretched my baby is; how she drank, how she passed out on the bathroom tiles,' says Handan.

'I'm thoroughly ashamed of myself,' says Behiye. She laughs. Her voice cracks.

'It's best to take a shower too. I'm going to Akmerkez with my mother to look at some things. Erim has invited me to their house this evening.'

'Is that so? You didn't mention you were going to his house.'

'Yes, yes. He was very insistent. To introduce me to his parents, I suppose.'

That jerk's parents were all that was missing. Erim's father has an automobile showroom. Handan had told her this at least forty times. Shitty rich family.

Behiye throws herself into the bath. She stands under the shower for a long, long time. In a state in which her sense of time was distorted. She couldn't quite figure out what was long and what was short.

When she comes out of the shower and finds she's alone in the house, she feels terribly relaxed. First she puts on a *Blink 182* CD in order to clear the slate. She wants to clean her ears with her bring-you-down/life-is-fucked-but-what-can-we-do music. On top of that she listens to *Limp Bizkit*: forces of dampness to rescue her soul.

She doesn't have the strength to make mushy pilaff. She eats a slice of toast with a little cheese. It seems to do her good. Good.

By this time it's four o'clock. They'll be home soon. They'll be back to change their clothes and drop off what they've bought.

She feels a wave of panic wash through her. Another whole day gone and buried. Again she'd done nothing; nothing to further their escape plan! She wants to go to Levent and find an internet cafe. Then the photographs: the photographs of her and Handan at the photography studio. They've been ready for some time. She didn't pick those up either, she didn't pick those up.

All of a sudden, Behiye feels as if not picking them up was a very bad thing, as if leaving their likenesses there was a very bad, very dangerous and very unlucky thing. Strangers could look at the pictures. Evil eyes. At Handan and Behiye. Could see how happy and beautiful they were, and do something.

The wave of panic grows and grows, it swallows Behiye and carries her along. She feels as if she's losing her grip on everything, as if she's losing her grip through laziness and fatness – it's happening. It's already happened.

Unexpected guest

• •

She grabs her jacket and rushes out. She has to run to the photography studio and rescue their likenesses. Before they're soiled, before they're finished. A moment before. Before a moment.

She jumps and hops down the stairs. She's pushing against the front door of the building when she sees someone coming towards her. She's found her! She's walking towards her, towards the door. She's coming – towards Behiye.

'Çiğdem!'

'Behiye!'

'What are you looking for here? How did you find me? Did something happen? What do you want?'

'Thank you very much, Behiye. It's been all of eleven days since we've seen each other, and look what you do when we meet! I'm dying of curiosity. Aren't you my friend? Can't I come and find you?'

'There's no news about Tufan, is there? It's nothing to do with him, is it, Çiğdem? Please, tell me the truth.'

'I swear there isn't, Behiye. He went to the course to look for you, he sent your mother to see us twice; this and that. He couldn't find any trace of you. Not everyone is as bewitched as my friend, all right?'

She takes Çiğdem and they go up to Handan's. Behiye makes tea.

'These people are poor; I mean, their house is really falling apart. And I thought they were something. Handan being so beautiful and all.'

'Not everyone lives in pleasure palaces like you, Lady Çiğdem. How did you find this place?'

'You've become more polite since I last saw you. Maybe you can beat me too while we have tea.'

'Look, I'm really not myself today. Last night was Handan's mother's birthday; I drank an awful lot. I've missed you. Only yesterday, was it, I thought of you. You came into our waters just like the *Titanic*, Lady Çiğdem.'

'Remember there were those kids at the course who went to school with Handan. I found out from them that she lives in the Petrol Complex in Nispetiye. So I asked around. There was a boy in the shop in back who knew the address. A boy named Cetin; I flirted with him a little and got the numbers.'

'Capable Çiğdem The Policewoman at work. So, what happens now that you've found me? What's this about counting the days since you've seen me? Are we talking about a passion here, Lady Çiğdemella?'

'Don't make fun of me, Behiye. You go mad, you steal money from your crazy brother and vanish from sight. The guy is after you, Handan isn't at the course, her phone number is out of service. Anyone would be curious. You may not realise this, Behiye, but you're my closest friend. I swear you have no feelings at all.'

The door opens in the middle of Çiğdem's speech about the spring of friendship; Leman enters with a very sulky face.

Behiye doesn't want Çiğdem to meet Leman. Why didn't she think of taking her to Levent or someplace? Her head has stopped working. The drinking really messed me up! Her head just isn't working at all. Or it's working very slowly.

Leman behaves very coldly to Çiğdem. And Çiğdem feels it. It's not as if she wouldn't feel it either.

'I'm a friend of Handan's from the course. I was passing and thought I'd drop by,' she stutters.

'Handan isn't home.'

She's acting like – what business do you have here? And to Behiye – all we needed was for you to start bringing friends around. She expresses all of this with just those few little words.

But Behiye can't bring herself to just send Çiğdem on her way. Nor is she in any state to make quick decisions. They act as if they're going to continue with their tea ceremony in the kitchen. They both feel like running away screaming; but they're stuck to their stools.

In the midst of this tension, the telephone rings. 'I'll get it, Behiye,' hisses Leman as she goes off to her room.

Ayhan Atacan, thinks Behiye. This, all this agitation about the telephone, it's all about Ayhan Atacan.

'Yes, sir. I'm her mother. Ohh, is that so. No, I wasn't aware. Yes, I suppose so. All right, sir. Yes, I understand. All right, thank you. I'll call you. All right. Good day.'

They listen to this cold and formal conversation with their ears perked. It wasn't Ayhan Atacan after all. Who could it be? Who would Leman speak to in this way? Who is it? What happened? What, what, what?

Leman comes to the kitchen as soon as she hangs up.

'That was the course director calling,' she says in a dreadful voice. 'Handan said she might sign up again, but right now her friend's brother is after her, and she begged for the money back. The stupid man didn't know what else to do, I think you know very well he returned the money, Lady Behiye. He called to tell me all of this. Is Handan going to sign up again: the course is completely full, but there's still room for Handan, and so forth and so on. Yes, Lady Behiye. How are you going to explain this disgrace? Until now my daughter has never lied to me, not even once. Handan doesn't know the first thing about telling lies. Do you have a brother after you; is that why you moved in with us? Go ahead, tell us whatever you have to tell us, let's hear your story.'

Seeing Çiğdem with her mouth hanging open, Behiye feels like slapping her one. If she hadn't come, Behiye might have got to the telephone first. If Leman had come home later, the director wouldn't have found anyone at home. The photographs are still at the studio. She didn't pick them up, couldn't pick them up, because of Çiğdem. Hadn't she felt that it was bad, that it was unlucky – hadn't this occurred to her? Hadn't she known it in her soul? Well, it had happened!

Leman is giving Behiye cutting looks. She's cutting her into little pieces. She's finishing Behiye. Behiye is finished, ruined.

Just then, something happened that never happens in life. Though it's something that happens constantly in Leman's life: her cell phone rings in her room.

She runs inside. Mr Şevket! Behiye knows all of Leman's tones of voice by heart. Now, in her room, she's talking in her Mr Şevket voice. She's telling him what happened. Explaining the 'secret' of why she's upset. The reason she sounds ill-tempered today isn't Ayhan Atacan's telephone call, it's the Course Money. This household calamity came in handy, after all. Behiye breathes easily.

'Get up,' she says. 'We're getting out of here.'

Çiğdem puts her bag on her arm, Behiye grabs her jacket from the sofa; they rush out of the house. A beautiful, fresh October evening is waiting for them outside. Behiye feels very happy with herself. It feels good to get out of that house and away from that witch Leman into an autumn evening.

'But what a beautiful woman she is,' says Çiğdem, her mouth still hanging open. 'I've never seen such a beautiful woman in my life. She's even more beautiful than *Michelle Pfeiffer*. Even more than *Cameron Diaz*. What a beautiful woman she is. But bad-hearted.'

'We'll find more blond actresses for you. So that you count them. Walk quickly, Çiğdem. There's a photography studio over here, I want to get there before they close.'

'Did you get the director to give you the course money? The man had their home number; he ratted on you. It's a good thing he didn't give Tufan the number. He could have.'

Behiye bites her lower lip. Çiğdem is very right. She thought she and Handan had torn up all the forms. That meant the man hadn't given up all of them. Then the story about Behiye's brother. Couldn't she have just told a lie? Everything has blown up in their faces thanks to Handan. They're in complete disgrace now.

Handan! Where are you? Where are you? Even your mother came home. Where are you, Handan?

Behiye feels an unbelievable Handan longing. Her eyes are filling with tears. She's like a madwoman, she knows this. One moment she's happy, the next she's in panic; then her eyes start tearing from longing and sorrow. Behiye is in a very bad state. Her nerves are frayed.

On the door of the photography studio, a sign reads:

OPENING HOURS
08:30-12:00
13:30-17:00

But this is a photography studio! It's only twenty past five, why is it closed? Why is it closed!

She gives the shutters a kick. A good kick. The people in the shop next door look at her.

She feels so much pain. So much pain that tears start to fall from her eyes. Tears of pain. Çiğdem finds some silly things to say to calm down the neighbours.

She's not going to be able to get the photographs. Or Handan. Handan is gone, and so are the photographs. Her foot hurts very, very, very much. She wants to shout: Handan! She wants to run screaming and shouting to the house to find Handan, to bury her nose in her neck. Handan! Handan! Is she too late for Handan too? Has she lost her? Where is she?

'Behiye. What's the matter with you? What's going on, the shop is closed, that's all. Don't be so upset, you can get the pictures tomorrow.'

She turns her head and looks at Çiğdem. Tears are running from Çiğdem's eyes and rolling down her fat, red cheeks. As she wipes away the tears with the back of her hand, more tears roll down. Çiğdem is crying her eyes out. She's crying for Behiye. This bothers Behiye. It bothers her a great deal, it hurts – both her foot and Çiğdem's crying.

'Fuck off, Çiğdem.'

'Behiye! What are you saying?'

'Fuck off! It's all your fault.'

'Behiye – I. Behiye – I didn't do anything wrong. I don't know their home number. I didn't give it to anyone. Behiye, what did I do? Behiye! Behiye.'

'I'm telling you to fuck off. I don't want to see anyone. Not you or anyone else. I'm the New Behiye. You have no idea. You have no idea about anything. The other me died. While you were sleeping.'

'You're breaking my heart.'

'I'm telling you for the last time: fuck off, Çiğdem.'

Çiğdem wipes away the tears with the back of her hand, but more tears keep falling, reminding her of a car's windshield wipers in a heavy rain. She crosses the street.

She stopped a taxi. Çiğdem jumped in. She's gone. She's gone. Now Behiye no longer has a childhood friend. Why should she have one? Is this childhood? Wherever her childhood went, that's where her childhood friend can go.

In any event, she hops back to Handan's house on one foot. But she's afraid to go up. The Witch Leman is there. Calamity Leman.

There's a little garden in front of the building. A garden

separated from the pavement by stubby plants. She throws herself down there. She wants the sky to grow dark and cover her. To close Behiye in.

A long time ago, it was a very bad day. A very bad taxi driver upset them a lot. She and Handan lay together on this grass. The grass did them good. It made them feel well. A long, long time ago.

A long time ago, with Handan.

It was yesterday.

But Handan was by her side, and now Handan isn't there. Handan is not by her side. She doesn't have the pictures either. She couldn't manage to get them either. They've been locked up too.

Handan!

Come rescue me. I'm sprawled here on the grass crying. Come take me away. Take me wherever you want to take me. Come get me Handan. I'm dying here. I'm dying of sorrow here on the grass.

Meat grinder

• •

'Behiye! My Behiye! What happened to you? Why aren't you at home? Why are you lying here? What happened, Behiye, did something happen? You've been crying. I can see it on your face. You've been crying.'

She flings aside the bags she's carrying and throws herself on to the grass. She saw her. She found her. How long has she been lying there? Behiye doesn't know. It might have been half an hour. She doesn't want to know. Three or four people came in and out of the building during that time. None of them noticed her. Only Handan. Handan came and found her lying on the grass. Handan! Handan!

'Handan.'

'What is it, dear, tell me what happened to you? Did something happen with my mother? Come on, let's go upstairs. It's getting cold.'

'Handan. I'm frightened. Bad things are going to happen; I'm frightened they're going to separate us, Handan.'

'Nothing bad is going to happen. Don't worry, don't be upset, Behiye. Come, my baby, come to my arms.'

Handan smell. Behiye is tired, very tired; but she's all right now. Only her head hurts terribly. Two skewers are twisting in her temples. That will pass too. Handan has come. Handan is babying her. Soothing her. Promising her good things.

'Everything will be all right, my one and only. You'll see, we'll get out of here. We'll have a completely different life. Be patient, there's not long left, my Behiye.'

They go upstairs. Leman isn't home. She must have gone out to the hairdresser's just after Behiye and Çiğdem left. To Sister Nevin, to Mr Şevket; she's at work.

She had a terrible fight with Leman at Akmerkez. She didn't want to buy Handan the things she wanted, tried to get her to buy cheaper things.

Handan brought up the *Jil Sander/Moschino* subject. They started going at each other about how Leman always got to buy expensive things, and Handan has to buy cheaper things. Later she bought Handan everything she wanted. Considering they didn't make a budget, didn't have a budget.

Later Erim called. They met him at Akmerkez. This evening he was going to his uncle's house with his mother and father. It was his aunt and uncle's wedding anniversary; Erim had to be there. He invited Handan and Behiye to come to their summer house sometime soon. It was a wonderful house with a swimming pool in Tuzla. They could have a lot of fun. Could could could. If only Behiye would come too. Burak was coming too. And Cenk and his girlfriend. Bla bla bla.

'So you're going to Erim's summer house tomorrow, Handan?'

'Yes, I promised, Behiye. Look how warm the autumn sun still is. We could swim, sit in the sun and so forth. How much fun we had in the university pool that night. We could have fun like that. Please come, Behiye, please come with me.'

'How could you say something like that? How could you compare our pool, that night, that dream, with that jerk's pool? You're polluting our pool, Handan. You're ruining everything we had together.'

Behiye goes and punches the wall. Her foot still hurts from

kicking the photographer's shutters. Now her right hand hurts terribly. Now it's complete. Symmetrical. Wonderful. Both of them are throbbing.

Handan opens her cat eyes, her big, sea-green eyes, as wide as she can. 'Enough, Behiye. Enough. I can't take it anymore. I'm tired of constantly making mistakes. Whatever I do I'm blamed for making a mistake. It was bad enough living with my mother, now I have you on my back. Why do you give me such a hard time? If you really loved me would you give me such a hard time?'

'Enough with the *Selami Şahin* lyrics, Handan. That's exactly how it is; people give those they love a hard time. Why give someone a hard time if you don't love them? Why would you bother if you don't love them?'

'Here you go putting me down again. You look down on me. So what if I haven't read as many books as you have. This much I know. Considering that you don't like me, considering that you're so full of resentment…'

'What?'

'There's no "what" about it, Behiye.' Handan has started to cry. 'I can't bear it. I really can't bear it.'

'You can't bear me. Me! Do you know what happened today? Çiğdem asked around and found the house. We came nose to nose at the front door. We came up here later; because I'm such an ass. Then Leman came home, then there was a phone call – guess who called?'

'Was it your brother?'

'The course director! You told him to give you the money, but that you would return. He found your home number and called your mother. That rat pig called here. Why did he have to call! The course is full. Why did he have to follow it up?'

Handan is holding her head in her hands. She's looking at her feet. She's crying and sniffling.

'I left our number with the man. I thought that if I could get you to agree to it, I might go back to the course, Behiye. I didn't want to drop the course. I want to study and get into Bosphorus University. I want to get out of this house, that's all. I only agreed because you wanted it so much. I wanted to go to the course.'

Handan struggles to get the words out. Now her crying has completely swept her away. She's crying loudly, from within, with great sorrow. With her whole body. A baby's crying. A baby cat girl's crying. If Behiye hadn't made her cry, would she have cried so deeply, would she have been turned so upside down? Would Handan have cried so much, so helplessly, so long?

'Look, here's what we'll do. We'll give that 1,000 dollars to your mother right away this evening. We'll say we're very sorry. I mean I'll say I'm sorry. I'll tell her it was my fault. Indeed it is all my fault. So, what about Australia, Handan? Do you want to go there, or have I forced you into this? Damn me. This is all my fault.'

'Don't curse yourself, Behiye. Don't put yourself down. Don't put yourself down so much. I'm making some preparations too. I have some plans of my own. I said some very bad things to you, I'm sorry, my one and only. I love you very much. You're the first friend I've ever had. Honestly. The first friend in my life. I'm sorry, Behiye. Forgive me.'

Handan comes and sits on Behiye's lap. Behiye's three aches, her head, her hand and her foot, are working overtime. Behiye can't bear the three of them at once. She needs to take some medicine. Or else she's going to howl like a wolf. She wants to howl 'Uuuuugh'. A howl of pain.

'My head, my hand and my foot are hurting so much! I need the father of all painkillers. Otherwise I'll start howling like the Wolfwoman of Istanbul.'

Leman has two drawers full of medicines. Handan is looking for *Apranax Fort*. That's the best. They find the box; but it's completely empty.

They decide to go to Levent to look for a pharmacy that's still open. The pharmacy in the market is open. They get Behiye some

Apranax Fort. At the *Küçük Ev* there Handan eats fried kofte and pilaff with beans. They share a cake and drink some tea.

Behiye still isn't quite herself yet. A hangover has a way of making you feel as if you're sinking through the floor. Handan's comments have mounted horses and are galloping through her head. Handan had said, 'I can't stand you.' She'd said, 'Enough already.' 'Enough already, I can't take it anymore.' Anymore. More. More. *More.* Ore.

She doesn't want to talk to Handan. Behiye knows she's in dangerous waters. She doesn't want to get into it with Handan. Now she has a seriously grave fear of losing Handan. It's her own fault; it's not because of the stars, or witches, or belly-dancers, or medusas or the forces of darkness. It's because of herself, *herself*, that she's so very afraid of losing Handan.

They walk a little in the back streets of Levent. The medicine has made the pain in her foot more polite, more tame. The pain in her hand and her head has passed completely. They've left Behiye in peace. Relax, Behiye. Don't go crazy. Relax. Be well. Be at peace. Please, Behiye. Please – this goes round and round in Behiye's head as if it were a prayer.

'Shall we go to Akmerkez, Handan? To the food floor. You could have a doughnut and I could drink another tea.'

'If you wanted to go to Akmerkez, why didn't you say so earlier? I could have eaten there. I could have eaten at *Burger King* or *Arby's*.'

Behiye doesn't want to go back to the house. She fears she'll find Leman's icy eyes and snake-like comments on the menu. Indeed, Handan's comments are from impatience. Intolerance. She's worn Handan out. On Handan Ground she isn't where she used to be. The ground is constantly moving away from her: erosion. She watches in terror as the ground slips away.

She needs to be calm. She needs to be jocular, sweet, indifferent. That's how she needs to be; but how can she do it? With the Handan Ground pulling away, constantly less area, less ground left; the ground getting smaller, lessening, how can Behiye calm herself? How can she be calm and jocular and sweet?

She's certainly in a panic. That's the truth.

Erosion Panic.

If that's the case she wants to lie on the ground and stamp her feet. Handan, don't leave me! She wants to scream, shout, weep, disgrace herself – that's what she wants to do.

They're in that frightful Akmerkez now. How many times, how many dreadful times, has Behiye ended up here in the past couple of weeks? There are people who pass their whole lives here, who spend all their time here. A veritable flock of people whose souls are filled with sand. The flock of the miserable.

The food floor makes her feel cramped. It feels narrow. She stares at the people around her. It grinds her soul to watch this miserable flock, these kids whose parents are servants in the Etiler area and who want nothing more than to be children of Akmerkez. As if it's gone through a meat grinder. She can hear the grinding sound in her ears.

At the table in front of them are two servants' daughters who've clearly been sitting there for hours. One of them has a smile on her, a smile that's been practised but is still a miserable failure. She's constantly looking up and smiling. She doesn't stop smiling. A smile that says – I'm open to all suggestions, come find me.

What could possibly find you, you miserable creature? I don't even want to think about what kind of disgrace is going to find you. I don't want to feel sorry for you, shred my soul, to have it go through a meat grinder and come out looking like worms in order to go to war for you. I don't want to.

I want you to get out of this disgusting place. I want you to flee screaming Help! Save me! I want you to run screaming out of this frightful, pitiful place and be free of it for ever. But that's not going to happen, is it? You'll remain here, on this floor, waiting for, inviting, whatever dreadful and disgusting thing might happen. You're not going to run down the stairs four or five at a time to throw yourself into the servants' quarters in the basement. You're not going to pull yourself together and say you're free of the place. I didn't belong there, and I managed to escape that frightful scene. Whatever I become, I'll be here. Whatever I turn into, it will happen here. This is my own place. I'm from here. This is what I am. Servant's daughter.

You're not going to say it. You're not going to say it.

Pitiful Akmerkez creature. You're not going to leave behind these dirty, airless, mossy waters that you've been wandering around in. Isn't that so?

'Behiye! Behiye!'

She turns and looks at Handan. Giving her what she thinks is a very cold-blooded, self-possessed, controlled look.

'Excuse me, Handan. What is it? Did something happen?'

'You're crying. You spilled tea on yourself. And you're crying. You're not even aware that you're crying, Behiye. I've been watching you for several minutes, and you're not even aware; what's wrong with you? You're in a very bad state. And you're not even aware of it. What's happening to you, dear? Tell me. Is it because of me?'

'Those photographs we had taken, Handan.'

'Yes, yes. We still haven't picked them up yet.'

'We weren't able to pick them up. It's become very bad, very unlucky. I went today with Çiğdem, but they closed early. Our photographs have been kept hostage there.'

'What do you mean they're being kept hostage? We can pick them up in the morning.'

'Will we? I mean, will we be able to?'

'Of course, Behiye. Is that what you were crying about now?'

'That and other things. You're right, though, I wasn't aware I was crying. I'm in a bad state. You're fed up with me Handan. I've tired you out. I've used up my ground. Everything slipped away from under my feet.'

'Come on, let's go home. You need to get some sleep. Everything will be fine tomorrow, Behiye, you'll see.'

As they're going out the side door of Akmerkez, they bump into Burak. The kids are going to meet up at *Home Store*. *Home Store* kids. First-class Akmerkez creatures. They can consume everything the place has to offer. They're not the ones who can only look with their tongues hanging out. They can have and finish everything on offer. As if they were in a very good position.

'We're going to have a cook-out too tomorrow at the summer house. I'm going to go buy meat with Erim in the morning. Is Behiye coming with us?'

Behiye wants to say 'Fuck your ancestors.' But she doesn't say it. Behiye doesn't say it. She gives him a dirty look, and storms out. That fat jerks think I'm going to go play clown for them this weekend and entertain them. A couple of pool numbers and so forth. Ha, ha, ha!

A little later, Handan comes running after her. 'You could at least have told him you weren't coming. You were rude to the boy.'

Behiye doesn't answer. She's put her soul through the meat grinder twice, three times, the way careful housewives prefer. Her soul is now in the shape of red and white worms. Her soul is sitting on waxed paper like half a kilo of ground meat. Behiye wants to vomit on her soul. To empty herself out completely.

And then throw her soul to the street dogs. So they can eat it and finish it off. Perhaps she'll be better off without a soul. Or else Behiye will go cartwheeling down the hill. If she can be free of her soul, perhaps a tree branch or a pylon or a bench will catch her and hold her. No matter how. How. Howl. Wolf-howl, soul-howl. Howl. Howl. No one will hear.

Drugged sleep

. . . .

The moment she got home, Behiye climbed into the pull-out bed. She was very tired, and felt as if she'd been beaten up. At the same time she knew that sleep was impossible. But she crawled under the covers, like a mouse. She doesn't want to meet Leman. Meeting Leman was all that was missing on this unlucky day. She covered herself well. Mouse Behiye.

Handan's words: Handan's first harsh words, the first time Handan had talked about being fed up, annoyed, disgusted. These harsh words had broken Behiye in two. The first time she's felt unwanted on Handan Ground. An unwanted person who was slowly becoming a nuisance.

I took refuge with you, Handan. So what? My Feeling You'll Be Rescued. You came to me. And I to you. My Feeling You'll Be Rescued. Will you go and leave me behind; will you leave?

At a very late hour, towards morning, Leman comes home. Behiye lies very still. She pretends to be sleeping Behiye. So that Leman won't say anything to her, won't throw her out of the house. Mouse Behiye.

But it's good; Leman won't come out of her room until ten or eleven in the morning. She came home very late; she'll sleep late tomorrow. Behiye will jump out of the pull-out bed early. She'll prepare breakfast for Handan. Then she'll run to the photographer's studio. She'll rescue the photographs. The photographs of Handan with Behiye, the ones that were left hostage because of Behiye's laziness. Laziness, lack of discipline, thick-headedness – Behiye wasn't like this before. She did everything on time. Even before it was time. She was in command of time.

Now she's lost her sense of time. Everything happens either very quickly, or very slowly. She can't make it in time. She either can't make it in time, or she waits a great deal – she doesn't know. At any rate, she's lost her sense of time. Behiye used to have an inner clock. Everyone has an inner clock. Behiye's clock is broken. Behiye, you have to repair your clock. You have to get a grip on yourself. Come to your senses. Broken Behiye.

Sleep is a well. When you're wandering around the darkness of the garden, you don't see it for your weariness. You fall into the well of sleep. You don't even know you've fallen in. That's how it is.

When Behiye opens her eyes she knows that she's slept for some hours. That she's missed the early hours. That Handan and Leman have already woken. She can hear their voices in the kitchen. They're already up. Behiye is late for the day again.

As she's running to the bathroom, Handan shouts, 'Good morning Behiye.'

She's afraid to go into the kitchen; but she has to. How much more can she avoid Leman when she's living in her house? She pushes herself, and enters the kitchen.

'Good morning, Behiye,' says Leman. In a Leman voice she's never heard before: neither cold nor warm, neither prickly nor soft. With such a calm, decisive Leman voice that's never been heard before.

'Good morning. I woke late again this morning.'

'Behiye, we have wonderful news for you. I told my mother about the course money; that we haven't spent most of it. I said we'd give it back. I said I was very sorry. My blue rabbit has forgiven us. And last night Mr Şevket – why don't you tell it, Mother. Tell Behiye.'

'Mr Şevket is going to pay the fee again for Behiye's course. All of the payments we owe, and all of our credit card debts are being paid off today. My new age has brought luck: we're free of all our debts. Now you won't think a bag and a pair of shoes are too much for your mother, Lady Handan.'

'Mother, you're really stuck on that. But I'm really very sorry about the course money. What we changed into dollars is still in Behiye's jacket. Mr Şevket needn't pay the school. I'll go and pay it with Behiye if I want to return to the course.'

'What do you mean, "if I want to return"? Didn't you pester me until I was able to come up with the money for the course? Didn't I have to go to the trouble of finding Uncle Cevdet and getting the money out of him? And you're a child who doesn't even know what a lie is. Or rather you were. This is all Behiye's influence. I am telling both of you openly to your faces. I'm not in favour of the two of you seeing so much of each other.'

Behiye feels like a pail of boiling water is poured over her head. She's throwing Behiye out! She wants her to leave the house. Where is Behiye going to go? Where does she have to go? She doesn't have a home. Her home is Handan Ground. She's being thrown out. Is she being thrown out? Where is Behiye going to go? Where?

She's finished her coffee. Leman gets up, putting her cigarette out in the ashtray Muki gave her for her birthday. She has a lot to do. She's going to go to the banks and pay off her debts. She's going to make her payments. And the water and electricity bills. Blahblahblah.

Let her get out of the kitchen.

Let her go. Let her go!

She's left the kitchen. Behiye is making toast for Handan. She burned her hand a little. But she doesn't have the strength to feel the pain of the burn. She cleans the kitchen like a kitchen robot. Leman has taken a shower and is getting dressed in her room. Handan kissed her mother and wished her luck. She went into the living room and turned on *MTV*. *Robbie Williams* and *Nicole Kidman* are singing a song together.

As she rubs the kitchen tiles, Behiye wants *Robbie Williams* to die. She wants to go into the television and poke out those frog eyes. That way maybe she could stop that annoying voice. Then the world wouldn't have to listen to the syrupy songs that come out of his crooked, thin-lipped mouth.

Handan goes into the bathroom later. She comes out the cleanest baby and goes to her room. She fills her little pink backpack and comes out of her room.

'Where are you off to, Handan?'

'I'm going to Erim's summer house today. They're going to pick me up in a little while; you know this, Behiye.'

'Your mother threw me out, Handan. She threw me out, you heard didn't you? But I can't go home. I don't have a home, Handan, I have no home left. I never did. I've never had a home.'

'Behiye, don't get yourself worked up. Leman is just being stubborn with you. She didn't throw you out. She'll forget in two or three days. Don't pay attention, please, Behiye. You're going to live here with me. I don't want to be without you. I'm accustomed to you. You're like a sister. More than a sister. Forget about Leman.'

'Are you going to stay there tonight?'

'Yes. I'm going to stay there. It's a long trip, it's hardly worth it if we turn around and come right back. I'll come back tomorrow night. Or maybe Sunday afternoon.'

'Whaaat? On Sunday; in the afternoon? Shit, Handan. What am I going to do in this house all that time? Leman threw me out this morning. What more could she have done besides spitting in my face?'

'Well then, come with me to Erim's summer house. You'll see, we'll have lots of fun. I'd rather not go without you.'

'Then don't go.'

Handan's cell phone buzzes. 'All right, Erim, I'm coming.'

'Look, Behiye, if you want to come I'll wait while you grab a few things. Otherwise I'm going. I promised them days ago.'

'I'm not coming. You go on.'

She kissed Behiye's cheeks quickly. She rushed out of the house. She's going down the steps. Sounds of her sports shoes going down the steps. Those sounds have stopped. Behiye can't stop herself from going to the kitchen window and looking down.

The car raced off. She memorised the licence number. Whatever use that will be. She wants to engrave on her forehead the licence number of the car that took Handan away. To stamp it. Handan went off in that car. She's leaving Behiye behind for the first time. She feels chased away from everything, she knows. But she's clinging with her fingernails to the receding ground.

She's ashamed of herself. But she can't go. She can't leave that place. She can't be without Handan. She can't. Shameless Behiye. Outcast. Outcast mouse.

Today is Friday. Today is Friday October 12th. There's reason to rush to the photographer's studio. It might not open on Saturday. But it might open. That photography studio has the least reliable opening hours. The pictures are there. Hostage.

She puts on her jacket. Indeed she's sworn not to step foot outside without her jacket. It's 12:30, but the studio is open.

She gives the paper to the buck-toothed boy there. A piece of paper concerning the photographs with Handan and Behiye. The photographs have a number: 1428-B.

The boy goes through the envelopes one by one. 'I saw your photographs. They were here yesterday.'

But the photographs aren't there today. They're not in the top drawer either. They're not there, or here. 'Ihsan might have put them away somewhere. When he comes back I'll ask him.'

'Why would Ihsan put our photographs somewhere else? Is there a reason?'

'There's no reason.' His front teeth stick out even more, making him look like an insignificant rabbit. That's the way his front teeth are. They jump out of his mouth.

Feeble-minded, buck-toothed boy. Behiye bites her lip to keep from shouting – get those photographs out from wherever you've stuck them. Find the pictures, man! Where the hell are our photographs? Find them quickly!

She just says, 'Find our photographs, brother.' But Brother Bucktooth understands that she's beside herself.

'I've looked everywhere. Ihsan will find them when he comes back. Leave your telephone number if you like; I'll call you.'

'I don't want to. You give me your number. I'll call and ask. Find our photographs. What right do you have to lose them?'

'But they're not lost...'

'Don't get me started!' Behiye leaves the shop. At an internet cafe in Levent she goes to the Australian Embassy website. The visa section has a lot, but a lot, of requirements. More important than anything, they want a notarised letter of consent from the parents of anyone under eighteen. Whatever.

Behiye sends a message: 'Where can I find the address of an Australian citizen?' It's like sending a message in a bottle.

She can't get an answer now. Everything there is closed now. Everything everywhere is closed. Closed. The photographs are lost. Closed.

Behiye can't bear it. Leman threw her out.

Cast out. Lost. Closed.

How will she get through today? How will she get through tomorrow? Handan is gone. Handan has gone. Cast out. Lost. Closed.

Here's a pharmacy right there. The pharmacy where she bought *Apranax Fort* with Handan.

'I haven't slept for days. Can you give me something to help me sleep?' she asks the assistant. A sweet boy assistant.

He can't give her anything that requires a prescription. He gives her a sleeping pill called *Unisom*. It's cheap too. That's good. Two million lira.

Behiye wants to sleep for one or two days. To sleep for one or two days. To be out of things for one or two days. Get these one or two days out of her life. To get lost. To be closed. To be cast out. To be Behiye. To not exist.

She keeps thinking that she hasn't eaten. The last thing she ate was part of Handan's sweet; she had three teas. She won't eat. Why should she? Let Behiye be lost. Cast out. There's no place for her.

On her way back she stops by the studio again. No, Ihsan hasn't come back yet. The buck-toothed boy shows his teeth again.

Behiye leaves.

Letter of consent. Whatever!

There's no one at home. Leman will come back towards evening to change her clothes. And she won't be out in the open on the pull-out bed in the living room. She'll be in Handan's room. She pops two *Unisom* into her mouth. She pops two more to make sure it will do the job. Four *Unisom* should put her to sleep for a day or two. She closes Handan's door and gets undressed. She puts on a long T-shirt. A T-shirt that reaches below her underwear. She gets into Handan's bed. Now she's rocking in a boat made of Handan smell. She feels a little sick to her stomach. A sponge is covering her brain.

The sponge started at the top and went down as far as her nose. Then down as far as her throat. A sponge covers her head.

Evidently she's begun to sleep. A sleep that's like a kind of stupor, that has taken her and led her down the darkest corridor.

She doesn't know how long she sleeps. She's not really sleeping. She's swinging in Handan's cradle as if she's been drugged. Behiye has fainted. She's not sleeping; she's really fainted.

The door has opened. The door has opened.

Leman.

Leman with her face in disarray. That's how she'll remember Leman later. Leman looking as if she'd been beaten up. A very drunk Leman. Very malicious. Very malicious.

'Girl, didn't I tell you to get the hell out of our house? What are you doing here in Handan's bed? Didn't I throw you out of this house this morning? Do I have to call the police or something? What is this? Get the hell out of my house. Get out!'

'Leman!' Behiye struggles to get the word out of her mouth. She's not really awake. It's more like she's having a nightmare. The kind where you can't run when you try to run, where you try to shout and no sound comes out.

'And she still says Leman. Who am I to you for you to be calling me Leman! Get out of my house. You've stuck to Handan. Getting that course money back, and so forth. What's your problem, girl? It's almost as if you were in love with my daughter. Leave my child alone.'

Behiye wants to say – so she can become a whore like you. For a few seconds she thinks she's said it. But she didn't. She feels as if there's a huge fist in her throat, and her voice can't get out. She's become mute.

Why?

It would have been better to be deaf. So she wouldn't hear these disgusting words. Or to have been blind. So she wouldn't have to see Leman's face. Or to have died. It would have been better for Behiye to have died.

'Leave my daughter alone, Behiye. Get out of our house. No one invited you. Now you're really being thrown out. Get your miserable things together and hit the road tomorrow morning. I don't ever want to see your face again. Leave my child alone. Get away from us.'

Behiye is still lying there with her head on the pillow, looking at Leman. Leman who's standing there killing her. A disgusting Leman. The ugliest Leman she's ever seen. The most disgusting Leman.

She imagines herself jumping up and slapping Leman across the face. With all her strength. She slaps Leman in the face. Then she grabs her by the hair and hits her head against the wardrobe. Against the wardrobe mirror. Pieces of broken mirror fall to the floor.

These images pass though her head one by one. They pass very slowly.

Anyway, Leman has gone off.

There are noises from the bathroom.

Leman left the light on. The light is in her eyes. She wants to get out of bed to press the switch. She wants to turn out the light.

But she doesn't have the strength.

Sleep has taken Behiye and thrown her down the well again.

Drugged sleep.

Behiye sleeps for hours. She sleeps in that house, in Handan's bed. In the house she's been thrown out. The drugged sleep of a mouse. Drugged sleep. Anyhow, she's asleep.

Stomach ache

• •

When she wakes, Behiye looks at the clock. The clock says five. What day is it?

When she lay down to sleep it was two in the afternoon. It was Friday October 12th. Towards morning Leman came into her room. She guesses from the state her face was in, from how drunk she was, that it must have been three or four in the morning.

During her drugged sleep, Leman ripped her down the middle. The rip is still there, in Behiye's middle. But the drugged sleep continued despite having been ripped. Behiye hadn't even been able to turn out the light – she hadn't turned it out.

So what day was it? Could it be Sunday?

Is it early Sunday morning; five o'clock?

The bathroom is right across from Handan's room. She has to rush to the bathroom. She has to pee right away.

Leman? Leman?

She's afraid of Leman; but she's also not afraid. She's very angry, very annoyed with Leman. She throws herself out of bed and runs to the bathroom. As she runs she screams 'Ayyyyk!' The way comic book heroes scream. Behiye didn't know she had it in her to scream like that. It just came out of her.

She peed. Then she washed her face; she left the bathroom. Leman is not around. She turns on the television and looks. It's Saturday afternoon – the time is ten past five. Her stomach is as upset. Her head hurts. Apparently four sleeping pills on an empty stomach is too much.

She goes and takes a shower. She gets dressed very slowly. She put *Linkin Park* on the CD player. So she can find her lost soul. But when she woke, or rather when she came to, Leman's words began to feel heavier within her. She realises their true heaviness. What heavy things Leman said to her!

Too heavy for Behiye to carry, to bear. Behiye is crushed under the weight of the words; she had no right to speak that way. The waves of resentment she feels towards Leman grow stronger, more violent. They crash against her shore.

She wants to go into that whore's room, pee on her bed, and cut all her underwear into little pieces. Pathetic, cringing acts of revenge. They'd bring Behiye even lower. She'd be even more ashamed of herself. Later.

But she wants to issue a threat to Leman. To mark Leman. To spray-paint a big red X on her door. You've been found guilty. You've been marked. An X that shouts 'your days are numbered'.

She wants to go to Akmerkez right away to buy the paint. She could fill her stomach too. Her stomach is so very bad.

She has to eat something. She has to eat something substantial right away. Behiye is certain of this. She grabs her jacket and rushes out of the house. She can still feel the weight of the 1,500 euros and the 1,000 dollars in her jacket pocket. A real weight. If they hadn't taken the course money, would Leman have told her to fuck off out of the house like that? In the end, everything, but everything, has to do with money. Would Handan have been so interested in Erim, would she have run after him like that, if he hadn't been a rich bastard? 'Erim's father has an automobile showroom. They change cars every two months.' How many times, but how many times, did Handan repeat this nonsense?

In the end, the whole Akmerkez phenomenon and so forth. It all had to do with money. Everything was because of fucking money. The Empire of Money and Penises. That's how Behiye feels. How this world of men and money has turned her into a pitiful ant, a bug, a frightened and outcast mouse. She feels it in her bones.

There's a *Küçük Ev* on the food floor at Akmerkez. She ate pilaff, and dolma with yoghurt. She didn't eat all of it, but she ate most of it. The food did her stomach good. And her mood. Behiye feels restored and healed.

She's not frightened of Leman after all. She feels ashamed of her girlish plans to take revenge by cutting up her underwear. She's going to go back to the house and listen to *Linkin Park*. Then *papa roach*, then *Sum 41* – she'll listen to whatever she has with her. She'll stomp on that inner mouse with her boots and kill it. She's going to get rid of that pitiful, insidious Behiye mouse for ever. Then that whore Leman will see what's coming to her.

Isn't it easy to catch someone unawares when they're in a drugged sleep and shout at them? To attack and poison them in bed. Even a jackal wouldn't do that. Even a vulture, a hyena, a tiger – 'Behiye, we're presenting you with an animal encyclopaedia' she murmurs to herself. Just like those jokes she used to make with Çiğdem.

Çiğdem! A burning smell comes from her heart. It was because of that snake Leman that she broke Çiğdem's heart, threw her out, hurt her.

Çiğdem, are you very angry with me? Did I hurt you very much? Very much, Çiğdem; will you recover? If I throw myself at your feet will you forgive me? My first friend, my childhood companion.

She buys a phone card and calls Çiğdem from a pay phone in the corridor outside the toilets. Çiğdem answers on the second ring. 'Hellooo, hellooo; who's calling? So you don't enjoy my voice? Shall we offer another one?'

Good. She's pulled herself together. She'll pull through. Çiğdem the spinning top. Waterfall of healthy soul. She's come to herself after all. Perhaps she knows it was Behiye calling, perhaps she felt it.

As she's standing there with the phone in her hand, she feels a sharp desire to call Handan. Handan. You sold me out, Handan! You jumped on the first rich idiot puppy you came across. Was that all it was? That ephemeral, that worthless? Weren't you my Feeling You'll Be Rescued? Weren't you announced to me under that plane tree; weren't you sent to me?

She doesn't call Handan's number. An unbelievable restlessness comes over her. She runs out of Akmerkez. A few people look after her, wondering if there's a thief or something.

She gallops to the Petrol Complex. She runs galloping, with her tongue hanging out. She takes the stairs two or three at a time. The lights are on in the house. She saw them from outside. Did Behiye leave them on? Has Leman come home? Or, or?

As she's turning the key in the lock, the door opens from inside. Handan is standing there. Beautiful Handan! She came to Behiye. She belongs to Behiye. She didn't go anywhere. She wouldn't go. They're Handan and Behiye. There's no other possibility.

'My Behiye,' she says, jumping on her neck. 'Where have you been? I was worried when I didn't find you at home. I was afraid you'd gone and left me.'

She lets the Handan smell flow into her, to heal all her wounds and scratches. She abandons herself to the Handan smell so that for once it can do her good. Handan has embraced her. She didn't sell her out; she came running back to her from that summer house. They're sitting in each other's arms on the sofa in the living room. They're where they should be, in the state they should be in. Handan and Behiye are in each other's arms.

Handan drops her lower lip. 'I'm as hungry as a wolf,' she says. 'I haven't eaten anything since last night.'

The hungriest baby cat girl in the world. She's always hungry.

Behiye has to feed her constantly. To cook for her. All kinds of food, and cookies, and cakes, and pastries. Their house will always be filled with the smell of hot food. With wonderful, appetising smells. Behiye will feed her baby cat girl six or seven times a day. There'll always be water boiling for tea; the kitchen will definitely have to be spotless when she sets the table for Handan.

Behiye feels herself tremble within. Behiye definitely has to be with Handan, to be with her, to feed her, to take care of her. To keep her full and warm.

But there's nothing left in the house. There are only a few cookies left over from Leman's birthday party, that's all. 'I'll make you a potato omelette, and some toast with cheese and tomato. If I brewed some tea to go with it…'

'My dear Behiye, my one and only. You're the only one who's ever taken care of me. To be with you, it's like being in a nest. You're my nest, Behiye.'

Handan smothers her cheeks and her neck with kisses. Those little girl kisses that only Handan knows how to give.

They're in the kitchen now. On happiness ground. Their little ship anchored in the harbour.

'Why haven't you eaten anything since last night?'

'Don't ask what happened to me, Behiye. I suddenly got very bored with that summer house, with those people, with Erim. They played *Play Station* until five in the morning. I felt terrible. I woke about twelve. Erim was still sleeping next to me. I packed my bag and left the house without making a sound. I only had a little money with me. I had to take minibuses, buses and ferries to get here.'

'Erim was sleeping next to you?'

'Don't ask. That's the big thing. Erim and I slept together last night. When I woke up I didn't want to stay there any more.'

'You slept with Erim? What do you mean?'

'What other meaning could it have, Behiye? We slept together,

I'm free of that business.' Handan is gobbling her omelette as she's talking. Filling her mouth with enormous bites.

'Handan!' Behiye wants to cry. It never occurred to her that Handan would go and sleep with Erim. Why didn't she go along? What an idiot, what a boor Behiye is. Blind Behiye. Fool. Stupid Behiye. Even the simplest, silliest things in life don't occur to her. Why does she want to cry now? Why are tears escaping her eyes? Because of Handan? It's clear that Handan is not the least bit concerned. What's happening to Behiye?

'Come on, Behiye. It happened. When he was assigning rooms, Erim's parents' room was left for us. Then when Erim came to bed towards morning; well, we slept together. You know, there was no blood or anything? It's not a pleasant thing at all, Behiye. I felt a stomach ache, that's all. I imagine my hymen was broken. When I was washing myself in the bathroom later this soft piece of flesh came into my hand. But as far as sleeping together, it's nothing more than a stomach ache. Perhaps because it was the first time. But it wasn't pleasant at all. It was over very quickly.'

'Are we talking about something you were required to do? What for? Why did you feel you had to do it? It's clear you experienced something disgusting.'

'It's not really disgusting.' Handan takes a bite of toast and swallows some tea. 'Let's call it an annoying stomach ache. It was going to happen in any event. Sometimes it was pleasant to kiss Erim. But sleeping with him wasn't. Anyway, it's over and done with.'

'I'm going to go crazy now! What's this nonsense about getting it over and done with? You opened your body to him, Handan. That idiot puppy entered you.'

'Look, let's put it this way.' Handan starts on her second piece of toast. She hands Behiye her empty tea glass. 'I mean, I kept telling you I had plans, I was making plans. This boy's parents are rich, right. I thought if I slept with him, if we started sleeping together we'd get married, then they'd buy us a house, and furnish it, a really nice place around here, in Etiler or Akatlar, furnished to our taste, and later a nice puppy.'

'What, Handan? I'm really starting to get curious.'

'Don't make fun of me, Behiye. I thought you could come live with us. We'd have the latest model car. We could study together, and I could get into Bosphorus University. We could study together at home. Erim's family could take care of us until we finished school. Then later...Then, Behiye, whatever happened would happen. Then we'd have real money, we'd have possibilities; we could go off to Australia. Or we could stay here and start our own business. That was my plan. To cage Erim.'

'Handan, did you think all of this – did you really think all these things?'

'What's wrong with that, Behiye? Millions of girls in the world think the same thing. What do you think they write about in those magazines?'

'So what happened that made you flee the battlefield after the first attack? You couldn't stomach it, could you? Couldn't you take the stomach ache?'

'One has to try it out. After we slept together I turned to Erim and said "Shall we get married?"'. Handan is laughing. The dimples are showing on the world's most beautiful laughing face. She's so sweet, so beautiful. Again, Behiye can't stop the crazy ache within her. It's an ache, it aches.

'So what did the matrimonial candidate say?'

'What could he say Behiye? "Girl, are you crazy. We only slept together once." That's exactly what he said. If I was in love with Erim or anything I'd have been terribly hurt. I don't know, it was all so funny, and...'

'And?'

'It seemed so boring to me.'

'Stomach ache.'

'Exactly. Everything seemed like a stomach ache to me. I thought I couldn't do it, I couldn't manage the situation, Behiye.

If I worked at it, I could have married Erim in a year or so. I could have brought it to that point. But I'm not going to. Do you know what I thought about all those hours on the road, Behiye?'

Handan's voice has changed. It's shrunk, got smaller. Her beautiful cat eyes are wet now. One teardrop has escaped from her right eye, and has rolled down to the corner of her pink lips.

'What did you think, my baby? What did you think, my baby cat girl?' Handan is on Behiye's lap now. She was stroking her hair. She's playing with her hair.

'I have a Leman fear, Behiye. I'm afraid of growing up to be like Leman. I'm afraid of becoming like the Sisters Nevin; but I'm even more afraid of becoming like Leman. I'm afraid of living my whole life thinking about men day and night. How frightened I am! I'm frightened, Behiye, I can't help it. But I'm so frightened, constantly, constantly.'

Handan has buried her nose in Behiye's neck. She's crying her eyes out now. 'Don't be afraid, my baby,' says Behiye. 'Don't be afraid, baby, you won't be like Leman. You won't be like that. Don't be afraid, my baby, don't be afraid, my one and only. I'll protect you. I'll protect you.'

They get up and go into the living room. Handan's tears have stopped. She went in and took a shower. She's a clean baby, and they're watching television now.

'Leman will probably come in a little while. I can't stay here, Handan. Last night, or rather towards morning, she threw me out of the house. She spoke very harshly to me.'

'She's drunk at that hour. She doesn't know what she's doing. She's not coming home tonight. She and Mr Şevket have gone to Polonezköy for the weekend. She won't be back until late tomorrow night. Don't take her seriously. Leman will forget everything; that's her temperament.'

'I'm tired of being in the house, Handan. Come on, let's go to Taksim. We can walk along Istiklal. Maybe we can listen to music somewhere. I'm so tired of being in this house; can we go out, Handan?'

'All right, Behiye. Let me put something on and we'll go out. If my one and only is bored, we'll go out. I feel completely swollen, Behiye. Not just my stomach, my whole body hurts. I feel like shit.'

'Watch your mouth,' says Behiye. 'You never used to talk like that. If you lie down with dogs you get up with fleas.'

'I woke up with fleas!' shouts Handan. She claps her hands happily as if she's discovered a secret code. Is Behiye ruining Handan's language, her soul; is the baby cat girl growing up and becoming harder because of her?

It's not just me, thinks Behiye. We finished high school. Then we found each other. Life is besieging us. Life is constantly pounding at our door. Where is life going to take us? Please let life take us somewhere nice. A nice place very far away. Have pity on us, life. Don't be bad to us. Embrace us; pity us. Why not? Huh, why not?

Incident

• •

They're in Taksim. They're walking down Istiklal hand in hand. They're walking hand in hand through the Saturday night crowds. Together.

They're not talking at all. Both of them are a bit tired, tired from what they've lived. But they're holding hands, they're together, and the weather is nice. They're drawing the autumn evening into themselves. They're drawing each other into themselves. Behiye is happy holding Handan's hand, even more than that, she's at peace. Handan's hand is so soft, so elegant. The world's most beautiful Handan hand. She wants to hold Handan's hand for the rest of her life. Behiye doesn't want anything more. Nothing more. To hold Handan's hand is enough.

Walking like this, hand in hand, Behiye's happiness doesn't stop; it increases. The happiness multiplies itself, grows bigger. Behiye is smiling as she walks. Her hand is in Handan's hand, and she's so happy. As her happiness expands, she's afraid she'll fly away like a balloon. Handan's hand is all that's tying her down. Otherwise she could fly away, somewhere up above.

All Behiye wants to feel now is this happiness within her. She doesn't want to be afraid, she doesn't want to be afraid of Leman; she doesn't want to be afraid of losing Handan, of the 'things' that could happen to her – she doesn't want to mar her happiness with fear. She just wants to be imprisoned in that moment's happiness: That's all she wants.

They're browsing through Behiye's favourite bookshop together. They're just browsing, Behiye isn't buying anything, or stealing anything. In the Terkos Pasaj there's a place that plays honest music. She heard about it from someone. They go there first. But it's still very early. There's no one there.

'Let's drink somewhere,' says Behiye. If they get drunk their evening will be extended, none of the fear birds could invade her.

In one of the back streets off Istiklal, they go down some steps to a bar and start drinking. It's deserted inside, but it's not completely empty. Handan drinks beer. Behiye drinks vodka. Vodka and orange, as she learned from Leman.

A group of boys comes up to them, and hangs out with them. A group of boys who can't take their eyes off Handan. They wear oversized T-shirts, and blue jeans that look forty times too big for them. They have rings in their noses, their eyebrows and their ears, and instead of belts they have chains coming out of their pockets. The kind of kids who hang out in the Atlas Pasaj.

None of them are bad kids. And two of them are very funny. None of the idiots who hung around with Erim were at all funny. They were just stuck spinning out stale jokes they memorized from *Cem Yilmaz* stand-ups.

'Don't start again,' says Handan. She's afraid of getting on to the subject of Erim and spoiling their fun.

Behiye drank four vodka oranges back to back. She drank very quickly. She drank away, in order not to get off the trampoline of happiness, so that her mood wouldn't be scratched and spoiled, and this and that.

Handan had two beers or so. Then Handan got bored, and then she got tired, and then she got hungry. After all, it was one in the morning. 'Come on, Behiye, let's go home,' she nagged.

Behiye's baby cat girl was tired and hungry. That's how babies are; what can she do?

They go into one of the sandwich shops at the beginning of the avenue. Handan ate a chicken sandwich and drank carrot juice. Behiye drank orange juice. She drank orange juice imagining there was vodka in it. That's how it tasted. It tasted of vodka.

They got into a taxi and went home. Handan was going to go to sleep right away. She was done in. She was so tired she was done in.

'I slept in your bed when you weren't here, Handan.'

'That's fine, Behiye.'

'I was afraid of Leman coming in and finding me on the pull-out bed. She still found me. She opened the door and breathed fire on me. Leman the dragon witch. A child's nightmare. Sister Leman towards morning! Lemanella, who'll slice you up with her words. The nation's most troublesome sleep witch.' Behiye laughs constantly as she spouts this nonsense.

'Come on, please, let's go to sleep.'

'Handan, I don't like sleeping on that pull-out bed. It's like sleeping in a train station. I don't know, like a bus stop or some public place. Would it be all right if I slept in here, on the floor?'

'It would be uncomfortable. Could I let you do that? Come and sleep next to me. We'll sleep together, side by side.'

Handan brushes her teeth and puts on her puppy pyjamas. Behiye puts on her sleep T-shirt, and they get into bed. Handan gives her a small kiss on the cheek. 'Good night, Behiye dear,' she says. She turns her back to Behiye.

Behiye puts her arm around Handan's waist. She listens to Handan's breathing. Behiye puts her nose in Handan's hair. Sleeping side by side like this tonight, shouldn't she stock up on Handan smell? Enough Handan smell to last for ever? Why should she? Handan isn't going anywhere. She isn't going. She'll always be there. With Behiye.

She wants to see Handan's face. But to see her face she'd have to sit up. She's afraid that if she moves she'll wake Handan. Perhaps she'll send her to the pull-out bed, saying we can't be comfortable.

Behiye's heart is pounding away. She's so happy she fears she'll crack down the middle. Split in two. But it's good. Good. Good. She's so happy. With her nose in Handan's hair. She pushes the hair aside lightly. She draws in The Handan Smell from the nape of her neck. Her heart is in her mouth. She's so delighted, so wild with joy, she can't sleep until morning.

Handan wakes up early and gets out of bed. Behiye pretends she's asleep. She pretends she's in a deep sleep. She falls asleep listening to the sounds Handan makes in the bathroom. She falls into a deep sleep. She sleeps without Handan and without interruption for several hours.

When she wakes it's twenty past one. Handan is sitting in the living room reading the newspaper with the naked women. Handan is dying of hunger. She hadn't wanted to wake Behiye. 'Come on, let's go down to Hisar. We can eat dumplings there. Can't we, Behiye, get dressed quickly and let's go.'

The place they went when she and Handan first met! Behiye feels terribly excited. She believes that everything is straightened out, that everything is going well and will continue to go well, that everything will go magically/luckily/wonderfully. Behiye wants to sing like a bird. To perch on Handan's shoulder and sing constantly.

She fills herself with nonsensical thoughts of happiness. Only, her head hurts from last night's vodka. Her head feels as if it's splitting open; but otherwise she wants to dance, play and sing children's songs. That good. That's good enough.

Because Handan is so hungry, she doesn't want to walk. They jump into a taxi. The roads are very congested. They get fed up in the taxi. The driver is a decent man; he doesn't do anything improper. Only with the October sun hitting the glass, and being caged in the taxi for forty-five, fifty minutes, they get fed up. And Behiye's headache and stomach ache are getting worse.

'You start eating, I'm going to go over here and grab some vodka.'

'What are you doing drinking vodka at this hour of the afternoon, Behiye?'

'That's what Leman said, that vodka is the best medicine for a hangover. I'm just going to have a few swigs to get rid of my headache. As medicine, I mean: vodka medicine.'

Behiye runs off and comes back with her vodka. They go to one of the tea gardens there. Behiye drinks her vodka furtively. She enjoys drinking secretly. She drinks and drinks, and laughs and laughs.

When they leave the tea garden she's amazed to see that she's finished half the bottle.

'You're like a child, Behiye. Is it proper to drink so much at this hour? Wasn't the vodka supposed to be medicinal? Weren't you only going to drink a little? Look, honestly, you're drunk, you're smashed.'

Behiye laughs away. She really is 'smashed'. She's found her heart, her soul, Handan, everything. It's so good. Behiye is so happy. That's good enough.

By the time they walked to Bebek and took a taxi home from there, it was a quarter past five. Behiye stopped drinking. But the half-empty vodka bottle was still in her hand, wrapped in newspaper.

Behiye wanted to sit on the grass in front of the building. 'Come on, Handan, this is our pool of grass. Let's jump on to the grass together. How many times you did me good by taking me out of here. Handan, there's something I never told you before. Do you know what you are? You're my Feeling You'll Be Rescued. Before you came, you were announced to me under a plane tree.'

'Come on, Behiye, let's go home. I don't have the energy to go into the grass pool. I'm tired, I've been tired since yesterday.'

When she hears this, Behiye feels as if she's been punched

in the stomach. She doesn't understand why, but that's how it is. Punched. In her stomach.

They go upstairs. As Handan is looking in her bag for her key, the door opens: Leman! She's planted in front of the door, raking them with a machine gun. Leman is killing them. There on the doormat.

Behiye feels like running, fleeing, from Leman. As her fear rises to her mouth, a terrible anger – huge and out of control, rises as far as her pupils. Now she too gives Leman a disgusted look. The war of looks. Witch Leman, you can't frighten me, extinguish me, can't turn my happiness to ashes.

'Are you back, Mother? I was expecting you later.'

Handan's voice is faint, fearful. There's neither 'my blue rabbit' nor pleasure at seeing her. She goes inside with a hangdog expression. To see Handan so frightened of her mother makes her feel as if a knife has been stuck into her. It wounds Behiye terribly.

'You're not happy I came home early, Lady Handan? Isn't this my own house? I'll come home whenever I feel like it.'

'Of course, Mother. I just wanted to say...'

'What did you want to say? Hasn't *she* gone yet? Didn't I tell you straight out? I don't want *her* in my house. Let her pack up her miserable things and get out! Come on. I've had enough of you. Bye-bye, Lady Behiye. Go home at once.'

Behiye is looking at Leman with eyes opened like crystal balls. She's looking at Leman as if she doesn't believe what she sees.

'What are you looking at that way, girl? You're making me uncomfortable, you're making us uncomfortable. I don't want you to influence my child anymore. Am I obliged to have you as a guest? Go on, Behiye, go and pack your things. You keep the thousand dollars. Let it be our gift to you.'

Behiye suddenly finds herself shouting at the top of her voice: 'Fuck you and your shitty thousand dollars. What's your problem, you disgusting woman? You couldn't turn Handan into the whore you are – that's it, isn't it? I've influenced her, I've done this and that – it's all bullshit. All bullshit. Don't start that bullshit with me.'

'Look, speak politely when you're speaking to me. Is that any way to talk to a woman your mother's age? Rude, disrespectful, frightful thing…' Leman was at a loss for words. She collapsed into an armchair and started crying. 'Go, I say. Go, get the hell out of my house. Or else I'll call the police.'

'You get the hell out of here. I'm not going anywhere. Wherever Handan is, that's where I'll stay. You get the hell out. Go to Nevin's whores' union or wherever it is you go.'

'Mother! Behiye! That's enough, both of you, that's enough!' screams Handan at the top of her voice.

Behiye runs into Handan's room and grabs whatever money is in her jacket pocket. She can't slow down, and puts her fist through the wardrobe mirror. The mirror broke into pieces. Blood pours out of her hand.

Behiye goes back to the living room and throws the blood-stained money at Leman. 'Take this money. That's the only language you understand. You only understand money, you worship only money, live only for money, don't you? Say it, say it, you money vampire! Take this money and leave us alone!'

Handan is crying her eyes out in the armchair across from Leman.

Leman gets up from where she's sitting and gets her bag. She goes out, slamming the door.

Behiye is looking at the blood flowing from her hand now. She doesn't believe what happened. How did it happen? It was great. Behiye was very happy. How did all of this happen? How did it happen? How? How?

She wants to run to Handan with a bestial scream. To shout aloud, Handan forgive me! To shout as loud as she can. But she just stands there. Perhaps this isn't real life; she's still asleep, having a nightmare.

She was so happy five or ten minutes ago. She wanted to

swim on the grass with Handan. How could everything change so much in an instant? How could everything be ruined like this? Could it all really have happened? It couldn't. None of this could happen in real life.

Her blood is dripping on to the upholstery of the armchair.

Handan is crying her eyes out. The drops of blood stand out on the cloth. Her hand is hurting too. If she was asleep, would her hand hurt this way? Handan is crying. Handan is in tears. This is real life.

Everything has fallen apart on her. Everything has fallen apart on her. What is she going to do now? How is she going to get out from under this? How?

Raid

. . . .

Behiye collapses on to the floor. She leans against the blood-stained armchair and sits on the floor. She sits on the floor. She sits. If she were to move, the living room would collapse on top of her, everything would collapse on top of her, as if everything was tied to her leg by a thread, and if she were to move, she and Handan would be trapped under everything.

In any event they're trapped under everything.

The world has collapsed on top of them. The world has collapsed.

Handan's cell phone starts to ring. Handan doesn't get up. The phone rings twenty times, thirty times. Very nerve-wracking. But Handan seems not to hear.

The person calls back. Again. And again.

In the end she answers. 'What is it, Mother? All right, I'm fine. Nothing has happened here. She's fine too. We're just sitting here. All right, Mother, I'm fine. I'm hanging up. Don't keep calling. There's nothing wrong. I'm going to sleep. Come on. All right.'

Leman is calling to check. Has the monster swallowed her daughter; has it harmed her princess? Mother Leman is calling.

In the end, Handan gets up and goes to the bathroom. It's in her nature to take a bath after anything bad or distressing happens. After anything good. At the beginning of the day and at the end of the day. Handan is constantly, constantly washing herself.

Behiye listens to the sound of running water. But she doesn't get up. She doesn't want to get up. She really wants to dig a ditch and get in. She wants to sink into the ground.

Handan goes into her room after her bath. She goes into the kitchen and gets the broom and dustpan. Handan doesn't understand this business. She can't manage to sweep up the broken mirror pieces.

'I'll come and sweep up, Handan,' she says, struggling to make her voice audible.

'It's all right, I'll do it. It's not a problem.'

Her voice is like ice. Handan's voice is icy. It's not a problem. The kind of answer she would give a stranger. She's thrown her out of her world. She's flung her out.

She heard the broken pieces being thrown in the garbage. It was very noisy. How noisy it was. Then Handan went into her room and closed the door. No goodnight. No goodnight kiss.

She's finished with you. Do you understand? Just get out of their house. Go into her room while she's sleeping and quietly get your jacket; then get out of their house. Leave them alone. Leave. Leeeave.

But Behiye can't survive. With that much pain. She'll shrivel. She'll burn. She'll smell burnt. She can't survive. It's impossible.

She was happy the moment before, and everything changed; couldn't everything change back in the same way? Couldn't things change back from being so frightful and hopeless to being happy and good and reunited with Handan? Could it possibly change so much? Since the whole world, the ground, Handan are receding from under her feet? Couldn't it all be given back to her? For Behiye? For poor Behiye?

Poor. Poor. Poor Behiye.

Now Behiye is sitting and crying and repeating, 'Poor. Poor.

Poor Behiye,' to herself. Her heart is burning. Her heart is on fire.
It can't stand much more of this pain. At one point it will snap. It
will scatter...

Poor. My poor thing. Poor Behiye.

Handan has turned out her light. She's sleeping now. Is she
sleeping now? Just last night she was lying next to Handan.
She was drawing in Handan smell, fearing she'd explode with
happiness. Today, here, she's looking at her hand, which hasn't
stopped bleeding, and she's afraid to move. She looks at her hand,
at the blood, because there's nothing else to look at.

Behiye can't stand it. How is she going to be able to stand it?
How will she bear it? Is this possible? It's too much for a person.
It's too much pain for a person to bear, to support. Too much
pain. Too much pain. Too much too much.

The disgusting vodka, wrapped in newspaper, is standing
at the entrance, right in the hall. Behiye is afraid to stand up.
Everything will collapse on her. As if everything hadn't already
collapsed on her. She crawls to the hall and gets the vodka, then
crawls back to where she was sitting.

She takes the bottle out of the newspaper. She needs alcohol
to clean her hand – it was so silly, just a passing thought, she
pours vodka on her hand. Her hand burns. Her hand is on fire.
It hurts as much as if she'd rubbed salt on to her wounds. The
burning, the fire, is good, though. Since she's burning inside,
since her heart is burning, let her flesh burn too. And her soul.
What is a soul? What is a soul?

She tosses her head back and gulps down the rest of the vodka.
Indeed, she doesn't quite know what she's doing. And she doesn't
want to know.

There's no way she can take this much vodka. Her stomach
is terribly upset. Her stomach is turning in her mouth. Behiye
bends over and vomits on the newspaper the vodka was wrapped
in. Disgusting! Everything is disgusting! Disgusting Behiye! This
is what you're made of after all: blood, vomit and pain. That's all

you are. That's what you're made of. You're made, and you're of. Made of. I hate the phrase. Behiye wants to vomit on the phrase 'made of'. If it was possible, she'd like to lay the phrase out and throw up on it. Throw up. That's much nicer than vomit. It's more definite. Definite. To throw up. Behiye threw up. Throw up Behiye. Get it out. Let Behiye get out of the game. Behiye has been shown a card of whatever colour.

How many hours did she sit there, entertaining a million silly thoughts, her heart aching/leaking/burning? Behiye doesn't know how many hours she sat there like that.

In the end she got up, gathered up the newspaper on which she'd vomited, and threw it in the garbage. Then she came and mopped up the living room. With her hand aching, with her hand burning with pain, she mopped and mopped the living room parquet. She mopped it amazingly thoroughly.

Then, with a sponge and detergent, she wiped off the armchair. Thank God the upholstery was a dark colour; thank God it was synthetic material. That's what it's called, isn't it? Synthetic material. Behiye's material is vomit, blood and pain. Couldn't one say that of Behiye?

Once she'd cleaned the armchair, the other armchairs and the sofa look very dirty. So Behiye set to work cleaning them. She cleaned and cleaned and cleaned. Then she cleaned the coffee table. And the other little tables. Behiye's cleaned everything else she found in the living room, she cleaned and cleaned.

Towards morning she was dead tired. She didn't pull out the pull-out bed. She lay down on the sofa without pulling out the bed. Behiye could be said to have passed out on the unpulled-out pull-out bed. Poor. Poor. Poor Behiye.

Handan's water noises again in the morning. She woke up to them. She rolled over and sat up right away. What is Handan going to do? Is she going to come and throw Behiye out of the house? Would Handan actually throw Behiye out? Would she throw her out of her life? Hadn't Handan come to her? Hadn't

Handan opened all her doors to her without conditions or reservations?

Behiye runs to the kitchen. She puts tea on the fire.

Perhaps if she makes tea, if she makes toast, if she acts as if everything is normal – cringing Behiye. Mouse. Mouse Behiye. Don't throw me out Handan. Don't throw me out of your life, Handan.

Handan's cell phone rings. She comes out of the bathroom and runs to her room.

'Fine mother. OK, Mother. All right. Nothing's wrong. Fine. OK, Mother. All right. All right, Mother.'

Handan comes out of her room, wearing the same pink mohair cardigan she was wearing when she first saw her, and with her hair in baby girl pigtails. The pink balls are bouncing in front. She stands in the kitchen door looking at Behiye, wearing a little cardigan that was more like a baby's than a young girl's.

Handan has tears in her eyes. Handan isn't crying. But there are tears in her eyes. She's put on the cardigan she wore the first day they saw each other.

Behiye starts to cry. 'I mopped the living room floor, Handan. I cleaned the armchairs. I even wiped off the money…'

'All right, Behiye.'

All right? Behiye?

'I'm making tea for you, Handan.'

'Behiye, my mother wants me to go to Sister Nevin's right away. She told me to go there right away. I'll go over and see what's what. Maybe she'll soften a bit. I don't know. You've ruined everything, Behiye. Behiye…'

'Handan!'

'See you.' She's put her bag on her back. Handan ran out of the house. She fled. She's fleeing Behiye now. That's what Leman wanted. She's fleeing. She's fleeing Behiye. She's going. Handan is going! Handan! Handan!

Behiye collapses on the kitchen stool and starts crying. What's she going to do now? Where will she go? Where? And Handan will come back home. She'll come back in a little while. Perhaps she'll get Leman to agree. Perhaps she'll get Leman to agree.

She gets her jacket from Handan's room. The box of *Unisom* is still in the left pocket of the jacket. She used four of them. There are still sixteen left. Sixteen small, round, baby-blue pills. Pills of Handan blue.

If she swallowed them all, Behiye would sleep very well indeed. She'd sleep and sleep and sleep. Perhaps while she was sleeping everything would straighten out. Perhaps Handan would soften her mother. Perhaps Leman wouldn't throw out someone who was sleeping so deeply. Would Behiye die if she took sixteen pills?

She wouldn't die. She'd sleep. She'd sleep a great deal.

She took the pills out one by one. Behiye looks at them. She brews tea. Nice tea. A nice tea is better than anything. A nice tea takes care of everything. According to Yildiz.

She thinks of her mother. How long, how long it's been since she's thought of her mother. She thinks about how she didn't drink tea because her mother enjoyed drinking tea so much: how tea reminded her, her mother. She's in pain. She's already in pain. Could she be in any more pain? I mean, is it possible?

She pours herself a tea. She throws the *Unisoms* in one by one. It's easier to take them that way. It's more pleasant. She throws in two sugars so it won't taste so bad. She starts drinking.

The doorbell rings. The bell at the front door of the building. Handan is back! Handan couldn't bear it, and came back! She's going to say 'my Behiye' and put her arms around her neck. She's going to suffocate Behiye with Handan kisses. Breathlessly, she presses the buzzer. She rushes out into the corridor.

'Handan!' she shouts towards the stairs. 'Handan! Have you come back?'

Sounds of two people climbing the stairs. 'Behiye, my daughter. Behiye, my child, Behiye!'

It's her mother and Tufan.

They've found Behiye. They've found Behiye. Behiye flees inside and slams the door in their faces. 'Go away! Get the hell out of here! Leave me alone! Go, go I say.'

She's shouting at the top of her voice. In a disgusting, broken voice. She's shouting. She's shouting.

'Open the door, you crazy bitch. Open the door I say. Don't close the fucking door on me. Open the door now. I'll kill you Behiye, you traitor! I'll pull out your carrot hair and throw it away!'

How Tufan shouts in his loud voice. Behiye wants to fall down and die. To fall down and die right there. And her mother has put on a headscarf. So she'll look like a good, suffering, family mother: overcoat and headscarf. Behiye is ashamed of her mother. She's ashamed to be ashamed of her mother in the middle of this tragedy. But she's disgusted by Tufan. She's disgusted by Tufan. She's going to finish Tufan off.

She runs inside and puts on her jacket. Tufan has begun throwing himself against the door. She holds the lancet tightly. Tufan is throwing his bear-like body against the door. He's pushing the door towards Behiye. He's broken the door. Tufan is standing right in front of her. Her mother is standing right behind him. Her mother is crying. She's covered her mouth with the edge of her headscarf.

'I'll teach you to slam the door on me. I'll teach you how to steal my money, you treacherous bitch! Crazy shit! You've gone too far, you've gone too far!'

Tufan grabs Behiye by the hair and starts hitting her head against the wall.

Her mother screams and shouts, 'Leave my daughter alone, Tufan! Leave my child alone! Tufan! Tufan!'

Behiye still has her hand on the lancet. But it's as if all her power has flowed out on to the floor, on to the tiles. Perhaps because of the sleeping pills. Perhaps there's nothing, nothing, left inside her. What can she fight back with? Where's her power, her strength; where's Behiye's hand? Where's her arm?

'Where the hell is my money?' says Tufan. He's let go of Behiye's hair. He's not hitting her head against the wall any more. Behiye collapses to the ground right there. She closes her eyes, her stomach is upset.

Tufan gives Behiye a kick in her stomach. A kick in her flank.

'God damn you!' says her mother, throwing herself to the floor. 'Don't you see the state she's in? Leave my daughter alone, I tell you.'

'I asked you where my money is.'

'On the coffee table,' she says with all her strength. She struggles to breathe. Or at least that's how it feels. She seems to be dying.

'The dollars aren't mine.' Tufan stuffs the euros in his pocket. 'Get up. Let's get out of this fucking house.'

'Behiye, what's wrong with you? Behiye, you look terrible. Behiye, my daughter, my child, you're nothing but skin and bones.' How her mother cried as she held Behiye to her bosom.

'Come on, Mother. Get up, we're going.'

They lift Behiye off the ground. Her mother takes her arm, and they go down and out of the building. Leman is waiting there in a taxi right in front of the door. She gets out of the taxi when she sees them.

'I had to break the door; I'm very sorry, Ms Leman,' says Tufan, full of admiration.

They put Behiye in the taxi Leman got out of. Her mother climbs in the back next to her. Tufan shakes Leman's hand, and gets in front next to the driver.

'To Çemberlitaş,' he says to the driver. 'I'll jump out at Zincirlikuyu on the way.' He turns around. 'I'm sorry, I lost control, Mother,' he says. 'She made me lose my temper. I didn't know what I was doing.'

'That's your sister, Tufan,' she says.

'What sister! She's nothing but trouble.'

'What's wrong with you, my Behiye? Put your head on my lap, dear. You can't keep your eyes open.'

'Thank God Leman had the sense to find us by getting Çiğdem's number from the course director. Otherwise how would we have found the girl? I was going to go to the police this week. I wasn't going to listen to you or my father. What a beautiful woman she is, though. She doesn't look at all like a mother. What blue eyes. Did you see her eyes, mother?'

'As soon as Sevil called and said "Behiye", my heart was in my mouth. Thankfully, we found my child safe and sound. Thank God we found my daughter. God knows how much I suffered in the last fifteen days. My prayers were answered, I found my baby.'

'We don't call people like this "baby", Mother. We call them "trouble". Brother, can you let me off here. Bye, Mother. I'll see you this evening.'

Her mother doesn't answer Tufan. She's stroking Behiye's hair. 'What kind of sleep is this, daughter? Did something happen, Behiye, answer me. Driver, take us to Haseki Hospital. I want them to look at my daughter. It's not normal to sleep like this.'

Behiye opens her eyes and looks at her mother. 'I'm fine, Mother. Please don't take me to the hospital. Let me sleep. I'm very sleepy. I'm sleepy. Don't take me to...'

'All right, my child. Fine, Behiye. You go to bed and have a good sleep. You're just skin and bones, my baby. My daughter. My Behiye.'

Her mother is crying. She's crying those silent Yildiz tears. She covers her mouth with her headscarf so no one will see.

'Motherhood is hard work,' says the driver.

'Don't ask,' says her mother. 'Only God knows how much I've suffered in the last fifteen days. Fire only burns what it touches.'

Fire only burns what it touches, says Behiye to herself. Fire burns what it touches, fire touches what it burns. Fire burns. Fire has covered everything, is burning everything. Behiye is burning so much, in fact she's not burning. She's falling. Behiye is falling. Out of the frying pan and into the fire. Into unknown places within herself. She's falling into herself.

City

. . . .

It all lasted nineteen days.

All of it: nineteen days.

From the moment The Feeling You'll Be Rescued came to her under the plane tree until the raid that tore her away from Handan's house, everything happened in nineteen days.

This fast, this brief.

Behiye didn't understand at all. She thought it was many many more days. Her whole life. New Behiye's life, that is.

Now she's counting the days she's been imprisoned in her family's house. Tufan had ordered that she be imprisoned in the house for a month. Her mother, and her father – miserable Salim – agreed.

Her mother doesn't go to the shop, she didn't go. She sits over Behiye as a kind of guard/nurse/pathetic policewoman. She's 'waiting for her daughter'.

Behiye is constantly sleeping, constantly sleeping and eating. She takes lots of *Unisom*. Then *Insidon*. She has a bit of help, that is. Çiğdem goes to the pharmacy and brings sleeping pills and tranquillizers. Behiye only sees Çiğdem. Çiğdem and her mother. From the moment Tufan comes home till the moment he leaves, she doesn't step foot out of her room. A few times she agreed to see her father. Otherwise, Behiye lives locked up in her room, in her family's house. She's forbidden to go outside. She's forbidden to go out for a month.

She counts the days. Thirty days is a lot of days. She counts them, but they don't end.

Four or five times, when her mother was in the toilet, or sleeping, she called Handan's house. The phone rang and rang, but no one answered. It rang and rang, but no one answered. Clearly, they turned off the sound and weren't answering.

Once, the phone was busy. Behiye's heart went into her mouth. Then again it rang and rang and no one answered. Evidently they were calling out. They don't answer the phone.

She called Handan's cell phone six times. Each time the same words stabbed her.

'The number you are calling is out of service.'

A few times she begged Çiğdem and got her to call Handan's house. 'I swear, they don't answer the phone,' she said. 'I let it ring about thirty times.'

She can't reach Handan. Anyway, Handan could find her. She could call Çiğdem and ask for her number. Handan could call Behiye. She could find her.

Perhaps she's also being punished. Perhaps she can't call Behiye. Is that the case? That's how it is. No, it isn't.

Behiye is afraid. She's afraid to call Handan, to leave the house. And on the day of the raid, Handan listened to her mother and fled to Sister Nevin's. She knew they were going to come for Behiye. There's no possibility she didn't understand. She knew. She knew.

Handan got tired of her. Fed up, worn out, done in. When she remembers their last night, Behiye gets goose pimples. She has to wait. To recover. To calm down. Then she'll find Handan. She'll explain. Whatever she has to explain. Handan will listen to her, she'll understand. It can't just end like this. Handan and Behiye can't end this way. It can't end this way, it can't be the end. It can't. Be.

She's still afraid to call Handan. She's afraid to leave the house, to get out of bed. She acts as if she's counting the days. And she is counting. She's madly waiting for Handan to call. Handan might call Behiye, and forgive her, and say how much she misses her. Then Behiye would go running. Whatever that lout Tufan did. It seems he promised Leman. Cringing idiot. Disgusting Tufan. One day Behiye is going to show him. For now, she's waiting.

She's waiting. She doesn't have the strength. She's sleeping. All right, with the help of the pills. She's sleeping, eating the food her mother makes; Çiğdem brings her cake and pills. Behiye sleeps and drugs herself. She knows how much she'll be in for the moment she steps out into the street. Handan. Handan!

She's built a concrete wall within herself. She's dumped truckloads of sand on her heart. She's buried her pain. She's counting the days. She's waiting. She's waiting. Handan! Could I forget you? Would it be possible for me to forget you?

At the silliest, least appropriate moments, she suddenly empties herself. She starts to cry. She cries like a madwoman. She cries for an hour or so without stopping. She's afraid of crying herself empty.

A month hasn't passed. But three weeks have passed. Isn't that enough? Twenty-one days. As of today, it's been more than twenty-one days since she was taken from Handan's house. Twenty-two days. Twenty-two days. Exactly.

In the afternoon she sits in the living room and watches a Turkish film. An old Turkish film: Sadri Alişik's film, *Mujgan*. Sadri Alişik is very much in love with Mujgan. Very, very much in love. But they separate. Then one day Sadri Alişik meets Mujgan on the street. They talk, Mujgan has a son, and she's named him Koray and so forth. There's a close-up shot of Sadri Alişik. 'Forget?' he says.

'Forget Mujgan?'

Forget? Forget Handan? Behiye starts to cry. Tears stream down her face.

She can't bear the excruciating pain she feels. She doesn't want to take two *Insidon* and one *Unisom*. She doesn't want to. She can't stand it.

She goes to her room and puts on her jacket. The lancet is still in the pocket. Waiting its turn politely. Or that's how it seems to Behiye.

Her mother is doing something in the kitchen. She sneaks to the front door, and goes out. She's outside now. She's outside for the first time in twenty-two days.

She has no money on her. Behiye starts walking. Sultanahmet, Eminönü, Karaköy, Tophane, Dolmabahce, Beşiktaş. She climbs up Barbaros Boulevard. Kislaonu, Zincirlikuyu, Levent. Her knees are shaking by the time she gets to Levent. Her knees are knocking together from tiredness and nervousness.

Petrol Complex. She's entering the Petrol Complex now. Behiye's heart is going thump, thump. Her head is spinning from tiredness and nervousness. Her head is spinning and her stomach is upset.

She rang Handan's bell. Ten seconds or so later the door opened. Behiye is going upstairs.

'Who's there?' Someone has come out into the corridor and is looking down. Muki!

'Ah, is it you Behiye? Leman, Leman! Behiye has come, Leman!'

Leman appears at the door of the flat. Leman. Leman.

'Behiye!'

Behiye is looking at Leman. Tears are streaming from her eyes. She can't help it. Her eyes are like two fountains.

'Come inside, my Behiye.' Leman's voice, face and clothes are in a terrible state. She's never seen Leman like this. Leman is finished.

Behiye feels as if she's in a cloud of cigarette smoke and alcohol. The house smells of cigarettes and drink. It smells terrible.

Leman sits in an armchair, with her bare feet tucked under her. There are purple rings under her eyes. Her eyes are red. And swollen. Her voice is completely cracked. Behiye understands right away that something frightfully serious has happened.

'Handan? Where's Handan? Where's Handan?'

'Handan is gone. Handan is gone.' Leman makes a wheezing sound. The kind of sound an animal would make. It's clear she's finished crying. She's cried so much; she can't cry anymore, she just wheezes.

'Where? Where has she gone?'

'She left us. She abandoned me. She ran off to Australia four days ago. She called around and found her father's relatives. They called her father, and Harun came. And they met secretly. They managed to get her a passport in three days. She has the same surname as her father. You know, children take their fathers' surnames. They didn't have to ask me for a letter of consent or anything. Harun took my daughter off. She's sixteen, after all. What can I do? My daughter ran away from me. She abandoned her mother; she didn't want me, Behiye. She didn't want me. She even said so. She said it right after you left. She said, "You shouldn't have done that. I'll never forgive you, Mother." She was fed up with me. Fed up, fed up, fed up.'

Leman struggles to cry as she wheezes. But she can't cry. Leman has cried so much her tears have dried up.

'My baby said she couldn't stand me any more. What did I do? What did I do to you, Behiye? What did I do to her? I felt as if the two of you were rolling off a cliff. I thought you two should be separated. You know what you did to me, Behiye. You know how you shouted in my face, how you broke the mirror and cut your hand. I was frightened. I don't know, I was frightened.'

Leman was congested. Muki brought her a glass of water from the kitchen. 'Don't cry, my Leman,' she says. 'Don't cry, my beauty. You're done in.'

'What did I do, Behiye? I loved my daughter. I loved my Handan so much. How can I live without her?'

Leman starts to howl. A cry of pain Behiye has never heard

before. Like some kind of animal sound. The scream of an animal that's lost its cub. Leman makes a sound she's never heard before.

Behiye makes a fist and puts it in her mouth. She can't bear Leman's howling. She can't bear Leman's inhuman screams.

Behiye is on the street now. She's walking. Levent, Zincirlikuyu, Mecidiyeköy, Şişli, Harbiye, Taksim. Behiye walks without stopping. She walks with tears streaming from her eyes.

At the beginning of Istiklal, in front of the false waterfall, the blind people have put an electric keyboard on a plastic table, and are playing music. There are big speakers planted on either side of them. The volume is turned all the way up, and they're playing and singing. They're playing and they're singing.

Behiye can't make out what they're singing. Her head is buzzing so much she doesn't know what they're singing. She can't hear the words.

The blind singer is nodding his head and smiling as he sings. Behiye doesn't feel like kicking the keyboard and the speakers. Kicking them to the ground. She doesn't feel like it.

Behiye feels pity for the blind. They're poor and they're blind; but at the same time they're in a good state, as if everything was going well, smiling as if everything is going like clockwork, that stubborn, persistent smile, holding on to their music and their songs, trying to stay on their feet.

Behiye's heart is burning. It's on fire. She wants to cry for the blind. It was disgusting of her to be annoyed with them. It was frightful. Now Behiye wants to cover the blind people's feet, to wash the blind people's feet with her tears. Pardon me. You're struggling to survive. Will you forgive me?

But why? Why is everything so bad? Who's deceiving these blind people? Who's making them learn these songs, who's making them sing? Who's telling them to pretend everything's going well, that everything's going like clockwork? Who's responsible for all of these things? Who?

Handan, who separated us? Why is everything so wrong? This bad? Hurts me so, burns me?

The streets are full. The avenue is very crowded. People are bumping into each other, struggling to walk. You don't exist in this city. You've gone. You've left me alone in this troublesome, evil city, this city where nobody wants me or accepts me. You left me Handan.

What am I going to do with this much evil? How am I going to clean up this evil city? How am I going to sort out what's bad and what's good?

Whoever has power is bad.

Whoever has power is bad.

In the square, Behiye collapses to the ground. She's so tired, she wants to curl up and sleep right there.

Behiye is so tired, she's finished.

All of the Behiyes she knows within her are finished.

'Handan!' she says, wiping her tears with the sleeve of her jacket.

Handan and Behiye.

They're finished. They're finished. Finished.

Wound

. . . .

1) The wound was caused by what type of trauma, object or instrument?
2) How many wounds are there? If there are more than one, are they the same type of wound?
3) What is the degree of damage caused by the wound?
4) Were any of the wounds fatal? Which of the wounds were fatal?
5) Is there any causality between the wound and death?
6) When did the wound occur?
7) Was the wound caused before or after death?
8) Was the wounding murder, suicide or accident?
9) How long did the victim live after being wounded?